ACT OF
VIOLENCE

ACT OF VIOLENCE

MARGARET YORKE

ST. MARTIN'S PRESS ❧ NEW YORK

Library of Congress Cataloging-in-Publication Data

Yorke, Margaret.
   Act of violence / Margaret Yorke.
     p. cm.
   ISBN 0-312-18522-7
   I. Title.
   PR6075.07A627 1998
   823'.914—dc21   98-16546
                                                  CIP

First published in Great Britain by Little, Brown and Company

First U.S. Edition: August 1998

10 9 8 7 6 5 4 3 2 1

ACT OF VIOLENCE

1

In prison, people don't talk about their crimes, unless to say they are innocent. Oh, you get to hear why some are inside – drugs, maybe, or debt. And you know about those who've made headlines in the papers. When they arrive after sentencing, everyone feels the tension. Lifers are put in the hospital wing at first, in case they top themselves. Some try it; some regret what they've done and want to atone. If they don't, or don't profess to, they won't be paroled. Most are released, eventually. After all, they've served their time and paid their debt to society. Like me.

Meanwhile, survival is the name of the game: getting through your time as best you can; keeping out of trouble.

Oliver Foxton glanced at his wife, who was looking through some papers, frowning. Recently she had been prescribed spectacles for reading, but rarely wore them. Was it vanity? Didn't executive women regard them almost as accessories essential to their image? He sighed. She was an executive now, but she seemed no happier than before she embarked on her career.

He felt responsible for her discontent. Ever since they met, his main aim had been to make her happy, but he had not suceeded. He was too old: that was one reason for his failure, but when they first married the age difference had been what had drawn her to him. She had dropped out of university after a damaging love affair about which he never learned the details. He had met her on a skiing holiday; he was staying with a group of friends in a chalet, and she was in another, with her brother and his wife, who had taken her along to cheer her up. Oliver was a competent skier, not fast, but neat. Not very tall, thickset, already secure in his position as a solicitor in Mickleburgh, he was the complete opposite of her discarded lover. That, and the rebound factor, accounted for Sarah's interest in him; it was easy to understand why he had fallen in love with her. He was ready to settle down, and she came along: young, pretty, bright and, at the time, rather brittle. The brittleness which he had hoped to smooth away had never wholly disappeared.

Like accidents, marriages result because those involved happen to arrive at what might be the wrong place, at the same time.

But it wasn't wrong for him. He wouldn't change that part of the story, only his own performance.

Back from the French Alps, he had immediately pursued her, and they were married in the summer. It had been hasty, he acknowledged now, but things had gone well at first; in fact, people thought they had an ideal marriage, and in many ways it was. They had a son and daughter, both now adult – Tim at medical school and Judy at university reading law. Oliver allowed himself to dream that Judy might one day join the practice.

The Foxtons lived in Winbury, a village three miles from Mickleburgh; they gave and attended small dinner parties, and Sarah undertook various voluntary activities, extending their range as the children grew older. For a while she helped a friend run a curtain-making business, soon acquiring expertise. Commissions fell away during the recession, and then the friend moved from the district. Sarah took a business course and now worked for a management consultancy, analysing statistics and advising on the reorganisation of small companies. Oliver wanted her career to succeed; if it did, she might find contentment, but so far this had eluded her.

They'd never had the struggle experienced by many newly married couples; he was already established in his family's firm, and money, though limited, had not been really short. They'd had holidays abroad, and had recently had a new kitchen fitted when Sarah had complained that theirs was out of date and shabby. If she wanted something for the house, she could have it; Oliver was generous, but she, in turn, was not extravagant. Their partnership excluded conflict, but nothing seemed to cure her perpetual unspecified dissatisfaction.

She was so cold.

That was it: she was distantly affectionate, dutifully so, but she was cold, and it must be his fault.

'How was your day?' he had asked her when she arrived home an hour after he had returned from the office. She had been to London.

'Busy,' she'd replied.

'Did the meeting go well?' He wished she'd tell him about it, describe what it was about, share it with him. Apart from wanting to meet her on her own ground, he would have been interested.

'I suppose so. We got our message across,' she said flatly. 'I have to go up again next week.'

Well, at least she'd told him that. She enjoyed her London trips, which had become more frequent lately. He must not ask her if she had had a pleasant lunch; he'd done this before and had been accused of prying.

He'd cooked the supper, something she rarely let him do. She'd seemed to enjoy the meal and even dropped a kiss on his head as she passed his chair; it was the sort of kiss a father might receive, he thought sadly.

He'd try no more this evening. Oliver rose quietly and left the room, going to his study where he put on a tape of *Don Giovanni*. Then he went over to the big square work-table he had recently installed near the window; on it stood the subject of his new interest: a Victorian dolls' house, which he was restoring.

Sarah was not so immersed in her papers that she failed to notice Oliver's departure. He'd be playing with that dolls' house again: what a puerile pastime for a grown man, she had thought, when he first brought it home, but now, as it was gradually returned to life, she saw how delicately he worked, how neat his big fingers were, how intriguing the result would be. She would not admit it, however; not to him, and not even to herself. She preferred to nurse her resentment.

In the train from London, she had run over in her mind the events of the day, the eager anticipation with which she had arrived at her meeting, a seminar with delegates from several consultancies and businesses. Clive Barry, from her own firm, had been there, and during the lunch break she had heard him in discussion with the managing director of a company for which they had aready done some costings. A new post was to be created within their organisation, covering much of the work for which they now employed an outside adviser. She'd apply. It would offer her a daily escape to London, and who could tell what she might yet accomplish, given such a chance? She might even have to spend occasional nights in town. Visions of her own tiny flat swam into her mind.

Of course, she told herself, she was always glad to return to Winbury in the evenings; she loved her pretty, comfortable house, but she would be happier if it were in some agreeable part of London. This was impossible, so working there would be the next best thing. Meanwhile, in a few weeks' time, she was going to a conference in Kent, and that would mean staying away overnight, the first time since starting work that she had done so.

Challenged, she would have said that she was fond of Oliver; it was simply that he had become dull: old and dull. After all, he was fifty-five. Clive Barry, for instance, was her own age, and many of the people with whom she worked were younger, like Daisy, the secretary she shared with several other senior staff members, who was only twenty.

For the first years of her marriage, Sarah had been too busy to indulge in regrets and had basked in being a youthful, pretty mother. Tim was born eleven months after the wedding, a plump, docile baby. Sarah ran things smoothly and was unaware that other new mothers among her acquaintance found her intolerably smug. Everything went well for her: the babies appeared as if to order, first a boy and then a girl, who both proceeded through infancy and childhood to satisfactory teenage years, causing only minor alarms. Sarah was a good cook and manager, and she always had reliable help, a woman from the village who came daily and did whatever was required, including looking after the children when necessary. Though past sixty now, she still came twice a week, and extra if required. This had made Sarah's career debut easy easy. No one suffered at home.

She had been charged with energy while she did her business course, and Oliver, aware that trying to restrain her would only make her more determined to go her own way, encouraged her to spread her wings, all the time fearful that, one day, she might fly right away.

Before he finished work that evening, Oliver, on impulse, had walked up the High Street to the market square, turned left by the church, and entered a narrow street where once there had been a butcher's; this had been replaced by a dolls' house shop, selling kits to build them, miniature furniture and artefacts, and books and magazines about their restoration and construction. He was looking for a replica stove to put in the kitchen of the house he was restoring. He spent ten minutes browsing without finding what he sought, but he bought a tiny plate of artificial fruit to set on the dresser. They knew him now, in the shop. The manageress gave him a limpid smile as she attended to an elderly couple who were disagreeing about how best to equip the thatched farmhouse they were building.

They were arguing, not discussing, Oliver decided, hearing bitter tones. The distinction made so much difference. The manageress excused herself from them, took his money, and he left, somewhat depressed. Returning to the office, he saw Miss Ellis's car parked in the yard behind his Rover. She was back early today. She worked in Fettleton, a market town ten miles away, but he was not sure what she did. She was a remote, withdrawn woman; they exchanged greetings if they met but never more. One of his partners dealt with her lease; there had never been complaints on either side. The new couple in the other flat were not home yet; their windows were dark. Perhaps they should consider fitting time-switches, he reflected, although with direct access only through the courtyard, the flats, which had been converted from the stable block of the house where the offices of Foxton and Smythe were situated, were relatively protected. Miss Ellis had not needed that advice; her lights came on automatically.

Oliver had lived in the area for most of his life, joining his father in the firm as a young man. Bill Smythe had died fifteen years ago, but Oliver had kept the name; the firm had had expanded, acquiring partners specialising in divorce, which formed a large part of their business these days. Litigation, wills and conveyancing still went on; people would always need lawyers. At the moment one of his clients had been accused of fraud and another of embezzlement. Foxton and Smythe did not handle many criminal cases, apart from motoring offences, so these made a change.

We haven't had a murder yet, Oliver found himself thinking.

He had driven home wondering what sort of mood Sarah would be in after her day in London. Perhaps he should have bought her some flowers instead of pottering about in the dolls' house shop. But she would only have said, 'What are these in aid of? It's not my birthday,' and assume he wanted sex.

He did, but only if allied to love. Flowers and presents could not win that; it had to come from the heart.

Rosemary Ellis had planned to rent a flat in Fettleton, where she worked, but when she saw that one was available behind the Georgian building which housed the offices of Foxton and Smythe, at the end of Mickleburgh High Street, she was immediately drawn to it, chiefly because of its seclusion. It was near the church, and not far away was a footpath along which one could walk to the river and across the fields. She had new neighbours now, a young couple who had taken the downstairs flat where previously a frail elderly couple had lived. They had moved to a bungalow; she had not fraternised with them.

From across the yard, if she were at home when he was there, she could see into Oliver Foxton's office. She liked watching him at his desk, shirt-sleeved in summer except when clients came in. They and his secretary would sometimes mar her view on the rare occasions when she had the chance to watch him from her hall window. It was enough; she did not ask for more, although if they met in the yard, where their cars were parked, that was a bonus.

She knew where he lived. She'd driven past his house, The Barn House, Winbury, a long low building made of the local stone, set back from the road at the end of a short drive. Beside it was a barn from which it must derive its name. She'd seen his wife – a pretty, smart woman, always in a hurry when occasionally she called at the office, but then Rosemary herself was rarely in the flat in working hours.

The new couple in the flat below, Ginny and Bob, had invited her to their house-warming party soon after they moved in. She was surprised and touched, though at first she was inclined to refuse, but she accepted, to be neighbourly; however, she would keep her distance. She bought them a plant in a pot, which they accepted with apparent pleasure.

The party was noisy; many of the guests were staff members from Mickleburgh Comprehensive, where Ginny and Bob taught, and some were the parents of pupils. Rosemary was handed a glass of white wine and introduced to someone called Guy, who asked her what she did, and without waiting for an answer, told her all about himself. He was an accountant, recently divorced, with two children at the school. Rosemary listened to his monologue, letting it wash over her. Of course he was not interested in her, but nor was she in him. She could not move away for she was hemmed into a corner and the room was crowded. At last Bob, circulating with the wine, rescued her.

'Sorry you got stuck,' he beamed at her. 'Guy's a bit of a pain when he starts talking about his obsessions. Have you met Kate?' and he left her with a thin young woman in black leggings and a short black skirt who turned out to be the head of drama at the school. Rosemary had no interest in the theatre; their conversation stumbled along as they failed to find common ground, and eventually, when Kate drifted away, Rosemary returned to her own flat without saying goodbye, her departure unnoticed. She heard the noise of the party throbbing on below until nearly midnight. Then there were farewells, the sound of car doors being slammed, and, at last, blessed silence.

The next day, a note thanking her for the plant and apologising for the noise, adding that that they did not often have late parties, was pushed through her door. She had not invited Bob and Ginny back.

Kate, however, she met again, a few weeks later, one Saturday. She was in the town bookshop collecting a book she had ordered when she saw the other woman in conversation with a boy who must be, Rosemary supposed, one of her pupils.

'Hallo,' she said. 'We met at Bob and Ginny's party. You're their new neighbour, aren't you? This is Jamie, my son.'

Jamie mumbled some sort of greeting.

'I'll be off, then,' he said, and slouched away, large and uncoordinated, in a big fleece jacket and grubby trainers. His feet were enormous.

'He's tall,' Rosemary managed. Kate did not look old enough to have a son older than a toddler.

'Yes, isn't he?' Kate looked proud. 'He's brilliant at music,' she said. 'He plays the cello.'

'Oh,' said Rosemary, at a loss for the right response. She was not musical. 'How nice.'

'Well, I mustn't hold you up,' said Kate, turning towards the door.

'Goodbye,' said Rosemary, glad to be released. On her own ground, she was fluent, but in a social context she was inept. Intimacy alarmed her and she avoided it.

2

The scene is as familiar to me now as it was when it happened. Shots of it were shown to the jury: the long winding path through the forest where she walked her dogs, the beeches in their summer leaf spreading out among the scrub, and, further on, glades of larches with their spiky foliage. There were places where the cover was dense, and patches where coppicing would clear out saplings.

I'd picked the spot, and waited for her, trusting that no one else would walk that way that day. I'd followed her before, looking for a likely place where I could lurk, observing her, planning it. We'd even walked there together, more than once, for we were friends. That was mentioned at the trial, blackening my character. If the dogs turned on me, I'd have to kill them, too, but they knew me. They would not recognise me as an enemy.

I was often at their house. I'd made love there, in her bed, while she was visiting her parents. Of course he felt he must be loyal to her, must stay with her, because there were the children. Choosing between us was too difficult for him, but whenever he told me that we must part, that I must stay away from him, all I had to do was press myself against him – I was tall, unlike her; we were physically matched – start kissing him, and he would respond. With her gone, the way for us was clear. That was how I saw it then. It seemed so simple. And it wasn't as if the children did not know me. I had often babysat for them.

No one would suspect me. I'd have an alibi and I'd express horror when I heard that she'd been the random victim of a prowler in the forest. It was unwise to walk alone down those dark rides and bridleways; anyone could be hidden there, among the trees, vandals on motorbikes at the very least.

She hadn't heard a thing, had suspected nothing until, in my strong boots, I came right up behind her and plunged the knife into her back. Then she had turned startled eyes towards me, and, in the instant, as I'd hoped, she recognised me, perhaps guessed the reason for the deed, uttered a faint gurgle, and collapsed. On the ground, she writhed, and so, to make quite sure, I withdrew the knife and stabbed her again, several times, until she lay still, blood pumping out. I hadn't expected that, imagining one thrust would be enough, but then a frenzy overtook me, lest she should survive. One of the dogs, Hector, uttered a bark and stared at me in puzzlement, and I got him, too, in case he started howling before I could escape. The terrier had run off and disappeared, and it was his barking outside their house, disturbing neighbours, that caused alarm, so that she was found within hours. I'd hoped she'd lie undiscovered for a long time. After all, the house was empty – he was at work, not due back until the evening, and the children were at their school, where I was working at the time, which was how I had met the family and obtained my babysitting post.

I'd expected the children to go home, find their mother missing and be alarmed. Then a search would begin.

I'd planned to drag her off the track, into the long grass and scrub, to keep her hidden for as long as possible, but when I realised that I would be covered in her blood if I carried out this scheme, I changed my mind. I stepped carefully away from her, and walked back the way I had come, not wanting to create a trail leading from the main track.

I met no one.

Then I went to see my mother. I knew she would be out that day, doing voluntary work she regularly undertook. I told her I'd arrived an hour before in fact I got there. She believed me. Why not?

Later, in court, her evidence helped to convict me.

I dropped the knife in a ditch on the way home, but the police found it. There were no prints on it. I'd worn gloves. They discovered who had bought it; the shopkeeper had thought it an unusual purchase for a young woman, though I had said it was for my father, a keen fisherman. Surely there were women anglers, too? The conversation had caused him to remember me: unfortunate.

In the end, I confessed, because she was pregnant. He'd cheated on me. I admitted manslaughter due to diminished responsibility, but my plea was not accepted. I received a life sentence, but at last I was released.

The boy with the knife in his bag walked down the road to school. Now he could prove he was a hard man. If anyone threatened him, he could win in a struggle. They'd back off as soon as they saw his weapon. If he wanted another boy's trainers, or his dinner money, he could get them, and no one would dare tell.

A knife meant power. You didn't have to use it, but knowing you had it gave you control.

The first tenant of the upper flat behind Foxton and Smythe's office had been Prudence Wilmot. When she was unable to decide where to live after the sale of her house in Wiltshire, the estate agent who had acted for her mentioned it as a possible temporary measure; its lease was handled by another branch of his firm. Prudence, whose husband had recently died, found the prospect of living in a small country town appealing; she could try it, and if she liked it, would look for a house nearby. This she had done, and now she lived in the High Street, near the market square, in a small terraced house.

Her husband had been in the diplomatic service and they had spent many years abroad in different postings; then, when they were enjoying their retirement, living in what had been her parents' house, the collapse of Lloyd's had brought financial catastrophe. Prudence's husband had had a stroke and died. Prudence, however, owned the house, and thus was saved from penury. While she was living in the flat she had time on her hands, and wrote an historical novel set in Athens, where she and her husband had spent some years. After several rejections, she found an agent and then a publisher; a second novel had followed, and a third; she was now writing one set in Florence. The income brought in by her books, though not large, was a welcome supplement to her budget, and she enjoyed the research. She worked on an old typewriter at a desk overlooking her small garden, easily distracted when unusual birds arrived on her lawn, and often going to check on her plants' growth. She lived there contentedly, without an intimate circle of friends because writing took up most of her time. Oliver Foxton had grown fond of her while she was living in the flat, and his firm had done the legal work involved in the purchase of her new house. When she moved from the flat, she had shown him the old, grimy and damaged dolls' house she had kept back when much of her furniture was sold; it had been in her family since her own childhood.

'It's silly to hang on to it,' she had said. 'Look at the state it's in. It's only fit for a jumble sale.'

'It's not,' said Oliver. 'It could be restored. It could be quite valuable, it's so old. Let me renovate it for you.'

'But I can't ask you to do that,' she'd exclaimed.

'You're not. I'm asking you,' he said. 'Indulge me.'

You can invent your life – your history. Who is to know if what you tell them is the truth? You're stating your version of the past, and it may be false, as in my case.

I have a new name, a whole new identity, and though it was all in the papers, sensationally described, it was nearly thirty years ago. I have been living as another person for a long time, moving around, it is true, but now settled here indefinitely.

After my release, I went to live in Wales and found employment as a post office clerk. Those connected with what they called my rehabilitation arranged this, and I stayed for eight years, doing charitable work in my spare time. I led – and lead – a blameless life and am of benefit to the community, not a danger. I have paid my debt to society.

There are others still inside who should be freed. Why not, when they have served long sentences? Some, like me, committed their crimes when very young, and as the result of passion; after years of incarceration they are new people, wholly altered. Confining them is most unjust.

My days are spent aiding others. I work conscientiously, discharging all my duties, more than fulfilling my obligations. I never talk about my crime, and rarely think of it.

It's better so.

Oliver had decided to furnish the dolls' house in the same style as when Prudence had played with it. Some dolls remained inside it: a father and mother, two girls and a boy, and several items of furniture which he cleaned up and mended. The house, Prudence said, was a replica of her childhood home. In those days her father owned a carpet factory and was prosperous. He had had the dolls' house built by a craftsman he knew and equipped it to mirror their surroundings, even to supplying their correct family, with her, her much younger sister and her older brother, who had been killed in the Second World War.

After his difficult evening with Sarah, Oliver spent nearly an hour working on the dolls' house. At the end of that time he had decided that he must devise a way to give her a treat – dinner somewhere, or a theatre. They could invite friends along, if she would be bored with only him.

He had not heard her go to bed. She was asleep, or seemed to be, when he went up.

It wasn't difficult to become a counsellor. All I did was advertise in the paper and put a brass plate on my gate, then wait. I'd done it elsewhere, before I rented a consulting room in Fettleton. I'd joined an association which required no qualifications, simply some statements as to education and intent; I was entitled, then, to proclaim myself a member.

I had the money to do it; having served my sentence, I'd built up funds in my various posts. I'd driven taxis, and worked in hotels, always keeping remote from other people. I never sought affection; it brought problems. Then my parents died – first my mother, of an illness, then my father. According to the lawyer who eventually traced me, people said he perished of a broken heart, because of what I'd done. How sentimental. I'd kept away from them after my release. Ever loyal, they had visited me in prison, but with little to say, though assuring me that they would always support me; after a while their visits grew fewer and fewer, and when I took on a new identity, we severed ties. It was not discussed; it just happened. However, they left me adequate funds to enable me to escape from office drudgery. Conscience money, I decided.

Enough counselling went on in prison for me to pick up much of the jargon, and I learned in the raw from those around me. I read various books to reinforce what I already knew; then

I was ready. It's easy to advise my clients; much of the art of counselling is simply listening, which isn't difficult though it can be excessively dull. Then I suggest ways in which they can confront their problems; common sense is often all that is necessary.

I don't like to think about the reasoning that motivated me all those years ago. What I did was wrong; I've admitted it often enough, and I had to show remorse in order to obtain parole. There was grief at the time, mostly his, and that of the children left without their mother – a role I had expected to assume. Mine was the sorrow of betrayal. There was the unborn infant, too; the papers made a meal of that.

He abandoned me, saying that he had never loved me. He took the two children overseas and, after a while, married someone else. Like me, he started again. Now it's as if he'd died, as though it had never happened. In fact he did die, not long ago. It was reported in the papers, with a reference to the case. I suppose these things never cease to haunt. He had manipulated me because he wanted me, perhaps as a boost to his ego, as I was so young, or perhaps he was simply a lecherous man who needed more than one woman.

Now I manipulate others, sometimes gaining considerable control. In addition to my straightforward consultations and on the strength of my professional reputation, I write an advice column in a trade magazine. I get satisfaction from what I do. I am an influence for good, and the past is expunged.

3

How was she to occupy Saturday?

Sarah, waking, saw that Oliver was already up. He'd be out gardening, she thought, or maybe working on that silly house. She supposed it was a good thing to have a hobby. People said so, and if you had one, you met others who shared your interest, possibly even life partners. There were amateur dramatics, for instance, and badminton or tennis. Sarah was not attracted to any of these activities; as a girl, she had not been good at games; nor was she musical, but she had been willing to fall in with the plans of others, one who was led, rather than a trail blazer. She embarked on an affair during her first year at university partly because the idea of romance was already in her mind, and she thought it was essential to acquire a boyfriend. When she was singled out by a young man who had a beaten-up old MG, and who was a rugger enthusiast, she was ecstatic. An emotional path had been mapped out for her, and with dedication she learned the rules of rugby, standing on the touchline, shivering in spite of her thick coat and woolly hat, cheering Harry on. She endured long draughty drives in his car, and his clumsy sexual fumblings, and, regarding her cooperation as compulsory, hoped that these would become more tolerable in time.

In the summer, when Harry took off for a backpacking holiday with a girl called Amanda, she was mortified. It seemed that everyone but Sarah knew of their romance; however, Harry had decided not to have it out with her but to slide away.

'What a heel,' said another girl, attempting consolation, but Sarah was too far gone to benefit from her words. 'You'll soon find someone else,' the girl encouraged. But Sarah did not want anyone else; she wanted Harry, the rugby hero, whom her parents had met when they came to see her one weekend. She was too keen too soon, thought her friend. But Harry had given Sarah status; his defection was, to her, a major humiliation.

Then she met Oliver, who offered her an escape which salvaged her pride.

Being in love with him, as she eventually decided she was – he was certainly in love with her – was much less upsetting than being in love with Harry. For one thing, she didn't have to watch rugger, or cricket, which in the summer had taken over as Harry's main interest. Nor did she have to drink too much, which she'd done to keep up with Harry and to help with sex. Oliver did not expect her to go to bed with him until after they were married; before then, he kissed her rather nicely and sometimes caressed her intimately, but he never attempted more. Once, when she had had a few drinks at a dance – dances didn't seem to exist now – and she had twined herself around him as Harry had liked her to do, he unwound her and said that it was time to say good night.

Sex with Oliver had not been a gymnastic contest, nor a power struggle. Slowly it became rewarding, and was so still, though now it had become a habit. She was bored with him. Perhaps, as time passed, everyone grew bored with their husband or wife. Verbal communication between them seemed to be dwindling away; Oliver would tinker with his dolls' house, or deal with the papers for the various charities with which he was concerned, and she would watch television and then go to bed. Lately, it hadn't mattered. She had her own papers to work on now. She'd found a new role, and she was meeting different sorts of people all the time, clients and colleagues.

Oliver was in the kitchen when she went downstairs. He had made coffee, and, after pouring her some, he suggested they might have dinner that night at a riverside restaurant they liked. Sarah was pleased, and she agreed to his proposal that they should invite the Stewarts to join them. The two couples had been friends for years; their children were much of an age. The parents met less often now that their families had dispersed; it would be a chance to pick up the threads. Daniel Stewart had been made redundant five years ago, and after being rejected by numerous firms to whom he applied for a job, had opened a second-hand furniture business in a former corn merchant's just off Mickleburgh High Street. Sarah called it a junk shop; very little of what he sold could be termed antique. He cleaned, repaired, stripped and polished, and sometimes painted, the things he bought up cheaply, often at sales. Midge, his wife, had started picture-framing in part of the premises and Oliver suspected that hers was the more profitable operation. The Stewarts, however, remained cheerful if impecunious; they were delighted at the prospect of dining out, and conversation was lively during the meal, with Sarah deploring the hours worked by young doctors – Tim was worn out, she said, and they seldom saw him. Midge enquired about Oliver's dolls' house, which had fascinated her when she saw it. Sarah thought this a pointless topic and began discussing a local road-widening scheme which was attracting protest.

The Foxtons had picked up the Stewarts from Deerton, the small village a few miles away where they lived in a slightly crumbling house built thirty or so years before in what had been the orchard of the rectory. After dinner, they drove them back, and Daniel invited them in for coffee. Sarah accepted, and Oliver assented; a delayed return home would postpone a post mortem on the evening, with accompanying criticism.

Midge led the way indoors, flipping on lights as she went. There was an air of shabby scruffiness about the interior; surfaces were dusty, and there was a pile of letters, some unopened, on the table. Bills, Oliver guessed. They went through to the sitting room at the rear of the house, where in daylight there was a view across the garden which was mostly apple trees, rough grass, and, in spring, hundreds of daffodils. Now, faded apricot velvet curtains were drawn across the windows. The room was chilly.

'Sorry,' apologised Midge. 'We didn't light the fire before we went out. We were at the shop till late.' The shop was open on Saturdays, and she had had several pictures to frame, promised for the afternoon.

Daniel offered brandy, and had one himself, but Oliver, who was driving, had had a glass of wine with dinner and would not risk going over the limit.

'Just coffee, please,' he said. 'Shall I make it?' He knew where most things were in this shabby, comfortable house.

'Would you? You are a dear,' said Midge. 'I'll light the fire. You'll have a brandy, won't you, Sarah?'

Sarah, suppressing a shiver, said she would.

Midge was on hands and knees busy with twigs and firelighters. The grate, which was not the open-hearth kind, as in the Foxtons' house, where ash intentionally accumulated, hadn't even been cleaned, Sarah noticed. Midge was such a sloven. It was surprising that Daniel didn't appear to mind. Oliver shouldn't be drinking coffee so late, she thought; it would keep him awake. Except that nothing seemed to do that.

'How many coffees?' asked Oliver, putting his head round the door.

'I'll come and help,' said Midge. 'The fire's going now and Dan will keep an eye on it. Won't you?' she added.

'Of course,' he said, smiling at her, sorry the Foxtons had decided to come in, but after all, they had paid for the dinner, refusing his attempts to split the bill.

In the kitchen, Midge and Oliver soon brewed the coffee in the cafetière which Midge said Mark and Jonathan, her sons, one an engineer in Scotland, the other at university, had given her for her birthday. They found cups and saucers, Midge scuffling past the mugs she and Daniel always used. You didn't serve coffee to Sarah in a mug, not unless it was elevenses in the kitchen.

'Sorry about the mess,' said Midge.

'I see no mess,' said Oliver, although by comparison with Sarah's, the kitchen was untidy, with crockery on the drainer and a tin of biscuits on the table.

'I'm a bit of a muddler,' said Midge.

'I don't think you are,' said Oliver, pouring boiling water into the pot. He gave it a stir. 'I always do that,' he said. 'I'm not sure if you're meant to. Stir it, I mean.'

'So do I,' said Midge. She smiled at him, then gave him a quick peck on the cheek. 'You're a saint,' she said.

Oliver looked startled, but he beamed at her.

'You're a corker,' he said.

'What a strange expression. I hope it's a compliment,' Midge replied.

'Oh yes,' said Oliver. 'It's meant to be.'

When they returned to the others, Midge bustled about, wondering aloud how long to wait before plunging the filter down on the coffee. Sarah was sipping her brandy. Her hair, which she had grown recently, and wore loose tonight, fell on to the shoulders of her scarlet coat.

She looked very beautiful, thought both the men.

And I'm the one who goes home with her, Oliver reflected. He had never stopped marvelling about this, blaming himself for any disappointments.

They had already brought each other up to date on their children's progress, and talk died away as they finished their drinks. Driving home, Sarah commented on Orchard House.

'What a mess the place is,' she said. 'Midge is a real slut.'

Oliver had feared this sort of conversation might develop.

'She works hard, and she hasn't got anyone to help in the house,' he said.

'She could find someone. She used to have a cleaner.'

'I don't suppose they can afford it,' said Oliver. 'Times aren't easy and they've still got Jonathan to subsidise.'

'Oh,' said Sarah. 'Are they really so hard up?'

'I think so,' said Oliver. He knew that Daniel owed money.

Sarah was silent. She was lucky to be able to afford to dress well and have more or less whatever she wanted. She did not say this aloud; nor, as they prepared for bed, did she mention any pleasure she might have derived from the evening.

'That sauce on the duck was far too sweet,' she said, as she turned off her bedside light.

Oliver, still cheered by his moment with Midge in the kitchen, had planned to slip his arm round Sarah tonight, testing her mood. This remark instantly cooled his ardour.

'I thought it was delicious,' he said. 'I'm sorry it didn't please you.' By his standards, this was a waspish remark. He leaned over to deliver a good-night kiss on whatever surface of Sarah he could easily locate. It proved to be her hair, and she did not feel it.

She wouldn't have minded an approach tonight, she thought, rolling over, her back to him. Of course, he never sensed how she felt. Unable to count her blessings, Sarah slept, while a few miles away their dinner guests lay linked together, mutually comforted, like nesting spoons.

4

Jamie Preston was spending Saturday night at his friend Barry Noakes's house in Deerton. Barry lived in Orchard Close, a group of seven modern houses in a cul de sac opposite the Stewarts. His parents had gone to a wedding in Sheffield and would not be back until late, so Jamie was keeping Barry company. Two of their friends, Peter Grant, who also lived in the close, and Greg Morris, whose shortest route home was through the Noakeses' garden, over the fence and across a field, had come to spend the evening. No girls were present; that was a restriction imposed by Barry's parents; there was to be no opportunity for licentious conduct. Barry and his friends, however, were content; they talked about girls and scuffled with them when they got the chance, but none was yet ready for a no-holds-barred session. They had hired three videos and settled down to enjoy pizzas cooked in the microwave and cans of Coca-Cola.

They were sprawled in the living room, watching a horror film which they were too young to rent legally, when the doorbell rang.

Barry opened the door, and saw four boys from the year above them at their school. They crowded into the doorway and before he could prevent them, they had pushed him out of the way and burst into the house, surging on into the room where the others sat in front of the television, empty Coca-Cola cans stacked neatly on the hearth at the side of the electric fire, their pizza plates piled on a coffee table.

The intruding boys had already been drinking. One of them, Wayne, had bought a six-pack of beer.

Their escapade had started as a dare, after they met at Trevor's house. He had been boasting that he could drive and would take them for a spin in his mother's car, which he could borrow without her ever knowing. She and his father had gone for their usual Saturday night out. They went clubbing and were always late home. The car would be back in its place when they returned. The whole evening stretched ahead of the bored boys, and here was a challenge. The four of them had piled into the Lada and their first stop was to buy another six-pack. Then they drove through the town and into the country, the passengers all drinking while Trevor displayed his skills.

Seeing Deerton indicated on a signpost, one of the others, who knew that Barry Noakes lived there and had heard his plans for the evening being discussed at school, told Trevor to turn off.

'There's a few having a party there,' he said. 'Let's join in.'

The others were pleased with this suggestion; it was much too early to go home. They urged Trevor on, though they were vague about finding the close and Trevor overshot the turning, stopping beyond it. They piled out of the car, giggling. There was a short argument about which was the right house; Peter Grant lived here too, and there were seven houses.

'We'll try them all till we find them,' said Paul.

This seemed a good idea. They started at the first house, on the corner, and Barry answered the bell.

Led by Wayne, the four boys pushed past him. Wayne had

a can of beer in his hand and he pulled it open, putting it to his mouth, staring at what the others were watching.

At first it was all right. The intruders stood for a few minutes, gaping at the television. Then Kevin spoke.

'What a load of shit,' he said, and began picking up cushions and throwing them at the screen.

'Wouldn't mind some food,' said Wayne. He looked at the soiled plates. 'Got any more of that? Had a takeaway, did you?'

'Sorry, no,' said Barry nervously. 'My mum left pizzas for us.'

'Your mum left pizzas, did she?' Wayne mimicked Barry's half-broken voice. 'Well, let's see what else she's left,' and, followed by Paul, he went through to the kitchen, where they opened the fridge. Paul took out a bottle of milk and drank some, then, looking at Wayne to make sure his action was observed, poured the rest on the floor and dropped the bottle, which rolled over under the table. Hearing their excited cries, Kevin and Trevor followed them into the kitchen and began emptying the fridge, throwing margarine on to the floor and standing on the packet. They found Lily Noakes's store cupboard and began spilling rice and flour around them.

'Hey, stop it,' Barry, following them, protested, trying to bar the way to other cupboards while Peter dragged at the invaders' jackets to pull them back. Wayne turned on the taps at the sink and began splashing water about, and then Kevin and Paul broke away, going upstairs, their feet covered in the sticky mess from the kitchen floor.

Jamie ran after them, shouting at them to stop, but they took no notice, pulling the beds apart, flinging duvets and pillows around. Then Paul leaped up on to Barry's parents' large bed, undid his zip, and urinated in a wide arc over the duvet.

Jamie was still yelling at them to stop, tugging at any part of their clothing he could reach, but, intent on their wanton destruction, Paul and Kevin ignored him, pausing only long enough for Kevin to hit out at him, sending him off balance, but he recovered and caught Paul round the legs as he zipped up his fly, bringing him down on the bed so that his face made contact with the sodden duvet. At this, Kevin rounded on Jamie, who presented a vulnerable target as he bent over, grasping Paul. Kevin pulled his hair and dragged him to the ground, where he kicked his head. Somehow Jamie managed to wriggle free, and, realising he could not defeat the two boys, he ran downstairs, but Paul and Kevin, their blood up now, went after him. As he fled, sounds of battle came from the living room. Jamie dragged open the front door and ran into the road, shouting for help.

He did not turn into the close but dashed across the road to a house whose porch light was on, Daniel and Midge having failed to turn it out after Oliver and Sarah left. Jamie ran up the path to the front door and rang the bell, then thumped the tarnished brass knocker, yelling as loudly as he could.

To him, it seemed like hours before Daniel Stewart opened the door and saw a blood-stained, frightened youth who gasped something incoherent about boys trashing a house in the close.

'Calm down. Tell me what's going on,' said Daniel, and the boy said a gang had gatecrashed Barry's house.

'They're wrecking it,' he said. 'They're fighting.'

'I'll come. Just a tick while I put on some clothes,' said Daniel, who had dragged on a towelling robe before answering the door. He raced upstairs, where he put on tracksuit trousers and top while Midge, woken too, sat up in bed asking what was going on.

'There's a fight in the close. Ring the police,' called Daniel. 'There's a young lad with a bloody nose outside.'

Jamie had not waited for him. Recovering his breath, thinking of Barry and the others, he ran back across the road to help his friends.

Daniel, following at a trot, saw that the trouble was at the first house, for the front door was open and he could hear cries. As he reached the scene a jumble of boys spilled out into the road, all fighting and punching one another. He couldn't see the one who had come to ask for help; in the dark – there were no street-lights in Deerton – they were just a mass of thrashing limbs. He reached into the scrum and grabbed a boy, dragging him back just as another adult male arrived from a neighbouring house and cuffed one of the boys around the head. It was impossible to tell who was on whose side, and the men tried simply to separate the youths. Two of them peeled away and ran back into the house from which all of them had erupted. Now Daniel and the other man had become the enemy, and as the attack turned towards them, even Barry shrank away, leaving only Jamie to oppose the other four. His blows seemed futile as he pummelled the backs presented to him, then tried to pull the boys away from the men. One of the men caught hold of Paul and held him in an armlock, and at this Kevin pulled a flick knife from his pocket. He thrust it into the midriff of the man, Daniel Stewart. The second man, punched in the guts by Wayne, was winded and had turned away. Kevin's victim released his hold on Paul, sinking to the ground, and Paul and Kevin started kicking him as he lay curled up, emitting wailing cries. Jamie did not realise that he was crying himself as he went on trying to drag Paul and Kevin away from the injured man. Then Kevin turned and stabbed him in the arm. The others had got the second man on the ground by this time and were kicking him, but then the doors of other houses in the close opened and lights came on.

'Beat it,' Kevin cried, and they sped back to the Lada.

They had gone before the police arrived.

The boys had disappeared so rapidly. One minute there had been the flailing limbs and tangled bodies, then the groans, and as the stabbed man collapsed, the other man, doubled over, had been brought down and was a target for the blows and kicks that followed. Moments later, as several neighbours appeared, there was the sound of the Lada being driven off with the engine revving loudly. The only youth remaining on the scene was Jamie, clutching his wounded arm. It was bleeding freely, and, without a jacket, suffering from shock, he was shivering. The gathering group of adults did not, however, see the blood, which his dark shirt was absorbing. Some turned threateningly towards him while others bent over the two men. The second one was soon on his feet and someone went to call an ambulance. Jamie retreated towards Barry's house, where Barry, horrified at what was happening but not brave enough to rejoin the fray, stood in the doorway.

'Friends gone without you, have they?' said one man, advancing upon Jamie, who, very frightened, backed into the house.

Hands dragged him inside and closed the door, and then the boys in the house saw that he was hurt. It was Peter Grant who fetched a towel and wrapped it round Jamie's soaking sleeve, making Jamie bend his arm against his chest.

Midge had not followed Daniel immediately. After she had telephoned the police, she had pulled on a sweater and trousers and gone downstairs. She put the kettle on. That was what you did in an emergency. Then she opened the front door. Strangely, as she realised later, the fight had not been noisy; there were no shouts or cries, but slowly a sense of foreboding filled her. She pulled the kettle to the side of the Aga, found a coat and a torch, and as she left the house a car tore past, travelling fast out of the village. She ran then, suddenly extremely frightened, yet expecting to see Daniel coming towards her, the louts having been despatched.

A man who she realised only later was Ted Grant was

standing, bent over, hugging his arms across his body. Someone else was stooping over a figure on the ground, who lay motionless, curled up in the foetal position. Then the police arrived. They had been very quick, someone later commented.

They took her to the hospital in their car, saying it was better so, for Daniel was dead. They were very kind. She noted that.

At the hospital, when they asked her who to telephone, she thought of Oliver at once. Only a few hours before, they had been laughing in the kitchen at Orchard House, brewing coffee, and now there was no Daniel.

With the front door closed upon the suddenly quiet scene outside, and unaware that Daniel Stewart was dead, Barry and Greg emphasised that they must give the police no names. Peter was less certain but he was busy administering first aid to Jamie.

'Kevin will murder us, if we do,' said Greg. 'And Paul. He was wild tonight.'

'He was on something,' Barry said.

'It'll clean up. The house, I mean,' said Peter, an anxious, rather studious boy. He was not yet aware that his father had been involved in the affray.

'But what about my arm?' said Jamie. 'Kevin had a knife.' He was feeling rather faint, more from shock than loss of blood, and though back in the warm house, he was still shivering. 'I can say it was an accident,' he added quickly.

At this point there was the sound of a siren outside and the ambulance arrived.

'You'd better go out there. Get the medics to see to you,' said Peter. 'I'll take you.' The towel he had wrapped round Jamie's arm was now soaked in blood. 'You'll need stitching,' he declared.

He put an arm round Jamie and led him out to where a
group of adults surrounded the figure on the ground, screening
it from both the boys. A police officer detached himself and
came towards the pair. There was no need for Jamie to explain
that he was injured; it was obvious.

'Come with me, son,' said the officer. 'Here's one you can
help,' he told one of the green-overalled ambulance attend-
ants.

Jamie, by then, was only too thankful to be told what to do
and taken care of. In the ambulance, however, the man who
had been attacked lay very still, his face covered.

'Is he dead?' asked Jamie. Surely people didn't die like that,
in seconds?

One of the police officers was travelling with them in the
ambulance.

'Yes,' he said. 'I'm afraid so. Stabbed. Like you, Jamie, but
you'll get over it.'

He'd asked Jamie his name immediately and had been kind,
but he knew that though wounded, Jamie might be an assailant,
his own knife in some way turned against him.

When the telephone call from the hospital woke him, Oliver
found the message incredible.

Sarah heard him say, 'Oh no! No!' and then, more calmly,
'Very well. I understand. I'll come at once.' As he spoke, he
was getting out of bed.

Sarah was instantly alert.

'What's happened? Is it Tim?' she cried.

'No – no, it's not Tim, nor Judy,' Oliver said, already pulling
on some clothes. 'It's Daniel. That was the hospital. He's been
stabbed.'

'Stabbed? How? Do you mean they had a break-in after
we left?'

'No. There was some sort of brawl in the village and

he went to investigate. I'm not too clear about the details but Midge isn't hurt. She's at the hospital. She asked them to ring us.' Oliver paused, and added heavily, 'He's dead, Sarah.'

'Oh, Oliver, no! Oh, he can't be!' Sarah gulped and her eyes filled with tears, which she blinked away. Sarah never wept. 'Oh, poor Midge! You'd better bring her here,' she said, immediately practical. 'I'll put the electric blanket on in the spare room.'

'Yes – do that,' said Oliver.

'What about Mark and Jonathan? Do they know?'

'The police will be dealing with telling them,' said Oliver. 'They're at the hospital – the police, I mean. I'll sort things out with them.'

'Shall I come with you?' Sarah asked. She did not want to; proximity to suffering was so upsetting. But poor silly, clueless Midge might need her. Sarah shuddered. In a flash, Midge had become a widow.

'It would be better if you got things ready for her here,' said Oliver. 'The business at the hospital may take some time. Formalities and so on. You're absolutely right. She can't go home on her own.'

'She'll be so shocked,' said Sarah.

'Yes.' No words were adequate. 'I'm off. I'll ring if we're going to be ages.'

'Right,' said Sarah, already planning sandwiches and coffee. Or maybe Horlicks. Coffee kept you awake.

Oliver bent to give Sarah a quick kiss and was gone before she could kiss him back.

What if Oliver, driving through the night, were in an accident? What if she never saw him alive again? He might have a heart attack – anything could happen. For the last twenty-three years he had been a steady fixture in her life. How would she feel if all at once he wasn't there? Frightened by these intimations of mortality, Sarah braced herself and banished them from her mind.

She put on trousers and a sweater, brushed her hair and tied it back, then went to find a new toothbrush and a nightdress for Midge, although by the time Oliver brought her back, it would scarcely be worth anybody's while to go to bed. Still, it was Sunday. No one had to work. Sarah could meet Mark at Heathrow, for surely he would fly back from Scotland. Turning her thoughts towards practicalities, she went to the kitchen.

Oliver, driving towards Fettleton, reflected that a police officer, possibly someone younger than Mark himself, might be knocking on Mark's door even now.

5

Kate Preston's was the third door to receive a pounding in the night.

She and Jamie lived in a small house behind Mickleburgh Sports Ground, where Jamie was a member of the junior rugby club.

Who on earth could be making such a racket in the middle of the night? She put her head out of the bedroom window and saw, illumined by the security light which had come on at their approach, two uniformed police officers, a man and a woman. What now, she thought, putting on her dressing gown and slippers, never for a moment connecting their visit with her son, who she believed was safely in Deerton with his friend, and, at this hour, sound asleep.

When the officers asked if they could come in she was alarmed. Had something happened to her parents, who lived in Devon?

They made her sit down before they told her that Jamie had been wounded in a fight.

'But that's impossible. He's at Deerton with his friend,' she said.

'That's where the fight was,' said the male officer, PC Roberts.

'He's not badly hurt,' said WPC Tracy Dale. 'It's just a flesh wound in the upper arm. He was lucky.'

While Kate tried to take this in, they told her that they needed to talk to Jamie, who was too young to be interviewed without a parent or a guardian present.

'Some lads came to the Noakeses' house and there was trouble,' Tracy Dale told her.

'Jamie wouldn't start a fight,' said Kate.

'Someone else got badly hurt,' said Roberts. 'We want Jamie to tell us what occurred.'

'I'm sure he will,' said Kate. 'I'll go straight to the hospital.'

'We'll take you,' said the officers.

Kate, feeling frantic, took two minutes to throw on some clothes. The police might not be telling her the truth about how badly Jamie was hurt. How could such a thing have happened?

'Are Barry's parents back yet?' she asked. 'They went to Sheffield, to a wedding.' Jamie and Barry were sensible boys; leaving them together for the evening, with Barry's parents due home that night, had seemed a reasonable plan. She should have had both boys over to her house, Kate thought, but, a lone mother, she encouraged Jamie to be independent.

'I couldn't tell you,' Roberts said. 'We've simply come to take you to your boy.'

'Was Barry hurt too?'

'I don't think so. Just the house,' said Tracy Dale. 'The other boys trashed it.'

Kate was silent as they drove on towards Fettleton. How could this be? Deerton, with a church and one pub, had a population of only about three hundred people. The village shop had closed some years ago; it was a backwater, with very few new houses. Other pupils from the school lived there; had some of them joined Barry and Jamie, maybe high on drugs or something?

'Jamie wouldn't start anything,' she repeated. 'He'd help a friend, though. Are you sure he isn't badly hurt?'

'That's what the man said,' Roberts told her. 'We haven't seen him. We've come for you.'

While Roberts and Tracy Dale were dealing with this aspect of the incident, other officers were in Deerton, seeking witnesses. The Scenes of Crime Officer and his team would be searching for forensic evidence from the site. They needed to find the weapon used; this was a murder enquiry.

Jamie, his wound stitched and dressed, had been pronounced fit enough to leave hospital and he was waiting for his mother to arrive. He was very white, trying to control his trembling when Kate rushed to him and hugged him, gently, because his right arm was in a sling.

'Whatever happened, Jamie?' she asked him, but he could only shake his head.

They were taken to a room near the casualty area, a place where bad news was broken, Kate decided. There, Roberts and Tracy Dale asked Jamie the same question.

He saw that he had to give some sort of explanation, but he told them very little. He and Barry, with Peter and Greg, had been watching a video when some other boys arrived, forced their way in and started wrecking the place.

'It got a bit rough,' Jamie said. 'This man came to sort things out. The fight was in the road by now.' He didn't want to say that his three friends had gone inside the house and left him to it. 'The man got in the way of the knife and so did I.' He did not mention that he had fetched the man. He looked at his mother. 'He died,' he said. 'The man.'

'Oh God!' It could have been Jamie who was killed.

'Have you got a knife, Jamie?' asked Roberts.

'It wasn't my knife. I didn't do it,' Jamie said, and the trembling began again.

'So you have got a knife. Where is it?'

'In my jacket. It's a penknife,' Jamie said.

'You can't think Jamie killed the man! Why, he's been hurt himself,' said Kate angrily.

'That could have happened in the tussle,' Roberts said.

'It did,' said Jamie. 'I told you, I got in the way.'

'You must know who the other boys were. The ones who broke in,' said Roberts.

'They didn't break in. They banged on the door and when Barry opened it they rushed past him.'

'If you won't tell us who they are, we've only got your word for it that they existed,' Roberts said. He spoke quietly.

Kate stared at him. She could not believe what she was hearing.

Nor could Jamie.

'Barry wasn't going to trash his own house,' he said fiercely.

'There were two other boys in the house with you,' said Roberts. 'Friends of yours and Barry?'

'Yes. They'll tell you what happened,' said Jamie.

'Had any of you been doing drugs?'

'No – of course not. That's sick,' said Jamie.

'You say so. What about the others?' Roberts persisted. Jamie might have had a blood test at the hospital; if so, it would show whether he was drugged up or not.

'My son isn't a liar. Why don't you listen to him?' Kate was furious.

'Please don't interrupt, Mrs Preston,' Roberts said curtly.

'I tell you, we'd just had some pizzas and were watching the video,' said Jamie. 'Then these other guys arrived.'

'If you tell us who they are, then we can talk to them,' said Roberts.

Jamie wavered. Then he set his mouth in a determined line. The others would have told their tale by now.

'I can't,' he said.

Kate understood. She was a teacher. She knew the code.

'Jamie's been badly hurt and he's shocked,' she said. 'Let us go now and you can talk to him tomorrow, when he's had some rest. He's not fit for this,' she added, 'and I'll soon find a doctor to say so.'

She was wondering if they needed a solicitor. Surely not! When she had a chance to talk to Jamie, she'd find out what had really happened.

'Very well.' Roberts knew he had pushed it as it was, but either Jamie was involved or he knew who was. 'We'll run you back,' he said. Roberts had considered taking Jamie to the police station to be interviewed in depth, even to be charged, but he'd get bail as soon as a solicitor was called. Besides, the boy did look ill. Innocent or guilty, he would not be judged fit for questioning.

In the car, Kate pressed Jamie's hand, urging silence. He was only too keen to keep quiet, and she felt him quivering with nerves beside her. Tears came to her eyes. Jamie, wounded, was the victim of some thugs, and this rude, callous policeman did not believe him.

When they were back in Mickleburgh, Roberts wanted to follow them into the house, but Tracy Dale stopped him.

'We'll see you in the morning, James,' she said. 'Get some sleep.'

Kate got him up to bed, tucking him in with a hot water bottle and a milky drink. Should she try to get the story out of him now, while it was all fresh in his mind? Would his resolution to stay silent strengthen if she left it?

'I tried to get him off that man, Mum,' said Jamie.

Get who, she thought, but did not ask. It might emerge.

'Did you tell the police that?'

'Not really. They were telling me what happened, sort of. By the time I'd been stitched up, they'd decided.'

And tried to stitch you into it, thought Kate.

They'd sort it out in the morning. She wondered about telephoning the Noakeses, who might know what had really happened, but realised that their house would be full of policemen. She would leave it till later.

She hoped Jamie would sleep. The hospital had provided a sedative and he had washed it down with his drink. She didn't expect to sleep again herself, but she went back to bed, managing to doze from time to time, while images of the past, her brief marriage, and her own childhood, spent in the Devonshire countryside where knife attacks and muggings were, at that time – and on the whole, now – rare, kept flickering across her mind.

Progress, she thought. Internet and schoolboys armed with knives.

Who was the man who had died? No one had supplied a name.

Jamie, surrendering to exhaustion and the tablet he had taken, had time to think that if he had not gone to fetch the man, he would still be alive.

'You were a bit hard on that poor lad,' said Tracy Dale as she and Roberts drove away.

'If his hand didn't hold the knife, he knows whose did,' said Roberts, unmoved.

'He'll tell. His mother'll get it out of him, when he's had some sleep,' said Tracy.

'We should have got his knife,' said Roberts.

'He said it was in his jacket. He wasn't wearing one,' Tracy said. The hospital had sent him home wrapped in a blanket, which Kate was to return.

'Hm. Wonder why that was,' said Roberts.

'Because he dashed out of the house, as he said he did, to lend a hand to the man who was killed, of course,' said Tracy.

'He knows more than he's saying,' was Roberts' reply, and Tracy knew it was the truth.

'I expect he left the jacket at his friend's house. He wouldn't have been wearing it watching videos, would he?' she said.

6

Trevor lay in bed listening for his parents' return from their night out, his duvet, in its red and black cover, pulled up to his ears. He tried not to think about what had happened in Deerton. It hadn't been his idea to go there; he'd simply accepted the dare to take the car. It was Kevin who had started the rampage, though Wayne and Paul had soon joined in. They'd somehow caught the mood from one another.

It was Kevin who had pulled the knife.

Trevor had one, a large one with a serrated edge. It was in his school bag and he felt good, knowing it was there, just as he'd felt good tonight, driving off, showing the others what he could do.

That guy they'd gone for would be all right. Kevin hadn't hurt him badly, and it was his fault for interfering. Trevor had punched him, but he hadn't touched the second man, nor kicked either of them hard. He'd thrown some stuff around at Barry's house but he hadn't seriously wrecked the place, and he hadn't gone upstairs. He didn't know what had happened there; he was in the kitchen at the time. If they were caught, though, he'd be in as much trouble as the others – more, maybe, because of driving without a licence, and not insured.

Would Barry and his mates blab on them? What about that

kid, Jamie Preston, who'd gone running off, squealing for help? He'd been in the fight and seen it all, even though the others had gone back into the house. They all knew one another; there was no chance of not being recognised. What had started as a bit of a laugh had ended up as big trouble. Trevor had meant only to show off and get respect, but Kevin had gone crazy, and Paul had taken something, silly sod.

If they all kept quiet, if Jamie Preston shut his face, it might just go away. Trevor guessed that Kevin and Paul, and maybe Wayne, would sort Jamie Preston, go round to his place and scare him shitless. He'd get the message. Everyone knew they were hard men.

He couldn't get warm, and as for sleep, he'd never felt more wakeful in his life. Trevor's mind kept replaying scenes from the night's events. There were questions, too: where had that man come from, the one Kevin knifed? They were on their way out, chasing after Jamie – Kevin had yelled, 'Let's get him,' but Trevor did not want to remember that – when the man arrived. If he hadn't interfered, they'd have gone with no harm done except a bit of mess in the house, which Barry and his mates could soon clean up.

Like many guilty people, Trevor sought to appoint blame anywhere but where it belonged. Those two men had brought all this on themselves. They'd not poke their noses in again in a hurry.

Could anyone have taken down the number of the Lada? It had been parked beyond the turning, so it couldn't have been seen except by someone standing in the road. That thought consoled him, but there weren't too many Ladas about; he hoped no one had had a good look at it. He'd got it back and parked it in the exact spot where his mother always left it, and it was totally undamaged.

He was still awake when his parents returned. Neither of them touched the bonnet of the Lada, which might have been

still warm. They went up to bed, confident that he was in, for
his trainers, which he was not allowed to wear indoors, were
standing neatly in the hall.

*I heard about it on the news on Sunday morning, and felt a
frisson of recognition, then a thrill which I suppressed because,
undeniably, a wicked act had been committed. The radio report
was sketchy: a man had been killed in Deerton, stabbed to
death while trying to separate some brawling teenagers. A
second man had been attacked but had not needed hospital
treatment. A youth, slightly wounded in the struggle, was
helping police with their enquiries. No more details were
given in the broadcast.*

*I could imagine it: the strange ease with which the knife sank
in, the sudden feeling of elation. This boy's experience would
have been the same as mine, even though his action had not
been premeditated, but if he had not been prepared to use his
knife, why carry it? My crime was different: mine was planned,
but it had not brought the result I had expected and desired. It
had not beaten her; in the end, dying, she beat me.*

*This boy, the guilty one: he'll be scared. If caught and
charged, he may be too young to be named. Perhaps he
meant to use his knife to wield power, impress his friends.
Image has always been important to young people; that's
what much of commerce is about. Very few youngsters come
to me for counselling; I prefer them to go to specialists in
their particular problems, but their parents are among my
patients, desperate because they can't control or understand
their children. It's no wonder, when they won't take time to
listen to them.*

*I'm consulted about office power struggles and the sexual
tensions that develop. People spend more time with their work
colleagues than with their families, or 'loved ones', as it is the
vogue to call them.*

Often they are not loved at all.

This dead man, this victim, may have had some loved ones; we'll soon hear all too much about them. Maybe they'll be exhibited on television, weeping and appealing for 'someone who must know something' to disclose the killer's name. Perhaps those exposures do shame relatives or so-called friends to name suspects.

This boy must be taught that he can't go about stabbing people just for kicks. He must pay his debt to society, but when he emerges after whatever sentence he receives, will he be redeemed, or merely hardened, ready for a life of crime?

I've never done it again. There has been no need. Since my release, I've avoided close emotional encounters. I can live without them, and vicariously, through the lives of my patients, I experience many things. They tell me their most intimate fears and secrets, and reveal their cravings. I simply guide their reasoning until they devise ways of dealing with what is causing them to lead unhappy lives, damaging to themselves, if not to others. I am powerful.

Sensational murder cases interest me. I'm sometimes tempted to attend trials of particular appeal, but I never give in to this impulse. It could be morbid, have a bad effect on me. Most of the time, I don't think about it. I can almost say it is forgotten.

The four boys involved in the attack, scattering afterwards, had not arranged to meet next day. Sunday mornings were usually spent in bed, though Trevor was reasonably conscientious about his homework. All four would normally arrive downstairs in time for whatever meal was going. In Trevor's house it was conventional, a roast, eaten at around two o'clock. More flexible arrangements operated for the others.

This Sunday, all four woke early. Trevor contemplated contacting Wayne, who had been less involved in the attack on the men than Paul and Kevin. He wouldn't mind a chat about it. Wayne would soon say there was nothing to worry about; it was just a breeze and no harm done. If they hadn't gone to Deerton, they'd have done something else and he might have been persuaded to drive to Fettleton, or even further, where the police could have stopped them and then he'd have been in real trouble. After consuming a large bowl of cornflakes, he walked across the town to Wayne's house, only to find that he had already gone out.

He did not know that Daniel Stewart was dead. None of the four learned that until much later in the day.

Midge, sedated, had eventually fallen asleep in the Foxtons' spare bedroom. Oliver persuaded Sarah to return to bed, where she drowsed, the upstairs telephone turned off, while he, in his study, was ready to answer calls if Mark or Jonathan rang after hearing of their father's death. The police, who would break the news to each of them, had been asked to tell them that their mother was spending the night in Winbury. There was no more to be done at present. Oliver could not believe that this dreadful thing had happened less than two hours after he and Sarah had left Daniel and Midge. It seemed to have been established that hooligan boys were responsible for the murder. This was not an inner-city area where difficult living conditions and rival gangs exacerbated crime; it had happened in a quiet village where episodes of drunk and disorderly conduct and minor theft were the usual reported offences.

Despair filled him as he thought about this manifestation of current youthful mores, and he reminded himself that such incidents were isolated: one did not hear about the law-abiding youngsters who were not part of this aggressive culture. But example was a strong factor; children aped their elders and if discussion was turned into confrontation, as happened in public interviews, while newspaper reports described objectors to anything as 'hitting out' at whatever it was they took exception to, it was hardly surprising that the pattern was absorbed and followed. A peaceable man, Oliver knew that some things must be fought for; he would stop at nothing to protect Sarah and their children, and there were plenty of public issues on which he held strong views, but he deplored the cut and thrust of public argument which seemed to have replaced debate.

He sat down on the small stool he had placed in front of the dolls' house. The downstairs rooms and four of the bedrooms were almost finished now. He had found a tiny scrap of sample carpet for the stairs and he would use straightened paperclips for stair rods. The original dolls had been wrapped in a soft cloth, and this had protected them; perhaps they were a little grubby, but he was fond of them and did not want to replace them with modern replicas. Midge had christened them the Wilberforces – Mr and Mrs Wilberforce and their children, Joe, Phoebe and Maud. He smiled as he took them from the drawer where he kept them while he was working on the house. Carefully, he put the father and the mother doll in the sitting room, and Joe and Phoebe in their respective bedrooms. Maud's room was not quite ready yet. He looked at them: Daniel and Midge, he thought, and their children, except that one of the boys had turned into a girl. Sighing, he removed the father doll and replaced him in the drawer.

Playing like this, he felt a sudden chill. What would Sarah say if she caught him? Besides, his analogy was morbid. He bundled up the other dolls and stowed them away. Then he began trimming the carpet to size, but his thoughts returned to Daniel, his friend, whom he would miss.

The police would want to speak to Midge in the morning. They hadn't really questioned her properly yet, but there was little she could tell them as she had arrived in the close after the boys had fled, and Daniel was already dead. They had had no chance to say goodbye, he thought. The post mortem was probably in progress now, but it might have been delayed until the morning as there was no real doubt about the cause of death. The inquest was likely to be opened on Monday or Tuesday but no funeral plans could be made because the defence, when someone was accused of being responsible, was entitled to a second post mortem. Poor Daniel, subjected to this indignity.

Unaware of Jamie Preston's role in the night's events, Oliver reflected that the rampage in Orchard Close must have been noisy to have woken the Stewarts, but their house was only just across the road. Midge might not be able to remain there. Oliver wondered what sort of insurance Daniel had carried; just enough to clear the mortgage, he suspected.

He went to the window and drew the curtains back. It was still dark, but dawn was not far off. Down there, beyond the garden, was the river. It was quiet in the house; he hoped the two women were asleep. Sarah had been splendid when he brought Midge home; she had not been over-fussy, nor sentimental. She'd given Midge a hug – a brisk one, not an all-enfolding one, but still a hug – and said, 'I'm so sad for you. Poor Midge,' which was just right. Then she'd bundled her upstairs and Midge had gone obediently while Sarah told her, 'You'll have things to do in the morning – horrid business things, and Mark and Jonathan will be arriving. You must get some rest. You won't want to make it harder for them.'

No, she wouldn't, and Sarah wouldn't let her. Midge, who still felt numb and stunned, allowed herself to be taken care of, just as if she were a child. There would be plenty of time to think about it all when she had to do so.

Two detectives in plain clothes, and driving an unmarked car, called at Kate's house at nine o'clock on Sunday morning. They had come to take Jamie, who was in the kitchen toying with some breakfast, to the police station for questioning. Kate must come too, they said, and they wanted Jamie's clothes from the night before. Silently, Kate found them and they dropped the garments into plastic bags which they sealed and labelled.

'We'll give you a receipt,' said Detective Sergeant Shaw. 'Where's his coat, then?'

'I don't know,' said Kate. 'And he didn't stab that man. He told those other officers, last night. He only had a penknife and he said it was in his jacket.'

'My jacket's at Barry's,' Jamie said. 'I rushed out without it when—' He was going to say 'when I went to fetch the man', but he didn't want to mention that.

'When what?' encouraged Shaw.

'When it all started,' Jamie said. 'When they trashed the place.'

'Want to tell us about it?' tried Detective Constable Benton, but Jamie shook his head.

'Hasn't Barry Noakes told you what happened?' Kate asked. These two were very different from the uniformed pair who had brought them back from the hospital the night before; the man had been a bastard, intent on bullying Jamie and pinning the blame on him.

'Not so far,' said Shaw, a stocky man with very short red hair. 'He's keeping stumm, like young Jamie here.'

Kate sighed. Jamie was frightened, and small wonder, but if Barry had said something, he would have opened up, she felt. She'd rung the Noakeses' house that morning, before Jamie woke, but could get only the engaged signal. She told Shaw, who said the receiver must have been taken off the hook.

'They aren't there,' he said. 'They're at a neighbour's house. Our forensic people have been going over it for evidence, and the Noakeses won't be let back till that's done. And then the clearing up will be quite a business, I can tell you.'

'Maybe Jamie's jacket's been found, then,' said Kate. 'And his knife. It won't have blood on it, I can tell you.'

Kevin and Wayne, passing Jamie's house, saw him and his

mother leaving in a car with two men who had to be policemen. Was he going to take the rap for what had happened, or would he split on them? And if he did, would he be believed? Everyone knew the police got things wrong and once they'd made their minds up, wouldn't shift.

Seeing him watching them from the car's rear window, they gestured threateningly.

7

On Sundays Rosemary Ellis went to church. This was habit, based not on conviction, nor on duty. It gave shape to her week and she liked to sit, respectably clad as ever, in a pew near the rear, where she would be inconspicuous and safe. Life had not always been safe. She had known fear and passion, but she wanted no more of either and so she sought to live at a distance from emotion.

It was a bright, cold day. After the long dry summer, when the trees had borne parched leaves which looked as though they would soon drop, at last rain had fallen and the autumnal colours glowed. Rosemary, letting the words of the service wash over her, contemplated driving into the country in the afternoon. Most historic houses open to the public were now closed until the following spring; she often visited such places at weekends and would imagine living in a mansion, one well endowed, with no need to entice paying visitors to troop round. She would cast herself back in time and become a wealthy Victorian matriarch or early feminist who had inherited these acres and this fine building. Servants, in these images, flitted past: maids in white caps and aprons, maybe a dignified butler with side-whiskers. It was a secure life, free from financial, emotional and physical anxiety. No one, in these dreams, died untimely of illnesses then fatal but now curable; no one starved or froze to death; no one went off to any war.

Sometimes, in these fantasies, the vague figure of Oliver Foxton hovered; he seemed so benign and reassuring, appropriate in such a setting, never a disturber of the peace she had designed. She did not picture an intimate encounter; everything was at a remove, as a pop star or a sporting hero or an actor might be idolised. Surrounding herself with phantom company did no harm and had no effect on her efficiency for she yielded to it only rarely, when she gave herself permission.

In church this morning, though, her musings were interrupted when shocking news was given of the local murder in the night. Some people, and she was one of them, had already heard it on the radio, but now it was brought closer as the vicar prayed for those affected: the bereaved family, and others who were concerned.

'Sadly, it seems evident that juveniles from the community were involved,' he said.

Rosemary joined sincerely in the prayers.

Jonathan Stewart, arriving in Deerton in his elderly Escort, had had to explain who he was before he was allowed to enter, for the area around Orchard Close was cordoned off and police officers were painstakingly examining the ground. With horror, he realised that they were searching for evidence connected with his father's death. The knowledge sickened him, and bile rose in his throat as he drove slowly through the gates and parked his car. He had often been alone here when his parents were out or away, but they had always returned, still solidly affectionate towards each other, partners in a successful marriage. Now all that was over. His poor mother! How must she be feeling? Jonathan himself felt dreadful and in dire need of comfort. He reminded himself that he must be the comforter now, at least until Mark arrived when they could share the task.

His mother might return from the Foxtons' at any minute. He'd tidy the place up a bit, light the fire, put the kettle on. First, he went upstairs to his own room which was heavily adorned with a variety of posters. His school trophies were arranged on shelves his father had put up. He flung down the bag into which he had thrown his razor and a few other things; he'd manage otherwise with what was here. His parents' bedroom door was open, and though the curtains were still drawn, he saw the unmade bed, his mother's nightdress and his father's pyjamas cast aside where they had shed them last night. The sight brought tears to his eyes. He went into the room, pulled back the curtains, and made the bed, tucking his mother's nightdress under the pillow on her side. Not knowing what else to do with them, he put his father's faded green Marks and Spencer pyjamas in the laundry basket. Still in the bathroom, he looked at his father's shaving tackle and toothbrush, and the aftershave he used, all on their usual shelf. Should he get rid of them before his mother returned? Would seeing them upset her?

Throwing them away would upset him; that was certain. Jonathan closed the door upon his dilemma and went downstairs. He'd ring Oliver, let him know he'd arrived.

On the telephone, Oliver spoke calmly, telling him that Midge was still asleep but that she would have to be woken as soon as the police wanted to talk to her. Detective Superintendent Fisher, who was in charge of the investigation, had already rung him and had agreed to come to Orchard House at half-past nine. He had told Oliver that the police had so far found no trace of the car in which the boys had driven off.

'Have some breakfast,' Oliver advised. He knew from experience that if you went without sleep, you could not function adequately if you also fasted, and pouring out cornflakes or making toast or whatever Jonathan might do now

would provide him with an occupation and distract him from
the police activity which must be going on outside the house.

He explained that Sarah was already on her way to meet
Mark at Heathrow and would bring him straight to Deerton.
Then he went to see if Midge was stirring. Though asleep, she
sensed his presence in the room and opened her eyes.

'Oh, Oliver,' she said, blinking at him drowsily, still affected
by the sedative. 'So it wasn't all a hideous nightmare, then.'

'I'm afraid not, Midge,' Oliver replied. He picked up the
dressing-gown which Sarah had left for her. Sarah thought
of everything. 'Jonathan's rung,' he said. 'He's at the house,
having breakfast. I expect you'd like to get there pretty quickly,
wouldn't you?'

Most of all, Midge wanted to burst into tears and be
comforted by Oliver, who reminded her of a gentle bear, with
his broad build and short button nose. She looked sadly up at
him. His once brown hair was turning white. A grey bear, she
thought. She mustn't give way now, though, if ever; Jonathan
needed her, and soon Mark would be arriving home. Home.
Home without Daniel, but still their home.

Oliver could see confusion on her face and he felt like
wrapping his arms round her and holding her close to comfort
her, but it wouldn't do to get emotional. Midge could do that
later, with her sons.

'There's coffee on,' he said. 'I'll make some toast. You must
have something.'

'Can I have a bath?' asked Midge.

'Of course. I'll ring Jonathan and say that's what you're
doing, and to expect us in under the hour,' said Oliver.

'Oh, thank you, Oliver,' Midge said. 'If I talk to him, I'll
only start to cry and that will upset him.'

No doubt it was the truth.

'I'll turn the water on,' said Oliver, and he did so, pouring
in some of Sarah's bath oil.

He delayed making the call until Midge had been in the bathroom for a few minutes, and Jonathan's voice now sounded steadier. He said he had opened the windows and aired the house, and that the police were crawling about on hands and knees in the garden near the road, and opposite.

That must mean they hadn't found the weapon yet. It might have been thrown over the stone wall which fenced off the Stewarts' garden from the road. It could be anywhere. Young lads rampaging wouldn't be thinking about fingerprints and might have left some in the house they had wrecked. Eventually there would be a line to follow; a neighbour might have identified the car they used. One or more of the boys would, in time, supply names, when they knew that Daniel was dead. The wounded lad had been aware of that, last night, but the police seemed to think that he could have been responsible. If so, the weapon, when discovered, might confirm his guilt.

Midge wouldn't be much help to the police. She hadn't seen a thing.

Kate said, 'Jamie, you must know who was involved in this. You must know who those boys are.'

They were alone in an interview room at Fettleton police station, given a final chance to sort this out between them.

'I can't say,' Jamie insisted. He didn't add, they'll kill me if I do, but he had seen Kevin and Wayne earlier, gesturing as he was driven off. Jamie's mother, who would have recognised them, had not noticed them. They could take revenge on her, if not on him. He'd tell if all the others did: not on his own. He needed to talk to them but how could he, shut up here at the police station?

'Jamie, a man who came to break the fight up was killed,' said Kate. 'This is very serious. You must tell what you know.' She did not add, if you don't, you may be blamed. Surely the police couldn't really suspect him? It was only their alarming way of trying to make him to tell them what he knew.

He did not answer, and she told herself to keep calm. There would be fingerprints on the murder weapon, when they found it, and Jamie's penknife would be in his fleece jacket, as he'd said. Their detective powers must have led them to that, in the Noakeses' house. Barry would have described what had happened; with his parents there, he would have told the truth.

Mother and son both had a sense of unreality, and Kate, who loved him, wanted to shake Jamie to rid him of his stubbornness. The stalemate was broken when DS Shaw and DC Benton returned to see what headway had been made. But they could get no further though they questioned Jamie patiently. He related how the marauding boys had entered the house and begun throwing things around, milk and stores from the cupboard, and he told how two had gone upstairs and started on the bedroom. He even said what one of them had done there, mentioning no name, and that he had followed because he was trying to stop them. But he would not say who they were.

Kate said, despairingly, 'He doesn't want to tell on schoolmates. That's it, isn't it, Jamie?'

'Sort of,' he said, studying the table top in front of him.

Kate saw that they would get no further now. She asked to speak privately to Shaw, who left the room with her while Benton stayed with Jamie.

'You don't really think Jamie stabbed that poor man, do you?' she asked Shaw, who didn't, but there was no other suspect. 'Surely Barry has given some information by this time?'

'Not so far. They're all banding together. As you've said, kids do,' said Shaw. 'It's early yet. The man hasn't even been dead twelve hours. One of them will crack, or we'll get a lead from something the forensic chaps dig up. The boy whose father came to help may weaken. His dad was winded and he's cracked a rib or two, though he said last night he was just bruised. He was kicked in the genitals, as well. That was what laid him out, I expect. But two grown men can't beat four lads armed with knives.'

Shaw knew that Jamie's penknife had been found inside his jacket, with nothing more incriminating on it than traces of pencil sharpening, and the blade that had killed Daniel Stewart was a long slim one; however, a lad could carry two knives, and if Jamie had another it might have been turned upon himself, but he was not one of the vandals; that had been established. As far as Shaw was concerned, Jamie was in the clear, although he had said nothing to prove that he had not been somehow responsible, however accidentally, for the killing.

'We'll talk to Barry's other friends,' said Shaw. 'And we're questioning all the neighbours, but so far nothing useful has come up. It doesn't seem to have been a noisy incident. They'd all got their tellies on, and such. Gate-crashing parties often happens, and that's when alcohol gets brought in. There were empty beer cans in the house and I don't think Barry and his friends were responsible for them. There will be prints on the cans and the innocent boys can be eliminated. Unless they moved the cans, clearing up, or trying to. Barry and his mates had begun that before we got there.'

'The other man – the one who came to help – he may have seen some of them,' Kate said.

'We'll hope so,' Shaw replied. 'But he's said they all had baseball caps on, and it was dark, with no street lighting. By the time he got there they were already in a sort of scrum.'

'And no one lost his cap?'

'Maybe he did, but as far as I know, it hasn't been found,' said Shaw. 'We'll be talking to the man again. Someone may be with him now. And Superintendent Fisher is meeting Mrs

Stewart this morning. Not that she'll have seen them. She arrived when it was all over, poor soul.'

'Just as well,' said Kate flatly.

She felt better after this conversation, but not much. Weren't you supposed to be innocent until proved guilty? That constable the night before had, she thought, been on the point of charging Jamie.

Rosemary learned who the suspect was from Bob and Ginny. They were about to set off on their bicycles when she returned from church. Both were keen cyclists and on fine weekends went for long rides into the country, stopping for lunch at various pubs. They were late leaving today, delayed by the dreadful news, as several other teachers, hearing what had happened and that some of their pupils had been involved, had been on the telephone. Wearing fluorescent jackets, they were pumping up their tyres when she walked across the yard.

'Good morning,' she said, formally. 'Off to the country, then?'

'Yes,' said Bob. 'We're later than we meant to be. You've heard what happened in Deerton last night?'

'Yes. It was mentioned in church,' said Rosemary. 'I believe the victim was trying to separate some fighting boys.'

The congregation, leaving church, had been discussing nothing else.

'Yes – and someone thinks they've arrested Jamie Preston,' said Ginny. 'You met his mother at our party. Kate. Very small, with short dark hair.'

'Oh, surely not?' Rosemary could not believe that the pleasant, gangling boy she had seen in the bookshop had been an aggressor in a brawl.

'He can't have done it,' Bob said. 'It's not possible, or if he did, it was a complete accident. I'm not sure he's really been arrested,' he added. 'But he was involved and he's been taken

in for questioning.' Hearing this rumour, they had telephoned
Kate but got no reply; then they had rung up one of her
neighbours whom they knew, who had seen two men who
looked as if they could be CID officers in plain clothes driving
off with Kate and Jamie.

'Oh dear,' said Rosemary. 'I'm sorry.'

She hurried into her flat, and Bob and Ginny, who had
wondered whether to cancel their outing in case Kate needed
help, went on their way. If Kate was not at home, they could
do nothing for her. They had made sure their answerphone was
on. If Jamie was charged, they would soon hear about it.

Prudence Wilmot had also heard the news and was shocked
and saddened. She had met the Stewarts briefly at the Foxtons'
when they had a summer party, and she had had some pictures
framed by Midge. She would send flowers to her tomorrow:
flowers for the living; she never sent flowers to funerals.

Depressed, she had two dry sherries before her Sunday
lunch instead of the usual single one. Then she cooked her
solitary chop.

8

Barry Noakes's parents, returning from their wedding party, were astonished when they were confronted by a police road block outside Deerton. Guilty calculations about how much he had drunk sprang into Cliff's head, and he expected to be breathalysed. However, when they had supplied their names, they were allowed to pass, and one of the officers on duty spoke into his radio. They were stopped again outside the close, which was cordoned off, and a uniformed officer came towards them.

'What's going on? What's happened? It's Barry – is he all right?' Frightened now, Lily Noakes, a pretty woman with rich copper-coloured hair, who had once won a beauty contest and maintained her glamour, sprang from the car, subconsciously aware that no fire engine nor ambulance was visible and that her house still stood.

'He's all right,' the constable assured her. 'But there's been trouble here. Barry's with a neighbour.'

'But—?' What about Jamie Preston? He was supposed to be staying over. A primeval cautious instinct stopped her asking more questions. Barry was safe, but something serious had happened here to account for the police presence. She could see that the place was swarming with uniformed officers, and the one who had spoken to her was now talking on his radio.

He turned to her.

'Detective Superintendent Fisher will be with you in a minute or two,' he said. 'He'll put you in the picture,' and soon a tall thin man whose pale grey suit hung loosely around his angular frame came towards them.

'What's going on?' Cliff was now as alarmed as his wife. 'Where's our boy?'

Fisher took them into their own house, where the forensic scientists had finished examining the sitting room. He would not let them go further.

'I'm sorry – you can see what's happened here,' he said, as Lily gasped and put a hand to her mouth. Her prized neat room was wrecked, and precious ornaments were missing. Barry and Jamie had never done this. 'I'm afraid the rest of the house is in a worse state,' said Fisher. 'Your boy and the friends he had visiting cleared up a bit in here before we arrived.' He told them that a group of young vandals, bent on trouble, had invaded their house, and that two local men had intervened and been attacked. 'There was a fight in the road. One of the men was stabbed,' he said. 'I'm sorry to say he died.'

'Jesus!' Cliff exclaimed.

'Who were they? Who was it died?' asked Lily in a whisper. She felt dizzy with shock.

Fisher related what was known: that Daniel Stewart had been killed, and Ted Grant slightly injured. 'One of the boys was stabbed, too,' he said. 'Jamie Preston. He was stopping over with Barry, I believe.'

'That's right. Oh dear! Does Kate know? Jamie's mother?' Lily asked.

'Yes. She's with him at the hospital. It's not serious,' said Fisher.

The man looked ill himself, thought Lily inconsequentially.

His face was pale and there were deep hollows under his eyes, but Neil Fisher had looked like this for years and was perfectly fit.

'Who did it? Who were these boys?' Cliff Noakes demanded.

'I wish we knew,' said Fisher. 'Barry isn't saying, but we can't interview him properly without you. None of the others will tell us anything. Perhaps they'll change their minds by morning. I certainly hope so.'

'But Mr Stewart! Oh, that's terrible,' said Lily. Poor Mrs Stewart, she was thinking: such a nice woman. At least she had those two sons; she wouldn't be on her own, poor soul. 'And Ted's all right?' she asked. 'Is he in hospital?'

'No. He wouldn't go, but I think he'll see the doctor today,' said Fisher. Ted Grant had admitted that his ribs were very sore; evidence of his injuries would be needed for the prosecution when whoever did this was in court.

'He was a good bloke, Mr Stewart was,' said Cliff, who was a plumber. He had done work for the Stewarts and was always paid on time. Some customers who lived in larger houses, with a grander life style, often kept him waiting.

Fisher had now been joined by a woman officer whom Fisher introduced as Detective Inspector Flower. Her colleagues called her Poppy and the pair, who frequently worked together, were known irreverently as the two Fs.

'We've found various sets of fingerprints,' she said. 'Barry and his friends, and you, of course, can be eliminated when we have all your prints for comparison. There were at least nine sets in the house and some of them will be alien.'

Alien prints. It sounded as if the place had been invaded by monsters from outer space.

'I want to see Barry,' said Lily. It seemed he'd had several friends round. She'd wondered about leaving him for so long on his own with only Jamie Preston for company, but she and Cliff were coming home, after all – here they were –

and the house wasn't isolated. Kate Preston hadn't seemed concerned.

'Of course, but he may be asleep by this time,' Poppy Flower said.

'When did all this happen?' asked Cliff Noakes.

'Before midnight. We got the call about ten to,' said Poppy. 'I don't know how long the lads were here. Barry and his friends weren't certain. They'd been watching videos.'

'Why did no one help them? she asked.

'They did. Mr Stewart and Mr Grant,' said Poppy. 'The fight was all over very quickly, Mr Grant said. The four boys ran off after he and Mr Stewart were hurt. By that time, several other people had come out to see what was happening. Three of the boys were quite large, they said, and one was smaller.'

'They left in a car,' said Fisher. 'Unfortunately no one saw what make it was, nor got the number.'

'Then they weren't from Deerton,' Lily said.

'It seems unlikely.'

'We'll talk to Barry. We'll see what he can tell us,' Cliff promised.

'They don't like what they see as telling tales, Mr Noakes,' said Poppy. 'That's the trouble. None of them's wanting to drop a mate in it.'

'Funny sort of mates, doing all this and killing someone,' Lily said. She was almost in tears, just holding on wondering what other damage had been done to the house. She could hear the forensic scientists moving around upstairs.

'Why do they do it?' Cliff wanted to know. 'Carry knives and that.'

'I wish I could answer you,' said Fisher. 'They think it's macho. They catch a sort of fever from one another and make each other worse.'

'Were they on drugs?' asked Lily.

'It's possible. Not necessarily,' said Fisher, thinking of the beer cans. 'More probably it's lads with too much time and energy and not enough to do, looking for excitement or making their own on a Saturday night. Maybe they were looking for a party to gatecrash and couldn't find one, so they hit on coming here.'

'Lads' stuff, eh?' said Cliff. 'No girls. Pathetic.'

'That lot probably can't make it with girls,' said Poppy. 'It's why they do this sort of thing. After all, the girls can choose, and decent girls aren't going to want to have much to do with lads who go in for rampaging.'

'It's sad,' said Lily, though she hoped Barry would leave girls until later.

Cliff and Lily got nowhere with Barry that night; he was still awake when they went round to the Grants to talk to him and kept saying he was sorry that he couldn't prevent the damage being done, but his real concern was for Jamie.

'He was trying to help the men,' he said. 'He was alone out there with Peter's dad and Mr Stewart. Only I didn't know then that it was Mr Stewart.' In the end they'd all left Jamie on his own.

Fisher had been listening to the conversation and had prompted its direction with an occasional question. At least he had now learned that Jamie Preston had been trying to help the men.

Barry might reveal more when he made an official statement later on, but it was a pity he hadn't told them that before. Not that Fisher was suspecting Jamie of being the perpetrator, however accidentally, but others did. Fisher, however, was the boss.

After Trevor dropped them off the night before, the other boys had separated, going to their own homes. Paul, still on a high, took some time to come down and then he told himself that he was safe. He hadn't stabbed that man; it was Kevin. Anyway, the old git was probably back home again by now; he couldn't have been badly hurt. Besides, it was his own fault. It would show him what was what, who was in charge, that Paul and Kevin and their mates weren't going to stand for being messed about. Kevin had a bit of a temper when he got excited, and he had had a knife. Paul had one too, but it was in his school bag, in case it might be needed. They must all just carry on as normal.

He felt better still when he heard from Wayne that he and Kevin had seen Jamie Preston being taken off for questioning. Wayne had come round to see him after parting from Kevin and he'd found Paul up surprisingly early for a Sunday morning, sitting in the kitchen with his headphones on, eating a thick piece of toast spread with jam and butter. They'd gone straight out into the back yard to talk. Kevin had said they'd better keep away from Trevor for the moment, since he'd been the driver. He wouldn't tell on them if he was caught, nor would they dob him in, and Jamie had better keep his mouth shut or they would shut it for him.

It was not until after midday that they learned that, between them, they were responsible for a man's death.

When Oliver took Midge home, he hung back while she went into the house and was embraced by Jonathan. The police had waved them past their cordon as soon as Oliver had told them who his passenger was, and identified himself.

The kettle was simmering on the Aga, and although she had only just had coffee at The Barn House, after their long hug and subdued murmurings, Midge, inconsolable, accepted more, and mother and son busied themselves with brewing it and pouring.

Only a few short hours ago, he and Midge had made coffee here together, Oliver recalled. He wondered whether to fade away and leave them on their own, but soon Sarah would arrive with Mark, and Superintendent Fisher was almost due. He could be useful, and it was soon clear that Midge and Jonathan needed him. Neither knew how to comfort the other and wanted to postpone the moment when they must.

'There'll be things to do. The police, you said.' Jonathan looked at him in desperation as they sat round the kitchen table.

'Yes. They'll want to know how Daniel got involved. I suppose you heard the racket those boys were making?' Oliver turned to Midge with the question.

'No. We didn't. We were asleep,' she said. After making love, a quick, tender session because both of them were tired. They would never do that again. It was over. Tears suddenly rolled down her face, and Jonathan clasped her while Oliver pulled tissues from a box on the dresser.

'Why did he go out, then?' Jonathan asked, when she was calmer. 'If it wasn't because of the noise?'

'Someone banged on the door and rang the bell. A boy. He wanted help,' said Midge. 'Dan put some clothes on and followed him over the road and I rang the police. I didn't follow straight away.' After saying this, more tears fell. Had she gone over sooner, she might have been with Daniel when he died, perhaps even, she thought unrealistically, have managed to save him.

When Fisher arrived, with Detective Inspector Flower, Oliver had to remind her to tell them about the boy who had come to the house. She couldn't describe him as she hadn't seen him, but Dan had said he had a bloody nose.

Fisher was gentle with her, and she had little to add to what they already knew.

'Did you see the lads drive away?' he asked.

'No. I heard the car roar off,' she said. It had been driven towards the centre of the village, where the road looped round and joined crossroads; it was not possible to say where it was heading.

'What about the boy who fetched your husband? Did he go with them?'

'No, he couldn't have. He wasn't part of the gang – he came for help,' said Midge. 'A boy got hurt. He went in the ambulance.' With Dan. She hadn't even shared that last ride with him. 'All the boys had vanished when I got there, and then this boy came out of one of the houses. He had a towel round his arm. I didn't know him. Another boy was with him – it might have been the Grant boy. His father tried to help Dan.'

All this was helpful in that it let young Jamie Preston off any hook PC Roberts had attempted to impale him on, but it brought them no nearer tracking down the guilty group. Poppy Flower had made notes of their conversation. To spare Midge, she said she would get them typed up and bring them out for Midge to read and sign. They were not going to make her go to Fettleton police station: not yet, at least.

The two officers had just left when Sarah arrived with Mark. She had food in the car, a cool box containing a pack full of chicken casserole, complete with vegetables, for the Stewarts' lunch. She knew Midge would have nothing suitable in her ill-stocked freezer, and those poor boys must be fed.

Oliver watched her proudly as she decanted the block and put it in a saucepan on the top of the stove, where it could begin to thaw. She put some other smaller packs in the freezer, so that they had more prepared food to fall back on. She was so capable, and she thought of everything in times of crisis, as was being proved at this moment, Oliver reflected. It was just as well that she was emotionally cool during this dreadful time when even he felt like weeping.

'We'd better leave you to it,' he told the family. 'We'll come back later if you want us. We'll ring up.'

'We will want you,' said Mark, a dark, stocky young man. He tried to smile. 'Thank you both so much,' he said.

On the short flight, he had had time to gain some control, and Sarah, at the airport, had been brisk and businesslike, giving him a hug and immediately telling him that his mother was all right and had had some sleep, and that Jonathan had arrived.

In the car, driving back, she told him what she knew.

'It must all have been very quick,' she said. 'I mean, there wasn't really time for Dan to know what was happening. He was stabbed and that was it.' But he had been kicked and punched. Oliver had told her that his injuries had been horrific. There was no need, however, for Mark to hear this now, even if he had to later.

'I'd like to kill whoever did it,' Mark said fiercely. 'Dad never harmed a soul.'

'No.' He was a bit of a wimp, Sarah had sometimes thought, but he hadn't been wimpish at the end. 'He was very brave,' she said. 'Going to the rescue.'

'Yes, but boys! You don't expect kids in Deerton to turn on you with a knife if you go to sort them out, do you?' said Mark.

'No. It's shocking,' Sarah said.

They had driven on in silence. What else was there to say?

9

From Deerton, Detective Superintendent Fisher went to see the Prestons while Poppy Flower dealt with Midge's informal statement. Kate, not long back from Fettleton police station herself, had begun cooking spaghetti bolognese for lunch.

Fisher introduced himself, producing his warrant card. So this was the man in charge, thought Kate; what now?

'I'd like a brief word with you and Jamie, if you don't mind,' he said, and added, seeing the despairing expression on her face, 'Don't worry. I suspect young Jamie's really quite the hero, if only he wasn't also such a clam.'

As he followed Kate into the sitting room, he caught a whiff of an enticing smell coming from the kitchen and it reminded him that he had had no breakfast. Jamie was half watching an old film on television. He started to get to his feet but Fisher told him to sit down again and asked after his arm.

'It's OK,' said Jamie.

Kate had sped out to turn down the gas, and Fisher waited till she returned before he said, 'Why didn't you say it was you who went to get help from Mr Stewart?' Peter Grant's father had now confirmed that Jamie had been trying to drag the attacking boys off the two men.

'No one asked me,' Jamie said. 'And if I hadn't, he wouldn't have been killed.'

Oh, poor Jamie, Kate thought: he was blaming himself for Daniel Stewart's death.

'Hm. Well, I don't think anyone else sees it quite like that, Jamie,' said Fisher. 'You weren't to know those lads had knives, were you?'

'S'pose not,' said Jamie.

'I'd imagine you'd want whoever did it to be punished,' Fisher suggested.

'Yeah,' said Jamie.

'So why won't you tell us who it was?'

No reply.

'It's because you don't want to drop your friends in it, isn't it?' said Fisher.

'They're not my friends,' Jamie growled.

'But you still won't name them?'

Jamie shook his head.

'If only you'd change your mind, you'd save us hours of work,' Fisher told him. 'We'll get them in the end.' He turned to Kate. 'Mrs Stewart told us that a boy came to the house asking for help, but she didn't see him. Her husband, though, said he had a bloody nose. Your nose bled last night, didn't it, Jamie? You got a punch on it. What a pity we didn't find this out sooner.'

Kate thought so, too. Immense relief flooded over her and she beamed at this bearer of good news, whilst wanting to shake Jamie for his folly and praise him for his valour.

Unable to persuade Jamie to say more, Fisher left, to try to piece together what information they had so far managed to retrieve.

Jamie, the prospect of arrest retreating, found he had an appetite.

'Smells good, Mum,' he said eagerly, as the door closed behind the departing officer.

The copper had said they'd get Kevin in the end. His nerve might fail, or Paul's. But they were iron men who wouldn't weaken easily. If he had told, they'd have found out and goodness knows what revenge they'd take, or get their mates to take. He had to protect his mother. His father's last instruction before he left to fight in the Gulf War, where he was killed, had been to look after her.

I went to church today. I got into the habit of attending services in prison. It looked good to the board of visitors and to the staff, and it helped to pass the time tranquilly, away from conflict, though most of the women inside revered me for the magnitude of my offence. Sometimes I'd talk to them about him – usually the younger ones – telling them about our hours together. I invented most of it, culling the romantic details from books and magazines which described all the things we might have done, but didn't. They believed everything. People will, if you speak with conviction. If the truth were known, we'd had so few times together. He was always afraid of being caught, but I grew skilled at tempting him when we had a chance, if she was out somewhere with the children. I needed only to touch him on a certain spot, on the back of his neck just below the hairline; an erogenous zone, it was – I learned that term later. It was amazing how fast I learned. I hadn't had another lover – something that astounded him and he said (but insincerely, as I discovered) made me mean so much to him. It all came naturally to me. I've never had a male lover since; it makes one much too vulnerable. Instead, I watch people, and I use power, carefully and selectively applied.

That woman – the new widow. There will be pictures of her in the morning papers. I expect she'll look pathetic – well, you would, after such an experience. I wonder if she's well insured. There are two adult sons, it seems, so she won't be alone.

His children will be long grown up by now. Sometimes I wonder about them. It was a late summer's day when it happened, the leaves still thick on the trees. Someone – a walker – had seen two figures walking in the woods. I had thought us quite alone. My shoes had mud on them but that proved nothing, as my counsel said; it could have come from anywhere at any time. She'd bled more than I expected. I'd read that if you struck a certain spot, in the back, the lungs would bleed internally. They said I stabbed her fifteen times. I don't remember that, so perhaps my mind really was disturbed, as I maintained to minimise my sentence. That was how the blood got on my clothes. I washed them, but it didn't all come out. It was long ago, before DNA testing was developed, and they could prove only that stains on my jacket, which I tried to burn, might have come from her. I didn't succeed in burning it completely, and the police found fragments in the grate at my bedsit.

He was in a dreadful state after she was discovered. He wouldn't let me near him to comfort him, though I went round to see the children. I used to like children: some children. I don't know what made the police suspect me. Maybe it was footmarks. It had rained recently and they made casts and matched them to my shoes. I'd worn heavy ones, suitable for walking. It wasn't wet enough for boots. Then letters were found. He'd kept notes I'd written him. You'd have expected him to get rid of them to protect me, but he didn't. He said I'd had a crush on him and pestered him, not confessing, for a long time, that we were lovers. The police took days to get him to admit that, and only succeeded after I kept insisting that it was true. I was proud of it. He'd wanted me, found me utterly desirable. He'd said so. He'd said she hadn't wanted sex for years, and that turned out to be a lie. What a two-faced bastard he turned out to be. I was glad I'd wrecked his life, because he had deceived me and destroyed mine.

It's hardened me. You don't survive so many years in prison without becoming tough and learning strategies to minimise the hardship. I took courses, passed exams, got in with a few women of a better type than the tarts and drug users. I had a woman lover for a while. She admired me because I was so strong. In the end I broke with her; she was too feeble, too demanding, and sex was not what I needed.

Before I found out he was dead, I used to think of tracing him, confronting him, seeing how he would react, but as he'd gone half across the world it seemed pointless. I'd expose myself, my past would be revealed and the respect I've earned through the effective practice of my work would be forfeit.

Inside, I learned the value of routine, and now I live my life by regulation. Up at seven o'clock, ten minutes' exercise to clear my mind, then fruit and muesli for breakfast, taken with herbal tea; caffeine is so bad for one, though I do enjoy a cup of coffee as a treat. I keep those hours even when I have no early consultation and need not hurry to leave my flat. My parents blamed themselves for what they called my fall from grace; they'd brought me up strictly and I'd done well at school, but I hadn't gone to college. Tertiary education was less universal then. I'd had various jobs and was working as a temporary secretary at the primary school where his children went when we met. It was a part-time post and so I could meet him when he snatched time off from his office. He worked locally. I was waiting to take up a purser's job aboard a cruise ship. It semed a good way to travel and capable women could do well, working for a shipping line.

I might have done it later, after my release, but by then I knew that I could no longer live close to other people, in a crowd. I needed space. I followed various other career lines

*before I chose to set up on my own as a counsellor, a decision
I have never had occasion to regret.*

'I didn't realise we had gang warfare in this area,' Sarah said
on Sunday evening. The whole episode had jolted her out of
kilter. So swiftly could death come, in hidden guise, in the
shape of a lad who had not, that morning, planned that by
nightfall he would be a killer. She could not explain her inner
panic to Oliver; all she could express was shock, and pity for
the Stewarts.

'On this scale, there isn't too much of it,' said Oliver.
'Gangs, yes, and punch-ups, and muggings, too. But not
a lot of this.' He wanted to reassure her, but these were
facts. 'Boys have attacked men who've tried to break up
their hooliganism. That's not uncommon, and people have
been injured. We don't hear about those incidents unless we
know someone who's involved.'

'It's dreadful.' Sarah did not like to think about violent
conduct. Suddenly her world seemed unsafe.

'Things have changed,' said Oliver. 'Some youngsters don't
learn to respect anything, these days.'

'And none of those boys will talk? None of the decent
boys?'

'Seems not. It's still early days. One will crack, or the
culprits' parents will get suspicious.'

'Would a parent turn them in?'

'Who knows? It would be a difficult decision,' Oliver said.

'What's going to happen to poor Midge? Will she have to
sell the house?'

'I don't know. I haven't got Dan's will. I hope he made
one,' said Oliver. 'They'll have to have a hunt through all his
papers.'

'And the funeral? When will that be? Next week some
time?'

'Most unlikely,' said Oliver. 'The coroner will adjourn the inquest, even if by then someone's been charged, while the police complete their investigation, and the defence will be able to ask for a second post mortem. They may want to try to prove that Dan had a heart attack, and then it wouldn't be murder, or even manslaughter.'

'So will the funeral have to wait till then? What if they don't catch whoever did it?' Sarah was aghast at this; poor Dan doomed to lie indefinitely in the refrigerator at the mortuary.

'The family will have the right to ask for a second post mortem, so that they can arrange the funeral,' said Oliver. 'If it drags on, I'll talk to Midge and the boys about that. Much better get it over.'

'I should say so,' Sarah agreed.

They were spending the evening by the fire together. It had taken the murder of their friend to keep Oliver from returning to his dolls' house restoration after dinner.

10

Oliver went to the office early on Monday morning, anxious to deal quickly with the post, and, by cancelling appointments, win time to help Midge and her sons if they needed support. At the moment, with detectives still busy in Deerton, the press had been kept at bay and the Stewarts were not answering the telephone. Mark had brought his mobile, and this was their means of communication.

The inquest was to be opened the next day, Tuesday. The coroner would keep it as brief as possible, and then adjourn it, to let the police get on with their investigation, but Midge would have to be a witness. He wondered if they would call the boy, Jamie Preston, who had summoned Dan to the close.

The Times had reported the murder on an inside page. Oliver could only imagine what the tabloids would do with the grim story and hoped Midge would see none of them. They'd send reporters to the inquest, for sure, and plaster her photograph, with imaginative captions, all over the front pages unless some sleazy scandal or other murder was thought more titillating.

At breakfast Sarah, who had an appointment in Birmingham that day, wondered aloud if she should cancel it; might she be of use to Midge if she cried off?

'You go,' said Oliver. 'It might be more important for you

to be free another day, if something crops up.' He thought that Midge, whilst grateful, might find her role as victim in receipt of Sarah's kindness too demanding; even in woe, Sarah would be critical. Yet she had been very upset the night before, reminding him of the vulnerable, wounded girl she had been when they first met.

He wasn't quite sure what she had to do in Birmingham. However, she was developing latent business abilities and he did not begrudge her the freedom to grow; in his view, that, not possessiveness and the exertion of control, was what constituted love.

He parked the Rover and walked across the yard to the office. As he did so, Rosemary Ellis came down the steps from her flat and went over to her car. He turned and gave her his usual pleasant smile, saying, 'Good morning.'

Rosemary's heart never leaped, but its beat quickened. What a fortunate piece of timing: what a bonus for her day! Her own smile transformed her square features, softening her face.

He forgot about her the moment he entered his office, but Rosemary's mind dwelt on him for several minutes. He was in very early today, she thought, not connecting him yet with the crime in Deerton.

Sarah, in the train, was relieved to escape from the sorrows of the weekend. She still felt stunned, unable to believe that she would never see Daniel again: his funny smile, his thinning faded hair and his lean shape. He was not a big robust man, like Oliver, who was so solid. Oliver would have been a match for a lad with or without a knife, she thought, and then she knew he wouldn't. Burly policemen, trained in combat, had been stabbed to death by villains. She shuddered, and she grieved for Midge who would find coping alone well-nigh impossible. She would have to train for some career, thought Sarah. At least she could help there, having done it herself, not that Midge would be capable of achieving as much. Resolved on this, she opened a file and scanned it. She liked to look important in the train and never read a novel. She seldom read novels anyway, unless they were being much discussed, preferring to browse through books on interior decorating or home management, even house design.

When she reached Birmingham, a short walk took her to the restaurant where she met Charles and Hugh, who wanted her advice on how to reduce staff without incurring lawsuits or losing efficiency, and at the same time increase their seating capacity. She inspected their premises, where lunch preparations were under way, and saw that the layout could be streamlined by minor structural alterations. The initial outlay would, in the long run, cut the wages bill. She made notes, took measurements, and said she would produce a scheme and cost it, and after lunching with her clients, suggested that the extensive menu could be reduced; a smaller choice, while maintaining their high standards, would reduce waste. Diners, she said, could sometimes be overwhelmed by too wide a selection. Charles and Hugh found her ideas stimulating and planned another meeting.

At the station, before catching her train home, Sarah bought an evening paper. *Quiet, have-a-go hero built life anew after redundancy*, she read. How did they get hold of such stuff? From some chatty neighbour, she supposed. Perhaps Daniel was a hero. How astonishing to think of him like that. She'd always found him rather dull: good, but dull.

She'd met a lot of men through her new career, a few of them moderately exciting, and whose conversation, when they discussed business, was interesting. Some were arrogant and pushy, and she had been propositioned, not always subtly, several times. She dealt with these suggestions by ignoring them, since administering a snub would, in her view, be an over-reaction.

Sitting in the train, in her scarlet coat and black skirt, a scarf at her throat and a gold bracelet on her wrist, Sarah knew that she looked good. What would she do if Oliver dropped dead? Pick herself up and get on with things, of course.

All the boys involved in Saturday night's affray had gone to school as usual, even Jamie, his arm still in a sling but more to protect it than from medical necessity. His mother was thankful he was well enough; she had classes she must teach and to be left alone at home all day, after such an experience, would be bleak. Barry, Peter and Greg would be there, too; resuming normal life, as nearly as was possible, must be best for everyone.

Kate's path at school did not cross Jamie's; he did not take her subjects. Both liked it this way; it wasn't always easy if your parents were on the staff, but Kate was popular and made her classes lively, so no one had a down on him simply by association. Some people didn't even know they were related.

He wondered if those four would turn up: Kevin, Wayne, Paul and Trevor. Surely they wouldn't have the nerve to show their faces, but then, if they stayed away, would they be suspected?

In the reports about the stabbing, which mentioned an injured boy, no name had been given because he was protected by the law for minors. When other pupils asked what he had done to his arm, Jamie simply said he'd cut it in an accident. His three friends kept quiet, too, but the staff, who knew the truth, speculated endlessly about which boys could have been responsible. Bob and Ginny, returning from their cycle ride the day before, had called in at Kate's and heard the welcome news that Jamie was in the clear.

'I've said nothing,' Jamie told his three friends when they met at break.

Nor had they, but they were all in trouble with their parents for failing to supply the names of the guilty.

'You were great,' Peter told Jamie. 'My dad knew a boy was trying to help but he didn't realise it was you, in the scrum. He says we're committing a crime by not helping the police.'

Jamie remembered the threatening gestures made by Kevin and Wayne the day before.

'They'll get us if we do,' he said.

'Not if they're arrested,' Peter said.

'They'd get bail,' said Jamie.

'Would they? After killing someone?'

'They didn't all kill him,' Greg pointed out. 'They'd let the others out, most likely.'

All agreed that this was probable. They knew of other youngsters who had got into quite serious trouble for thieving, even breaking and entering, and who had been swaggering around without a care in no time, after not even being cautioned.

'The police will catch them in the end,' Peter said. 'They've been searching the road outside our house, looking at every blade of grass by the hedge and so on. They'll find something. Or someone will have seen the car.'

'It was probably stolen,' said Barry. 'You bet they nicked it.'

Peter's father had done what he could to describe the miscreants, but they were already attacking Daniel Stewart when he arrived, and he did not see their faces. One was shorter than the rest, and all were wearing jackets. Only one boy, and that was Jamie, had had no jacket on; if he had, his arm might have been protected. It was dark in the road; the porch lights from Barry's house and his own were the only illumination on the scene. As far as he could tell, all the boys wore some form of headgear: baseball caps, he thought.

'The police will talk to every boy in the school. You'll see,' said Greg.

And they set out to do so, starting with those in the same year as the four boys whose names they knew.

Kevin and Paul met, as they did most mornings, on the way to school. Walking slowly along, they agreed that to have stayed away might draw attention to them, but that they would keep apart during the day, and avoid Trevor and Wayne. Usually all four spent some part of the day together, but to do so now would emphasise the fact that they were a quartet. It seemed that Trevor and Wayne had the same idea, for they, though they did not avoid each other, kept their distance from the other two.

'It didn't happen,' Trevor told Wayne. 'If we keep our heads down, it will go away.' Neither of them had used the knife. Neither had anything to fear unless that berk Jamie Preston talked.

'He won't,' said Wayne. 'Me and Kev saw him going off with the cops yesterday. We let him know he'd better watch his step.'

All four had rationalised the night's events. They hadn't set out to fight, only to have a bit of fun at Barry's, knowing he and some of his mates were on their own, and it was Saturday. That old guy had come round poking his nose in and had got in the way of Kev's knife, which was in his hand because he might need to protect himself against the interference. Not one admitted any shame to another; to do so would be weak. None admitted to the surge of excitement he had felt when the violence escalated and they were all in there, punching and kicking. It had been a stupid accident; that was all.

None of their parents suspected anything, but all were surprised when their boys stayed in that night, each upstairs in his room, allegedly busy with his homework.

11

By Monday night the police were no further forward with their investigation. Almost every boy in the same year as Barry and Jamie had been traced and interviewed, but though some were unable to explain their movements on Saturday in an altogether satisfactory manner, so far there was nothing to connect them with the crime in Deerton. More checking would be done, and Detective Superintendent Fisher had arranged with the headmaster that he would address the school assembly in the morning. Several known troublemakers were questioned, but none of their prints matched those found in the ransacked house.

And there was no sign of the knife.

'We need one of the four musketeers to weaken,' said Fisher, who had thus christened Barry and his friends, as they were all for one and one for all. 'If young Jamie Preston's wound had been more serious, they might have been scared enough to talk, although God knows one wouldn't wish that on the lad.'

'He certainly knows who stabbed him,' said DS Shaw. 'He may let something slip to his mother.'

The dead man's clothes might yield traces from his killer, whose own clothes would be stained with blood. Find a suspect and you would find the evidence, Fisher thought, but a likely candidate had to be in the frame before such proof could be established. Ted Grant thought all the boys were wearing poplin type jackets, which did not readily leave fibres, nor attract them, but they would mop up blood. However, there were plenty of traces at the Noakeses' house, including urine-soaked bedding.

So much detection involved slow, careful checking; flights of fancy rarely led to arrests.

Mark Stewart left Deerton early on Monday morning to drive up to the Lake District, where his paternal grandparents lived, to tell them what he could about Daniel's death. They had wanted to come down to Deerton, but had been persuaded to remain at home because they could not help at present, and they would provide fresh targets for the media. Midge's parents lived in Spain, where money went further and the sun shone much of the time. Midge had telephoned them on Sunday afternoon, catching them after their siesta, and they had volunteered to fly back at once, but she urged them to stay where they were.

'Or you come here, pet,' said her father, a former market gardener who now grew fruit and vegetables in his sunny garden, and sold some of them.

'Later,' she said. 'In the spring, maybe, when this is over.' She might be strong enough to face their kindness then; not yet. She promised to let them know as soon as there was any news and explained that much of the time they were leaving the telephone off the hook as they were receiving so many calls from reporters. They'd understand that; they'd see the English papers when they went into town; her father often bought one. Now he'd make a special trip, most likely.

Poppy Flower came to see her after Mark had gone, to report progress – none – and to explain about the inquest the next day. She was sure a boy would talk eventually, but that could mean a day or two, and meanwhile they hoped the knife would turn up, or some mother would discover blood-stained garments being washed in secret.

But Kevin had slipped out on Sunday night and dumped his jacket, wrapped in two dustbin liners, in a bin outside a row of shops. It would be cleared away on Monday morning.

Midge and Jonathan went to the workshop after Poppy Flower's visit. There was no queue of irate customers lined up outside, wanting to know why it was not open, but fresh bills had landed on the mat. Jonathan retrieved them. He and Mark had had a brief discussion in which they shared concern about the business and its solvency, recognising that they must discover the true position in the next few days. More unpaid bills were stashed in the desk. There were also outstanding debts from customers who owed money.

'Things aren't too good in here,' said Midge. 'No one wants to buy our stuff though Dad did a lot of repairing.'

'Is there much of that waiting to be done?' asked Jonathan, who might be able to do the simpler jobs. His father had become extremely skilled.

'Not really. Dad was pretty much up to date, I think,' said Midge. 'There's some framing. Nothing that must be done today. I can manage the repairs, you know. Maybe not to Dad's standards, but I've helped him. I'll only take on easy things in future.'

'Mm.' Jonathan didn't know how to say it. She couldn't manage on her own.

'I'll see how it goes,' she said. 'I've coped when he had flu.'

'Let's put a notice on the door saying we'll be closed tomorrow, anyway,' said Jonathan. 'We'll have to sort all the papers and stuff. We can do a bit of that now, and maybe pick out anything that's promised, so we can tell the customers, if necessary.' It was too soon to make decisions. His mother hadn't really taken in the finality of his father's death, and nor had he. Then there would be the funeral and all that. Oliver had quietly explained the situation and they had agreed, if no one was arrested, to ask for the second post mortem to be done as soon as possible. Poor Dan must not be left where he was longer than was unavoidable.

Those little shits. If Jonathan could get his hands on who had done it, he would willingly strangle them with his own bare hands.

'Maybe we can sort things out at Christmas,' he said. 'Mark'll be back for a bit, and Judy will be around.' He paused. 'I could skip the rest of term,' he said. 'You shouldn't be all on your own.'

'You mustn't do that,' she said. 'I'll manage.' At the moment she couldn't imagine it, but she would have to do it.

'Pity Sarah's got a job now. She'd have helped – kept you company,' he said.

'Yes, but she makes me feel incompetent,' said his mother.

'How silly. You're marvellous,' said Jonathan, and gave her a hug which nearly made her crumple. 'You're just as capable as she is, if not more so, only you don't make a meal of it, like she does, for all to admire.'

Midge had to laugh at this shrewd assessment.

'She's never satisfied,' Jonathan went on. 'Not even with Saint Oliver.'

'Maybe she'd like the challenge of a devil,' said Midge, surprising him. Perhaps she would; it was a novel thought.

Kevin hadn't meant to kill that man. Or had he?

He thought about it briefly, walking away from school. He'd got a knife, and so, when he was thwarted, he had used it. He was a hard man. Pity only a few guys knew that, but it couldn't be made public as the stupid git had snuffed it. Kevin felt not one speck of remorse or shame for what he had done, nor any pity for the suffering he was causing. He didn't give the aftermath a thought. He swaggered on down the road. That man in charge, Superintendent Fisher or some such, had addressed the school that morning, describing what had happened and asking anyone with information to come forward. It would be in strict confidence, he said; Detective Inspector Flower would be in the headmaster's office, waiting. She stood beside him, Detective Inspector fucking Flower. Seeing her, Kevin had adopted a serious expression; she might be seeking signs of guilt but she wouldn't find them on his face. He could trust his own mates to fake innocence, but what about those others, those four who knew the truth?

On the whole, it had seemed wise to bunk off as soon as he got a chance to slide away from school unseen. The police couldn't interview you without a parent or guardian there if you were under sixteen, and he was, for a few more weeks. Perhaps teachers counted as guardians. He wasn't sure about that, and he didn't mean to find out now, as everyone knew the police could put words in your mouth and make you admit to things you hadn't done.

If that silly old fool hadn't come interfering, they'd have driven off and no harm done. Those kids would have had some explaining to do about the mess in the house but they could have cleaned up most of it in no time. He hoped Jamie Preston had taken note of the warning he and Wayne had signalled on Sunday morning. They'd been cautious, making sure the two police officers were looking ahead and that only Jamie, staring at them from the window, had seen them. It was lucky they had had the chance to warn him. He was a kid without a dad, no one to stick up for him; he'd take heed.

Kevin was a bit bothered about the knife. What could have happened to it? He'd thought he'd shoved it back in his pocket, but it must have dropped out. He hadn't worn gloves, so if it was found and had some blood on it, he could be in big trouble, but he'd never been fingerprinted; the police didn't know about Kevin Parker. They couldn't trace the knife to him.

It had all got a bit heavy, out in the road, but Kevin wasn't going to let it get to him. He'd act normal – not too angelic or folk would wonder – but he'd keep within bounds for a bit. He'd liked being the leader; he'd shown the others what he could do. He'd had power. He hadn't meant to cut the kid: of course not. Jamie Preston had just got in the way.

It did not occur to him that if luck had been against his second victim, he could have been responsible for two murders, not just one. And he didn't think of it as murder. It was an accident.

This morning a woman came to talk to me about her husband. She suspected that he had a mistress, and I coaxed her to talk about the reasons for her fears, and to consider what separation, which she was contemplating, would mean in practice. She cried a great deal, which irritated me, and I told her she was weeping for her father, who had died when she was ten, and that she was seeking to transmute her youthful unresolved grief into current anxieties. I didn't suggest that she had been abused in childhood; many counsellors go down that road and it's too easy a way out. All most of my patients need is a listening ear, because friends don't have the time these days, and nor do doctors, and few priests or parsons are pastorally oriented. I give my patients value for their money as I sit facing them in my consulting room with its plain white walls and leather chairs. I gaze at them, maintaining steady eye contact, and I have a box of tissues handy, even coffee keeping warm.

They feel better when they leave, after paying my fee of forty pounds a session. They've had my undivided attention for the period of their appointment, and often their problems can be dealt with by the sort of advice given in the agony columns of magazines. Sometimes I make notes on a pad placed on the desk in front of me. I keep a file on every one of them, and I know many secrets. I've got plenty of scope for blackmail.

It's doubtless true that this woman's husband has found someone else; who can wonder at it, looking at her? I'll foster her suspicions, nourishing her flickering desire to declare the marriage over, but I'll make her understand the economic disadvantages for her, and the inevitable difficulties for the children – there are two teenage girls. I'll point out that as she is still mourning her own father, so will they mourn theirs if he leaves, and that they may decide to lay the blame on her. It will take us many expensive sessions to reach this conclusion. By then the husband may have acted independently and the choice will not be hers. Whatever the result, she'll need support through the period that follows, and she'll pay me for providing it. I will need to calculate what she can afford; those unable to pay my fees can go to the Citizens' Advice Bureau for practical advice, at no cost to themselves. My patients must pay for the indulgence which I offer.

I have male clients, men who are impotent, or gay – what a misnomer when often they are seriously sad – and can't accept it, or can, and are wondering what society will say. Some men who consult me have wives obsessed with becoming pregnant when the very thought of having an infant to complicate an already difficult or over-intense relationship terrifies them. Sometimes I want to shake them, tell them to face up to their obligations, be men, as they sit before me, whimpering, pale caricatures of masculinity, wanting mothers. Don't men ever grow up?

Some men have paranoid delusions that the whole world is against them, and I direct them to list the good things in their lives, and then the bad, and weigh them up. Often I can see how those in a failed relationship will refuse to take responsibility for any part in the breakdown, when both parties are obviously to blame. Lack of communication is frequently the real trouble,

*but at least one partner is trying to communicate with me.
By using the correct language, the appropriate terminology,
I render them more articulate.*

*I don't want to lose the easy patients; they, after all, pay my
bills. I don't refer on the more difficult ones unless I think they
are unstable, deranged enough to harm physically themselves
or others; these are outside my remit and I urge them to
consult their doctors and seek psychiatric help. Such people
rarely come to me because they are reluctant to admit they
have a problem. The ones I see are those who could redeem
themselves. Some have lives which are extremely drab; some
stories are pathetic; and there are tragedies: women who think
they will lose their husbands' love if they cannot reproduce,
and, occasionally, the bereaved.*

*Treatment can become addictive. Patients return because
they see me as their friend, perhaps their only one.*

Prudence Wilmot had recently installed a fax machine. It was
still a novelty to her, but it was useful when communicating
with her American publisher and her family and friends who
were overseas, most of whom had access to this rapid means of
communication. Oliver had told her that she should link herself
to the Internet, where e-mail would open up a whole new world
to her. Prudence was not sure she needed a whole new world;
the one around her was enough.

'Have you done that?' she asked.

Foxton and Smythe had not.

'I often hanker for the old world,' Prudence had confessed.
'Where people had good manners and life did not rush past so
rapidly.' She had sighed. 'In my parents' generation, it was
travel that developed at amazing speed. The first car took the
road in their infancy, and they lived to see men land on the
moon. In my generation, it's the revolution in communication
that's so difficult to keep up with. What do we do with all this

time we've saved? And do we really communicate, if it's all done by electronics?'

Oliver had agreed that she had a point.

On Monday morning, she walked along the street to the florist's and ordered white and yellow flowers to be sent to Midge. Why was she called that, she wondered; some childhood nickname carried on, she supposed. Emphasising that she wanted no heavy purples, no russet shades, she paid and left, and when she reached home she wrote Oliver a message which she faxed. He could attend to it or not, as he liked; telephoning would be a definite interruption.

VERY MUCH REGRET THE TRAGEDY YOUR FRIENDS HAVE SUFFERED, she wrote, in bold block letters so that they would transmit clearly. LET ME KNOW IF I CAN HELP. BROAD SHOULDER, TIME AVAILABLE, ALSO BEDS IF RELATIVES NEED THEM. ASSUME GUILT NOT YET ASSIGNED. It was like a telegram of old, she thought, feeding it into her machine.

Oliver smiled when he received this missive. He had brewed himself a strong cup of coffee, earning a reproof from his secretary who said she would have gladly done it for him, and took time off from going through the pile of mail to reply.

MANY THANKS, he faxed back. ASSUMPTION CORRECT, BLIND ALLEY. MIDGE AND SONS STUNNED BUT COPING. DITTO FOXTONS. MIGHT CALL UPON SHOULDER LATER.

Prudence had once told him that one of the consolations of age was the acquisition of new friends across the generations, and the freedom to enjoy the company of men to whom, twenty years before, if one was of the same generation, one might have been attracted.

'With,' she said, 'devastating problems and possibly dire consequences.'

Oliver understood. He could chat to Prudence to his heart's

content without Sarah raising any objection. She wasn't even his mother, whom until her death Sarah had resented, though she never interfered and had been very generous to them.

When he had taken on the restoration of the dolls' house, Prudence had been touched. As a child, she had loved playing with it; it had stood on a cupboard at a level with her face, and she had spent hours arranging the family of dolls inside, putting them to bed and getting them up, sending the father doll off to work, just as her father had departed daily, and the small boy to school. When her sister was born, a baby doll had appeared, representing Emily, who later had taken the house over. Embarking on his self-imposed task, Oliver had revealed unexpected talents and a dextrous touch. She knew that he enjoyed it. All that would be on hold, now, she thought, while he helped the Stewarts through their crisis. As, of course, he would.

12

Sarah walked across Fettleton station yard to her car, which she had parked near one of the pay machines, beneath a light, obedient to advice about avoiding vulnerable situations. She had never felt at risk in Fettleton, but after Saturday night's events, she knew that danger could lurk anywhere, and cars had been broken into here, their radios stolen and any articles left visible to thieves. The station itself closed down at five o'clock; after that you had to buy your ticket from a machine, and if you needed help or information, there was no guard or ticket collector to approach. Oliver had insisted that she carry a mobile phone, now that she was travelling around, and she was amenable; she did not want to be stranded with a puncture or a car that wouldn't start.

There were no problems tonight. The car started and she drove off through a mist of gently falling rain which had replaced the earlier frost. What would it be like to make a train trip every day to work? She must pursue the possibility of the job she had heard discussed in London last week, just a day before Daniel was murdered. It seemed an age ago.

The house was empty when she reached home. She had expected Oliver to be there and because he was not, she felt aggrieved. There was one message on the answerphone:

Judy, deeply upset by what had happened to the Stewarts, was coming home, and Oliver had left a note to say he had gone to meet her at the station.

Shedding her smart coat and skirt, putting on slacks and a big sweater, Sarah decided that this was confirmation of her theory that there was an interest between Mark and Judy that went beyond the scope of their childhood friendship. Oliver had not agreed. It would be difficult to nurture a romance when they were separated by several hundred miles, he suggested, though of course it was quite possible. He suspected that it was Jonathan with whom Judy had a strong bond. They were close in age, and had always been great friends. He said nothing of this to Sarah; he knew she had ambitions for her daughter, whom she pictured, if she completed her law degree, marrying a barrister who would become a silk, perhaps a judge, not a mere provincial solicitor like Oliver.

Sarah poured herself a glass of wine and went into the kitchen, where she began putting together a pasta meal, enough for three. Judy would be hungry.

But only Oliver returned. He had left Judy at Deerton. He invented placatory messages from Judy to her mother, and ate his portion of the pasta with appreciation. Sarah had had a lavish lunch in Birmingham; he had had sandwiches in the office. During dinner, he asked about her day and listened while she told him a little about it, refusing to let his mind stray towards the Stewarts and their plight. But Sarah's basic soundness soon surfaced, and she asked how things were with the stricken family.

'They're all still stunned,' said Oliver. Midge had looked like a little ghost, and both the boys, a sturdy pair, had pale drawn faces. Judy had burst into tears as soon as she saw them, and there had been hugs all round, and tears from everyone, though Oliver had turned away to hide his, which he blinked away, unnoticed.

He told Sarah that Midge and Jonathan had been to the
workshop and discovered that the business was in deep financial trouble. Daniel had managed to hide the full gravity of
the situation from Midge, although she knew that things were
tight. A copy of his will, dating from when the couple married
nearly twenty-five years ago, had been found at the house, and
the solicitor who made it had been traced. Oliver had spoken
to him; the will was valid. Everything was left to Midge and,
if she predeceased him, in equal parts to any future surviving
children. It was straightforward. The question was, had he
anything, except debts, to bequeath? There were other papers
to be gone through. Mark, back from his lightning trip to see
his grandparents, said he would get on with this as soon as
possible, but there was the inquest the next morning.

It was all very depressing, but at least there would be no
legal complications about settling the estate. A partner in the
firm which made the will was named as executor; he was dead
now, but a colleague had taken on his clients. The firm would
communicate with Oliver, who would, he had told them, act for
the family in any way that would be helpful. In view of what
had happened, the other solicitor, based in Norwich, where
Daniel hailed from, was only too thankful for this offer.

There might be some delay with probate due to the manner
of Daniel's death, but at the moment all such questions were
purely academic.

Oliver told Sarah some of this.

'Couldn't he have managed things better?' she asked.

'He couldn't foresee that he would lose his job at the age
of forty-four,' said Oliver. 'He kept working. He worked
bloody hard.'

It was rare for Oliver to swear. Sarah felt surprise.

'What will Midge do?' she asked.

'It's too soon to make plans,' said Oliver. 'We'll have to
see how things work out.' He thought she might have some

quixotic notion that she owed it to Daniel to continue with the business; she would have to earn her living, but she couldn't do what he had done, as Jonathan was already aware, and she would not be able to afford to pay a carpenter to help her.

'She'll never find another husband,' Sarah said. 'Not a chance.'

Oliver could scarcely believe that he had heard her correctly. He was furious, but he swallowed more wine and took a deep breath.

'I'm surprised to hear you put forward such a solution to her financial dilemma,' he said. 'And what about her grief? I should think remarriage is the last thing on her mind.' How could she be so insensitive?

'It's the only answer for someone like her,' said Sarah, undaunted by his reaction. 'She's ineffective. She'll never cope alone.'

'She may astonish you,' said Oliver grimly; he was now determined that if he had anything to do with it, she would.

He rose to clear away their plates. There was fresh fruit to follow; Sarah made puddings only at weekends.

Later, when he went into the study to fit the new coal range into the kitchen of the dolls' house, he thought of Midge as he had last seen her, showing Judy the flowers Prudence had sent which had been standing in a bucket of water since their arrival. Judy had offered to arrange them. Midge had been grateful, smiling at Judy, welcoming her, when perhaps she did not really want her in the house just now. Jonathan did, however; that was obvious. He said he would run her back to Winbury later. Oliver had another vision of Midge as she had lain asleep the previous morning, in their spare bedroom. He had felt an urge to take her in his arms and had thought his impulse sprang from pity. Did it?

At all events, whatever Sarah thought, Midge, in the language of today, was eminently fanciable.

*   *   *

Much of Sunday had been spent by the parents of Barry, Peter and Greg in the company of the police. The Noakeses were eventually allowed to begin cleaning up, and were discovering the extent of the damage. Cliff declared that redecoration throughout would be needed, and new bedding in their room. The police had removed the duvet, but they left the rest. Photograph frames had been smashed and stamped on; papers had been flung from drawers. Cliff and Lily Noakes were worried about how much would be covered by their insurance.

Peter's father, Ted Grant, had been persuaded to let the police doctor look at him, and his bruised ribs were photographed for evidence of assault. He saw the sense of this. The doctor said he had cracked several ribs and sent him for X-rays, which proved that one was broken. There was no specific treatment; time would heal them and the bruises. When he was back at home again, he and his wife, Gwen, tried to persuade Peter to name the boys responsible, but he remained silent.

'They'll do it again. Whoever had the knife's still got it, and now he's used it once, what's to stop him stabbing someone else?' demanded Ted.

'It'd have been all right if Mr Stewart hadn't come along,' insisted Peter. 'We'd have seen them off.'

'You weren't succeeding, were you? That was why young Jamie went for help.' By now it was generally understood that this was how Daniel had become involved.

'They were leaving,' Peter said, but they had left the house only because they realised Jamie might be fetching help.

Ted had guessed that was the reason for their flight.

'And Jamie came back, when he could have skulked in safety at the Stewarts' place,' he said. 'If Mr Stewart hadn't come, they'd have done for your pal Jamie.'

Peter knew that this was very likely true. He stared at his feet, not answering.

'I wish you'd say, Peter,' said his mother, who had been listening to them both in anguish. She understood Peter's curious warped loyalty, and she understood, too, that he was frightened of reprisals. These boys, whoever they were, were capable of anything, as had been proved. She could scarcely believe that all this had happened while she and Ted were watching television, with Peter, as they thought, safely in their neighbours' house three doors away.

'You may think you're brave, keeping stumm,' said Ted, who was an electrician, working on his own. 'There's other sorts of courage, like doing the right thing when it isn't easy.'

He couldn't believe that this had happened on his own doorstep. Boys could be wild, and high spirits could lead to recklessness, but this was vicious, mindless violence. Leaving out the fact of murder, and the attack on him, what had happened in the Noakeses' house was horrible.

Greg's mother took the same line. She had two daughters as well as Greg, and was divorced from Greg's father, but she had a boyfriend who stayed overnight in Deerton when he could. He was a long-distance lorry driver and was often on the road. He'd been at their house on Saturday and that was one reason why Greg had gone out. He didn't like to think of Rick in bed with his mother and found it difficult to be civil to the man, though Rick was always pleasant enough to Greg and his sisters, and generous to their mother. Greg suspected that he had another family in Leeds, which was where he was based, and he was perfectly correct.

The parents of the miscreant boys had no suspicion that their sons were involved. The murder was discussed in each household. It was the sort of shocking crime you didn't expect in a small village. Stabbings happened outside pubs and clubs when people were drunk and got into fights. In Kevin's house on Sunday, over the meal the family had together after the pubs closed – his parents liked to go down to the local around one o'clock on Sundays – it was the main topic while they ate the pie his mother had made. She was a dinner lady at a local primary school. After saying that he hoped Kevin would have nothing to do with lads like that, his father, a telephone engineer, wondered aloud if he would finish a job he was doing in the allotted time. He'd run into problems with the installation.

Except for Paul's mother, the parents of all the boys had jobs; none was neglected. They only rarely played truant. None of the four fitted the profile of a shiftless, deprived adolescent who was programmed to commit crimes. Wayne and Trevor, though doing better at school than Paul and Kevin, had not achieved enough to give them confidence, and both found it difficult to handle teasing and practical jokes. Neither had any major interests or enthusiasms. They would join others in looking for a laugh, but a laugh might be an act of petty vandalism. Until now, none of the four had been involved in anything serious; on Saturday, very briefly, all had found being on top exhilarating.

On Tuesday morning the inquest was opened and, as expected, adjourned after evidence of identification had been given and the circumstances of Daniel's death outlined. The knife had pierced his heart. As no one had yet been charged with the crime, the family had to understand that the body could not yet be released. It was so cruel. Midge, horrified at the prospect of further assaults upon it in another post mortem, agreed that they should wait for a few days, at least, before insisting that it be carried out.

'People don't think about these things when they go around stabbing people,' Midge sobbed, collapsing.

'People don't think about others at all when they use knives. They are governed by their violence,' Neil Fisher told her. And, at times, a prior plan; sometimes aggressive self-defence was their only instinct.

Oliver, needed in court by a client who had been charged with dangerous driving, had had to leave them after the inquest. Judy had gone back to Deerton with the Stewarts, and, once home again, Midge succumbed to a storm of noisy grief triggered off by the bureaucratic red tape. Judy sat her down in front of the fire with a box of tissues while Jonathan went to make some tea. Mark had another thought and rummaged in the sideboard in the dining room. Surely Dad had some brandy somewhere? He found a bottle, nearly full, and poured them all, including Judy, a tot. The girl sat awkwardly beside Midge, wondering how to comfort her. She patted her hand.

'He was great, Dan was,' she said. 'He's always been there, in my life. I won't ever forget him. He was fun. He made us laugh. Remember the firework parties when we were young? How we used to sing, dancing round the bonfire? It was Dan who started all that.' He had been more lively than her own father; quick-witted and amusing. 'He was so alive,' she said, and she too began to cry.

This enabled Midge to regain control. She blew her nose on a tissue, then sat up straight and told them all that they must resume their own lives.

'We'll finish sorting out Dad's papers and things,' she said. 'We'll decide what bills to pay and all that, and I must carry on with the business. We can't make any proper plans until the police catch that wicked boy. I'll need you then – all of you,' she said, including Judy, who would be hurt if she were left out, and who anyway was dear to Jonathan, as was obvious. And to Midge. She was not at all like Sarah. 'I've got to get used to being on my own,' Midge continued. 'I can do more framing and cut down on the furniture part. I won't buy in any more at present. We'll see how things go. Oliver will have some ideas about the best way forward.' That was the phrase. Politicians used it all the time. Sometimes, though, the road wound and twisted; you could not always forge straight ahead.

At the moment, all she wanted was to be alone, to weep and wail and spill out her anguish without having to exert control. But Mark and Jonathan had also been bereaved; they had their own loss to deal with. Sudden death, if not murder, happened all the time and people survived, and so would she, if only the agonising ache which filled her chest would dissolve. The pain was so intense that she wondered if she was having a heart attack, and then she understood that this was what was meant by heartbreak.

In the kitchen, finding lunch from among the frozen items Sarah had provided, Judy told Mark and Jonathan that she was sure her parents would gladly have Midge to stay indefinitely, but they all agreed that this would be only a temporary solution. Daniel's parents might come down, but that would mean more work for her. It would be different if there was any practical way to help; at the moment, with the police investigation apparently achieving nothing, it seemed that there was deadlock everywhere.

Midge had gone upstairs to wash her face. Returning, she realised they were discussing her and went to tell them that they must stop worrying. She was afraid that, to fill their time, they would start wondering what to do with Dan's clothes, and at the moment she could not bear the thought of discarding so much as a pair of his socks.

'You must all resume your lives as soon as possible,' she repeated. 'Now, what have you found for us for lunch?'

Sarah was right. Food was essential and the need to eat it filled the time as another hour of the unending day dragged by.

*   *   *

Later, when Jonathan drove Judy back to Winbury, there was no one at home. Sarah was at her office and Oliver was still dealing with his recalcitrant motorist.

'Your mother enjoys her job, doesn't she?' said Jonathan, kissing Judy in the hall.

She put her arms round him. Funny that Midge and Daniel, both willowy, had two such sturdy sons.

'She certainly does. She's good at it. She's quite ambitious,' she said.

'How does Oliver feel about it? She'd never worked before, had she?'

'He's pretty proud of her, I'd say. I think he's sometimes felt guilty about snapping her up almost straight from school, before she'd had time to turn into her real self,' said Judy.

'She seems real enough to me,' said Jonathan, who admired Sarah without ever feeling drawn to her. She was a very confident woman, he thought, unlike his own diffident mother.

'She was only nineteen when they got married,' Judy said.

'Things were different in those days,' said Jonathan. 'And there wouldn't have been you and Tim if they hadn't.'

'No – funny, isn't it?' said Judy. 'We'd have been other people. Or not existed. Weird.'

'Unimaginable,' said Jonathan. He loved Judy and when they were apart he missed her, but he knew they might end up with other partners. On the other hand, they might separate and, eventually, come together again, like streams of mercury. Neither would put chains upon the other; not now, not ever.

'I wonder how Dad's getting on with his house,' said Judy. 'Have you seen it?'

'What house? Has he bought a seaside bolthole?'

'It's in the study,' Judy said. She led him there, and Jonathan saw the old dolls' house on its table. She opened it to reveal its three storeys, the staircase, now neatly carpeted, the various bedrooms, the bathroom with its old-fashioned fitments. 'He hasn't fixed the lights yet,' Judy said. 'But he's done a lot this term.'

The dolls were arranged in different rooms, the children in bed, the father in his study, the mother in the kitchen. Until recently, the house, in human terms, had been unfurnished; now, much of it was fit for habitation.

'Good heavens!' Jonathan exclaimed. 'Where did he find it?'

'It was Prudence Wilmot's. It turned up when the stuff at her old house was sold. She couldn't bear to part with it,' said Judy. 'Dad's fixing it.'

'Prudence Wilmot – that's who sent the flowers?'

'Right. Prudence used to live in one of the flats behind the office. She and Dad are great mates,' she said. 'It's nice for them. She's at least seventy,' Judy added, seeing his expression. She took the child dolls out of their beds and arranged them downstairs, appropriately, and put the mother in the drawing room. 'They must be up by now. It's tea-time,' she declared, and closed the house.

13

'We may have to fingerprint every teenage boy in the area,' said Fisher, when by Tuesday evening they were no nearer lining up a likely suspect. 'I wonder if we'd be able to set that up at the school or will we have the parents shouting about their kids' rights?'

He pondered to himself. The headmaster had been very helpful, but had been unable to name possible tearaways. He had suggested the offending boys might have come from Fettleton, where there were several notorious gangs. Fisher had discounted this idea. The boys were known to the four he called the musketeers; that meant that they were local.

'The innocent lads will cooperate, whatever we set up,' Shaw remarked. 'It's only the guilty who'll give trouble.'

After the Noakeses' prints and those of the three visiting boys had been identified among the rest found at the ransacked house, four unidentified sets had been discovered. One set had been on a discarded beer can; four clear fingers and a thumb; others were less distinct, but sharp enough, on items thrown about the rooms, particularly the kitchen. There was plenty of proof, once they knew who to test, and they would find all four boys in time; Fisher had said so on television, asking for those who knew anything to come forward. There would have been some blood-stained clothes, for instance. All this delay, and stress, not to mention cost, could have been avoided if only the four musketeers would talk.

It was decided that if they were no further forward by the morning, as was most probable, they would seek to set up the mass fingerprinting operation on Thursday, obtaining whatever clearances were necessary. But not every boy would be in school. The guilty might bunk off; still, a list of absentees could be useful. Because the boys they sought, or some of them, were almost certainly under sixteen, the police must be meticulous in what they did to apprehend them. The smallest technical oversight could lead to the acquittal of a guilty individual.

After this depressing conference, Fisher left his subordinates to continue the door-to-door interviewing of every boy qualifying as a possible suspect. Many pupils, like Barry Noakes, lived in villages around Mickleburgh. It was a slow and tedious job, and irritating when the lad to be questioned was not at home. Most seemed to have busy social lives and their parents did not always know where they were, or how they had spent Saturday evening.

Fisher went to see Kate and Jamie Preston. Jamie was the most promising prospective source of information.

Opening the door, Kate was not too dismayed to see him. She did not find this thin man with the lined face intimidating, but she did not underestimate his intelligence. He was alone, which reassured her.

'Come in,' she said. 'Jamie's upstairs, doing his homework.'

'How's his arm?'

'He says it itches. I suppose that means it's healing,' she said.

She led him into the sitting room and gestured to a chair, then sat down facing him. The room was small and pretty; like her, he thought, fancifully. Fisher lived among severe, functional furnishings in a modern flat in Fettleton. Framed prints of various theatrical productions adorned Kate's walls; there were flowers on a table, and a pile of books on the floor.

'Has he said anything?' asked Fisher.

'About who did it, you mean? No.' Kate shook her head.

'It's possible they've been threatened. Jamie and the other three,' said Fisher. 'Those young villains won't hesitate to beat up these other lads if they split.'

'I know,' said Kate. 'The kids at school won't ever tell, if there's bullying or some trouble of that kind. Not that there's a lot at our place. It's pretty good, on the whole, but you always get the bad apples.' She hesitated. 'I told him they'd all be safe if whoever did this was arrested and locked up, but he said they'd get bail.'

'It's not very likely,' Fisher said. 'But on the other hand, only one boy stuck the knife in. Whoever else was involved might get bail, depending on his luck. I'd oppose it very strongly, for their own protection as much as anyone else's. People would find out who they were and the lynch-law factor has to be considered.'

'I'm so angry about it,' Kate said. 'I'm in a real rage. Jamie might so easily have been killed, like that poor man.'

'I'm angry, too,' Fisher told her. 'Why should decent boys get dragged into this sort of thing because of some evil little toe-rags who don't give a shit about anyone except themselves?'

Kate stared at him, astonished.

'You really do care, don't you?' she said.

'Of course I do. All coppers do. Well,' he qualified, 'most of us. We care about innocent bystanders getting killed.' And all too often, police officers were the victims.

'Shall I get Jamie down to talk to you?' Kate asked. 'Or would you like to go and talk to him?'

'I can't legally interview him without you there,' said Fisher.

'You can go and talk to him, though, can't you? Like a friend?' she suggested. 'He means to go into the army, like his father,' she added. 'He's interested in tanks. And he plays the cello.'

'I don't know a lot about tanks,' said Fisher. 'But my father was in the army in the war. In the infantry.' He'd lost a leg, but Fisher did not tell her that.

'Then you've got a bond,' said Kate. 'Try it.' She smiled at him. 'I'll put the kettle on,' she added. 'For when you're done.'

Jamie might make some casual remark that would give Fisher a lead, but it was unlikely; the boy would be on his guard. However, if he didn't resent the superintendent's presence, he might let something slip to his mother later.

But he didn't. Fisher spent only a short time upstairs, and when the two came down together, Jamie had a Pepsi while Fisher drank a cup of coffee with Kate.

Fisher had given him his personal card, with the telephone number of the direct line to his office. Jamie had accepted it and put it in a drawer in his room.

It was a long shot, Fisher thought, but it might yield something, if the weight of Jamie's knowledge grew too heavy for him.

After Fisher left, Jamie was tempted. He felt terrible about the man who had been killed. If he, Jamie, hadn't chosen that door to bang on – had gone to a nearer house, even Peter's across the road – that man would be alive. But Peter's father might be dead instead. And would Kevin have pulled the knife if the man had not arrived? It might have been Jamie himself who was the target, he knew; they had left the house to come after him. The more he mulled it over in his mind, the more confused he became. Kevin ought to be punished for what he'd done, but then there was the question of revenge. The gesture he and Wayne had made on Sunday was explicit. It was lucky the police officers hadn't seen them; they might have gone and asked what they were doing, and the boys would have thought Jamie had named them.

Jamie knew that witnesses could be frightened off from giving evidence; it had happened at school on a minor scale over some thieving, which had gone unpunished because no one would speak up for fear of reprisals, and no one split on those who used or dealt in drugs. Like many others, Jamie didn't want to know; he walked away.

That copper, Fisher, had been cool. He'd glanced round Jamie's room and talked about football, seeing a poster on Jamie's wall, but said he liked cricket himself, though that was less popular with his colleagues. He said it was sometimes difficult to take a line that wasn't the same as your friends'. Jamie heard the hidden message, but Fisher didn't keep on about it. He'd seen Jamie's cello standing in the corner and said he used to play the saxophone. Then he'd handed Jamie his card.

'We'll get those lads in the end,' he said. 'But you and your mates could make it easier for us. Point us in the right direction.' He'd paused, and added, 'Your mum's got the kettle on. I'd quite like a coffee. How about you?'

Jamie had followed him down the stairs and had listened while Fisher and his mother drank their coffee and talked about plans for Christmas. Fisher said that crime was sure to flourish over the holiday period.

'Unless it snows,' he said. 'That keeps thieves indoors. And if they do come out, sometimes they leave footprints we can follow.'

Kate had laughed. She said that she and Jamie might go down to stay with her parents this year, instead of inviting them to come to Mickleburgh.

While she was seeing Fisher off, Jamie returned to his room.

He closed the door and lay on his bed, eyes shut, while the horror of Saturday night washed over him. Why had he run to that particular house? Because he saw its porch light shining, and it was away from the close, where he would be penned in if Kevin and his gang came after him. He'd wanted to put space between them. How could he know that they would turn on that man and pull a knife on him? Kevin hadn't taken his knife out in Barry's house. Thank goodness! In that small space, he'd have done dreadful damage, waving it around. All Jamie had wanted was to stop them destroying the Noakeses' house; he'd seen fights enough at school, but he hadn't understood that vandalism could whirl up into a real battle, as it had in the road. His memory of pitching in himself was vague; he'd tugged at a boy's sleeve and he had pummelled Kevin's back. Then there had been the sharp stinging pain in his arm as Kevin had swung round.

Jamie could see them all: he could hear the laughs and jeers while the four boys set about their destruction of the Noakeses' house; he could see the scowls and hatred in their faces, and then there was their united attack on that one man, and he remembered Wayne punching Peter's father in the stomach, and when he was on the ground, kicking him in the ribs and in the balls. Peter's father – a broad, burly man, much bigger than the one who died – had groaned. He must have seen their faces, but then it was so dark and all the boys were in similar clothes – jeans and black or navy anoraks.

He'd almost told Fisher who they were. The man was decent; he didn't question him, or threaten. He hadn't come on all kind and sentimental, and then turned hard, which was what was supposed to happen when you got arrested. He wasn't like that other man, the night it happened, PC Roberts, who was sure that Jamie was the murderer. If he told anyone, it would be Fisher.

Later, his mother tapped on his door and, at his murmur, entered. Jamie was still lying on his bed.

'How about getting undressed?' she said. He looked very white. Was he having an attack of conscience, or was it delayed shock? Maybe a bit of both.

Meekly, Jamie let her help him take off his shirt; then he went to the bathroom where somehow he got into his pyjamas, one-handed.

'Forget it all for tonight,' was all she said, as he turned on his radio with its snooze button.

'At least that man didn't have any little kids,' said Jamie.

'No. His children are grown up,' said Kate. But there is a widow, she reflected. 'Good night, Jamie. See you in the morning.'

'See you in the morning.'

People said that with confidence, trustingly, or 'see you', meaning 'see you soon', but fate could intervene to render it impossible. There was no 'soon' or 'in the morning' for Daniel Stewart. Kate knew what sudden bereavement was; when Jamie's father was killed, it had happened to her, and at a distance, and sometimes she thought she had still not accepted it, but on occasions, hearing of broken marriages, she had asked herself if theirs would have lasted. Could it have survived the stress of his career?

She thought so. She had known, in theory anyway, what she was taking on when they married; she was aware that there would be separations, frequent moves, and that his life would often be at risk. But when they were together their closeness grew, and now Jamie was beginning to look so like his father, much more than when he was a little boy. Since being widowed, she had not wanted a relationship that might harm her bond with Jamie and bring difficulties to their lives. Failure could threaten their security, and as it was, they managed very well. She was a teacher before she married, and a brief retraining course equipped her to resume her career. At first they had lived in Devon near her parents, who had been a great support during the early years. Without them, things would have been much harder, and her parents, elderly now, were still glad to have her and Jamie visiting at any time.

They would be shocked and anxious when they knew their grandson was involved in Saturday's act of violence. Though the names of none of the boys were mentioned in reports about the murder, there were photographs of Barry's parents outside their vandalised house. It would not need much sleuthing skill to identify that family, and, by connection, others. So much for privacy. At least no reporters had lined up at Kate's door. Jamie had not yet been flushed by a brash journalist who would want to talk to Kate and quote her, or offer huge sums of money for her story.

A neighbour in Deerton had been found to pay tribute to Daniel Stewart, describing him as a quiet man, always ready to help with village events and who worked long hours at his business in Mickleburgh. Someone knew that several years ago he had been made redundant from a position with a furniture factory which was taken over. He and other staff were disposable as the new owners brought in fresh faces; he had started his own repair workshop, funding it, it was hazarded, with his redundancy payment.

Poor man. A nice man. Kate sighed, reading this. Tomorrow she would try to talk it through with Jamie again.

In the morning, after a restless night, she woke with an aching head, and to a silent son.

On Wednesday, at midday, Peter and Jamie walked into town together to buy chips.

Each evening, Peter's father had lectured him, to be told that you didn't grass on your mates.

'Funny sort of mates,' said Ted Grant, 'gate-crashing the Noakeses' house and breaking the place up.'

'They didn't mean to kill Mr Stewart,' Peter said. 'It was an accident. He happened to be there.'

'Like I did,' said his father. 'Trying to help.'

'Yes – well—' Peter could not look his father in the eye.

'He had a knife,' said Ted. 'A flick knife. I saw it in his hand. Not a penknife.'

Peter did not answer. He knew that other boys at school had knives.

'Think about it, Peter,' said his father.

While they ate their chips, Peter and Jamie discussed the situation, and Jamie reported Fisher's visit of the previous evening.

'He's all right,' he said. 'He didn't hassle me. I feel bad about it.'

'So do I,' said Peter.

'He gave me his phone number,' said Jamie. 'I suppose he meant so that I could ring him privately.'

'Will you?' Peter wished he would, and take the load off him.

'I'm afraid of them getting at us – and at my Mum,' said Jamie. 'She's on her own.'

So were lots of other mums, thought Peter, Greg's for one, though she had that Rick bloke.

'I could do it,' he said, reluctantly. 'I could disguise my voice and say I wasn't you.'

'They'd trace the call,' said Jamie.

'I could use a phone box. One near the school. Then they'd know it was a pupil, but not who.'

'You'd have to wipe the telephone, to get rid of fingerprints,' said Jamie, for the police had all theirs, the four of them.

'No wonder criminals get caught,' said Peter. 'There's such a lot to think of.'

'They don't all,' said Jamie. 'The police need tip-offs and stuff.'

'Let's give it another day. Maybe two,' said Peter. 'And if the police haven't managed it by then, we'll think about it seriously.'

Having reached this compromise, both boys felt happier.

14

Violent crime fascinates me. I buy, as well as The Guardian, a tabloid paper which reports, in lurid terms, the most horrific crimes. Perhaps, in the way that I help my patients transpose their troubling impulses and emotions into acceptable channels – gardening, tapestry, charity work, even sport or jogging – I am vicariously laying ghosts.

I have dreamt about it, seen her trusting back turned towards me, the little dog running at her heels, the larger one ahead, and the appalled expression on her face as she stared at me, understanding my action and that she would die.

It was wrong. I know that. I've said so often enough, but it's difficult to feel regret. If my efforts to deflect suspicion had been more successful, the killing would have been blamed on some itinerant mugger and, in time, when he had recovered from his guilt, we would have married. Although her being pregnant put a different slant on things; he had deceived me most dreadfully. As it was, if he had not gone overseas, I would not have been able to keep away from him. I would have traced him – that would not have been difficult – and I would have watched him, tried to infiltrate his life, been what is these days called a stalker. Once someone has been as important as he was to me, they *cannot be forgotten, even if what I felt for him afterwards was contempt.*

I might have sought to punish him. Perhaps I did it anyway.

I'm accustomed, now, to being close to no one. Perhaps I never was; the only deeply serious relationship I ever had, and that proved false, was with him. I was an adopted child, something I did not know until my adoptive brother – I thought he was my real brother – told me when I was thirteen. He'd heard an aunt and uncle talking about it, though to be fair to them, they were not aware that he was within earshot. He'd challenged them, asked for the truth, been told it and been sworn to secrecy. Of course, the next time we quarrelled – this often happened – he broke the news to me, mocking me, taunting.

Then my parents – as, for want of a better term, I still called them, and sometimes think of them, even today – told me a charming tale of how they chose me – ME – this particular infant – from among a dozen others. In those days, before the advent of effective contraception for unmarried girls and legalised abortion, babies for adoption were readily available. Their family unit enlarged by my arrival, they promptly produced their own natural son, followed by a daughter. They assured me that they loved me just as much as this younger pair, my mother – a secretary before her marriage – gazing at me solemnly, holding my unresponsive hand, while my father, managing director of a prosperous manufacturing business, remained silent, falsely smiling, nodding now and then to endorse her words.

I felt differently towards him after that. If he tried to hug or kiss me, I saw it as a sexual threat – though I understood my revulsion only later, when I studied psychotherapy in prison, reading it up compulsively, not realising then that I could turn it into a career.

It helped me to understand my actions. I was not to blame. I had been betrayed, first by my natural mother who had abandoned me, then by my adoptive parents who went on to have their own children, and finally by Lionel.

He was the one I should have killed. He destroyed me; but I destroyed him too: I must remember that.

I have rebuilt my life. I'm a respected member of society, practising an honourable profession, doing good. I keep a low public profile, not anxious to become too notable in the area in case I am asked about my life, although I have a blameless history since my release, and one that can be verified.

When it became possible to trace one's real mother, I set the operation in train. It took time, but I located her some years ago. She's still alive, and now a wealthy widow. I've written to her, giving no address, posting my letter in London, wanting to disturb her. How shaken she would be to learn what I had done. Her respectability would be shattered. I enjoy knowing that I have the power to do it. Though I have assumed a new identity, it could all be proved; DNA testing would confirm our relationship beyond all doubt.

I feel remarkably incurious about my natural father. Strange.

Now I'm wondering about the widow of the man stabbed in Deerton. What are her thoughts? How is she feeling? Bereft, yes – but what does that mean? Abandoned, rejected? If she consulted me, I would suggest she feels resentment because he left her alone, late at night, to intervene in a dispute between some loutish boys. According to reports, that seems to have been what happened. He could have stayed at home with her, letting the boys sort out their own quarrels. Is she angry because he chose to interfere, and was killed for his pains? If not, she should be; it would be a natural reaction but she would think that it was wrong. Exploring her guilty feelings would be good for weeks of sessions.

Deerton is not far away. I might post my card through her door.

I'll wait for a while and see what happens. It won't be difficult to discover some background so that I can amaze her with my insight. I already know that she has two adult sons and they will be affected, too; they will feel increased responsibility for her. She and the dead husband had a business in Mickleburgh, selling antique furniture or something of the kind. I will look into that. It will be months before there is a trial, if the boys responsible are ever traced. Probably they will be: one of them will give himself away. The stabbed boy would make an interesting study, but though he may have nightmares, and conflicts of conscience over giving information about other boys to the police, the authorities will elect to counsel him; he will not come my way, however badly he is troubled as a result of the incident.

I could teach that woman, Marjorie Stewart, known as Midge, how to be strong. What a silly name. Is she like a gnat, darting about? Probably I'll get in touch with her, but not yet.

This afternoon I have a male patient whose problem is a failing relationship. He's been married once, and was divorced; then, too quickly, he entered into this new partnership with a woman with three small children. He sees himself as their saviour, and perhaps he is, moving in with them, providing money, a stepfather figure. He had no children from his marriage, and I asked him why this was. Had he been against having a family, or had his wife? I was curious to know. It just hadn't happened, he had said, though his wife had undergone fertility treatment – drugs to boost ovulation, he had explained, looking embarrassed; they hadn't got as far as attempted test-tube conception. When I think of my own unwanted birth, I feel disgust; nature loads the scales so unfairly. I feel disgust, too, when I hear of temperature-taking, charts, the obsession that makes begetting a child the sole reason for intercourse – though some churches tell us this is what it should be. I told my patient that it was no wonder his marriage foundered under such a strain. Now I see clearly that he cast himself in the paternal role that nature denied him, living out his fantasies through this other woman's children, but she resents him disciplining them and the eldest, a boy of seven, is openly rebellious. My patient wants to have a child with her, but she won't agree; she isn't confident that they will stay together.

Nor am I. I must decide this afternoon whether to point out ways in which he can improve things, by making concessions to her wishes and by ceasing his stern reprimands to the children. After all, it is her house, and he is the interloper. He's tried showering the children with gifts and treats, and seems to see-saw between extremes in his attitude towards them. He hasn't explored his own essence adequately, his inner core; he doesn't know what sort of man he really is. Shall I help him to find out, effect a positive result, or shall I introduce him to a construct, to an artificial concept of what he wants to be, teach him to adopt that role, and plan his future going on from there? He's already had four sessions during which I've tediously noted down his history and listened to his self-pitying monologues. What has he done to deserve these two raw deals, he enquires, when others can be happy? I've asked him if they really are. All life is compromise, I say, and one has to decide how much of it to practise. His current relationship is surely doomed, but it could be prolonged for some weeks, if not months. He says it's difficult to meet potential partners, and I'm sure that's true. Various newspapers run Lonely Hearts sections, but I hesitate to recommend answering those advertisements. You never know who will reply. After all, I could insert one and no respondent would know that I have served a prison sentence on a charge of murder, and am still on licence. A woman making an appointment to meet a man this way might be entering a danger zone. On the other hand, two lonely people who might be compatible could meet by such a means. It is a gamble.

Having to miss the inquest irritated Sarah but there was no need for her to go; she had not been present when Daniel died, was not involved except as a friend, and had no excuse for missing work that day.

'It won't take long,' Oliver had told her, when she expressed doubts as to where her duty lay. Today was a normal one, in the office; there was no outside commitment. Even so, she telephoned Orchard House, offering to cancel everything and come, to be reassured by Mark.

'It'd be better if you can keep in touch with Mum after we've left – Jonathan and me,' he told her. 'That would be a big relief to us.'

'Of course I will, Mark. You can rely on me,' she said.

Mark knew he could; her job meant that she was probably too busy now to try to take his mother over, which might have been a risk. In fairness, Sarah wasn't a monster and she could be very kind, as long as what she did was recognised; her kindness did not operate invisibly. He didn't know how long he and Jonathan should stay. Sooner or later, their mother must be left, but their father had been dead for only three days. How was he getting on? Was he used to it by now? Was he truly at peace and sleeping, as Mark hoped? Surely he couldn't be in purgatory, or limbo, as some religions would insist? Troubled by the prospect of eternity, Mark settled for oblivion.

He wondered what his mother believed about all this. If she broached the subject, he'd pick her up, develop a discussion, but he wouldn't start one.

Would the police ever catch those guilty boys? Surely the other lads would tell, the Noakes boy and his friend Peter Grant? Mark was not too old to have forgotten schoolboy ethics, but this was serious stuff. He accepted that the boy who stabbed his father might not have had the intention of killing him, and Oliver had warned that a plea of self-defence might be entered and sustainable. It would be alleged that Daniel had over-reacted and misjudged the degree of the affray in progress. But he'd had no weapon. He hadn't taken a shotgun with him; he didn't own one. There had been cases where householders protecting their property with guns were accused by apprehended burglars of assault, if not actual bodily harm, and convicted.

He decided to talk to the two boys who lived in Orchard Close, Barry Noakes and Peter Grant, and see if he could persuade them to reveal a name. They'd be back from school around four-fifteen; the bus would drop them at the crossroads and they'd walk home from there. He'd waylay them, invite them in, and lure confidences out of them through a softening process. That would be a better tactic than going to one of their houses and having to get past the parents. Ted Grant, who had given evidence at the inquest, might still be at home, nursing his injured ribs, but Barry's father and mother wouldn't be back from work until much later. Mark knew the form; he and Jonathan had attended the same school.

Accordingly, he prepared to meet the boys that afternoon. After the inquest they had all come home and had a quick lunch; then Jonathan and Midge had gone into Mickleburgh to look through the workshop books in detail. Mark's task was to bring order to the papers in his father's desk at home. Apart from the copy of his will, unearthed from a faded folder, they had already discovered outstanding domestic bills, some of which must be paid at once or Midge would find herself without electricity or the telephone; Daniel had been staving off disaster by instalments. With the consent of the solicitor in Norwich, Oliver had arranged to open a client's account for Midge to deal with any outstanding payments which the bank would not honour while Daniel's affairs were sorted out. Mark suspected that Oliver was guaranteeing this account himself; he must find out for certain, for he, Mark, could put some money into it. They could not be under an obligation to Oliver for long. Jonathan might be able to do something about the money owed to the workshop by chasing up the customers who had not paid their bills. Mark sighed. There was a lot to do, and yet not enough. They could not draw a line beneath their father's death: mourn, and hold the funeral. All depended on the police discovering who had used that knife.

He sauntered up the road, a sturdy young man with brown hair and a small scar on his cheek from a fall from a tree when he was ten; he had broken his collar bone at the same time. He felt totally exhausted, physically and emotionally, after the long drive to Kendal and back the day before, and two near sleepless nights filled with anxiety and grief. Soon he saw, coming towards him, two boys. They were talking together, quietly, not joshing each other, or kicking stones, like boys on their way back from school so often do: they were holding a serious conversation.

Peter and Barry had parted from Greg and several other schoolmates further along the road, where their ways divided. They did not immediately recognise Mark; he was just someone in jeans and a dark fleece jacket. They were walking slowly, reluctant, in Peter's case, to go home, where his father might be waiting to have words with him. Both knew their parents would be pressing them to talk to the police. They were planning to go to Barry's house, where there would be no parents yet.

'Well – Barry – Peter,' said Mark confidently, coming up to them and addressing them collectively, for he was uncertain which was which. Except for university vacations, and short visits, he had not lived in Deerton for years, and could not safely identify youngsters who had turned from children into adolescents in that time. On the other hand, it was reasonable to suppose that they might know who he was, but he took no chances. 'Maybe you don't remember me,' he said. 'I'm Mark Stewart and it was my father who was killed on Saturday. I'm wondering if I could have a word with you. Both of you,' he added.

The boys exchanged glances. They could refuse, could run home; he couldn't force them. But they were both unhappy about their ethical dilemma and he might devise an escape route for them. He was closer to them in age than their parents, and he was looking at them in a friendly way. He wasn't angry.

'Can't do any harm, I suppose,' said Peter. 'I'm sorry about your dad.'

'So'm I,' said Barry, who felt responsible for the whole tragic business because it had begun in his house. 'He was all right.'

Mark wanted to ask how Peter's father was. He hadn't had a chance to speak to him at the inquest as Ted Grant had gone off with the police, who were going to show him numerous school photographs to see if he could pick out any of the offenders. Unsure as to which boy to address, he turned to walk with them to Orchard House and, gazing ahead, said, 'Your father tried to help, Peter. He got hurt, I know. How is he?'

One of the boys, the slightly taller one, replied.

'Says his ribs still hurt. Says he'll be all right, though,' he answered. Ted had displayed his bruises to his son, wanting to break his silence, and very nearly succeeding.

They had reached Mark's gate, and he led the way up the short path to the front door, which was unlocked. He opened it and ushered them ahead of him.

'There's no one here, only me,' he said. 'Go on in.'

To both boys the house, though larger than theirs, seemed very shabby. The window paint was peeling; the striped paper on the walls in the hall had faded; the carpets were worn. Their own modern homes were kept in spanking repair and, except for their rooms, which were often untidy, were spotless. Both fathers redecorated at least one room every year. The two boys stood awkwardly together, waiting for what was to follow. Mark said that he was going to have a cup of tea, and would they like one, or would they rather have coffee, hot chocolate, or fruit juice? He didn't think there was any Coca-Cola. Both said they'd love a cup of tea, which quite surprised him. He thought few youngsters drank it, these days.

'Let's go into the kitchen, then,' he said. 'I'll put the kettle on.' Before he went to meet them, he had brought it to the boil. Now, telling them to sit at the table, he raised the lid on the Aga and moved the kettle on to the hot slab. 'There are some biscuits in that tin,' he said. 'And a cake in the other one. Help yourselves. Knives are in the drawer there.'

The cake was courtesy of Sarah: a gooey chocolate sponge, with butter icing. The boys were unable to resist it, and Peter cut them each a slice.

'Some for you?' he asked Mark, knife poised.

'Yes, please,' said Mark, and while the tea brewed, he found plates for everyone.

The boys were relaxing. Put food in a boy's stomach and, if flagging, he would revive. It was one of Mark's grandmother's dictums and she had followed the prescription when he arrived in Kendal the day before, to good effect.

There was silence for a few minutes while the tea was poured and the cake consumed. Mark, who wasn't hungry, sociably ate his piece and felt better straight away. He poured himself a second cup of tea, and cut another slice of cake for each boy.

'It must have been horrible that night,' he said. 'Those boys just barged in, didn't they, Barry?' He addressed the shorter, tubbier boy, who had a snub nose and freckles and a rather trusting face.

'Yeah,' he agreed, cautiously.

'You weren't expecting them?'

'No.' These admissions had already been made to the police, so repeating them could do no harm.

'There were four of them?' This was the number estimated by Peter's father and the forensic experts. Mark didn't know if the boys had confirmed that to the police, so it might be useful to hear them do so now.

'Yeah,' Barry repeated.

'And they started wrecking the place straight away?'

'Yeah.'

'They pissed on Barry's mum and dad's bed,' Peter burst out. 'Scumbags.'

'Was that what made the other boy – Jamie – go for help?'

'We couldn't get them out,' said Peter. 'We tried. Honest, we did.'

'I believe you,' Mark said. They'd been taken by surprise – almost ambushed – by tougher, if not older boys; Mark concluded that as soon as they realised that Jamie had gone for help, the cowards had fled, and met his father as they left. He had been in their flight path, like the victim of a bee sting.

'They go to your school, don't they? The other boys?'

Peter and Barry did not answer.

'I take it that means yes, or you'd have said no,' said Mark, who, not being a policeman, was bound by no rules as he conducted his interview.

'Did you see the make of car they drove?' he asked.

'No,' the two boys said in unison.

'We were in the house,' said Barry sheepishly.

'Jamie came back after fetching your dad,' said Peter. 'He needn't have. They went for him while my dad was still running across the road.'

This was a full sentence. Mark, encouraged, asked another question.

'Your dad might have been killed, like mine,' he said. 'And

so might the boy who was hurt. Jamie. He's a friend of yours, isn't he?'

'Yes.'

'Those boys might do it again, and someone else might get killed, if they're not caught,' said Mark. 'The police haven't found the knife. That means whoever used it's probably still got it.'

'He could get another one, if he hasn't,' Peter pointed out. 'That's easy.'

'Yes – well—' This was off the point. 'He's used it once. He could do it again,' said Mark. 'How are you going to feel if he does, knowing you could name him now and he'd be arrested?'

Neither boy replied.

'You'll feel you were to blame,' Mark told them roundly. 'And you would be. You could mention a name to me, and I could pass it on, not saying where I'd heard it. Then the police could question that boy and they might find the knife. And they could take his fingerprints. There were plenty in your house, Barry. When they know who to talk to, they'll find proof.'

'They'd guess it was us. They'd know. The others would get us – not – not—' Barry pulled himself up short. 'Not the one with the knife. The others. 'Cause in the end, they'd go down too, if he got caught. But not at first.'

'You think he'd drop them in it?'

'He wouldn't want to take all the blame,' said Barry.

'One of them must have stolen the car they came in,' Mark said. 'Isn't that right?'

Neither Barry nor Peter knew who the driver was, or that the car was not exactly stolen.

'Maybe,' said Barry.

Mark knew that the police were checking up on cars stolen in the area that night. One might be found which would yield helpful evidence. How could he trap these confused, decent boys into making a slip, giving the tiniest hint? He racked his brains.

'I suppose lots of people at school have got knives,' he said. 'Serious knives, I mean.'

No reply.

'As I've said, if they do hurt someone else, or kill someone, you're going to feel pretty bad about it, aren't you? I think you feel quite bad already. You'd better go home now and think about it. You can give a name to me, as I've said, and I'll tell the police if that makes it easier,' he told them. 'But you might have to have the guts to stand by that later.' Then he added, 'Jamie had a lot of guts that night. So did your dad, Peter, and mine. Where's yours, now? All you have to do is give me a name. They'll be arrested if you do. Just one name.'

For one would lead to the others.

Neither boy spoke. Mark escorted them to the door. He had given them the message; now their consciences must do the rest. Silently, they trudged away, Peter turning at the gate to say, 'Thanks for the cake.'

If either was going to crack, it would be Peter, Mark decided, going in to clear up the used crockery before his mother came home and found out what he had been doing. If she looked in the cake tin, she would marvel at his greed.

15

Oliver, having pleaded what mitigation he could devise for his unhappy client, though there was very little, and managed to placate him in the matter of his fine and suspension, returned to the office by way of Daniel and Midge's workshop. He knew that she and Jonathan had planned to go there this afternoon, but they might have lost the impetus when they went home after the inquest. However, they were there, Midge putting tacks into a picture frame, Jonathan sitting at the desk, confronting piles of paper. His attitude was one of despondency; as far as he could tell, the financial position of the business was disastrous; trying to stay solvent, his father had been juggling funds but several balls he had had in the air were about to crash, and the bank might get restive. The recession had affected the business, which was overstocked because Daniel had bought up items at various sales, hoping to make a good profit when they had been repaired and smartened up; what he had not considered adequately was the inevitable slow turnover. Until a year ago he had employed an accountant but had ended that to reduce outgoings. Jonathan had been forced to conclude that this might have been a mistake, especially as the cost could have been offset against tax, and he was in despair about how to put things right. His father hadn't even got his records on computer, a matter Jonathan, a modern young man, found extraordinary. All this mess, he thought, looking at the various heaps of bills and peevish letters, could have disappeared. This wasn't strictly true: the bills would still arrive, but Daniel could have filed everything away on disk with memos to himself.

Oliver's arrival was a big relief. Perhaps he would break the bad news to his mother. Jonathan looked up at him.

'It'll take days to sort things out,' he said. 'Just look at this,' and he showed Oliver a sheet of paper on which he had listed the sums his father owed.

'I can't guess what the stock is worth,' he continued. 'Though it will be possible to calculate what was paid for it.' He had a feeling that Mark's labours at Orchard House were going to produce a similarly dismal catalogue. The only part of the business which showed a healthy profit was Midge's framing, but its scope was limited because of the prohibitive cost of more advanced equipment and a wider range of styles.

After looking up to greet him, Midge had carried on with her work. Oliver cast a glance in her direction and raised an eyebrow at Jonathan, who shrugged.

'Still dazed,' said Jonathan. 'We all are.'

Oliver, who had helped Daniel with the acquisition of the workshop premises, knew that the lease ran out at the end of March. It was renewed quarterly, in advance, but it seemed safe to assume, from Jonathan's gloomy demeanour, that the rent was not paid up. Midge couldn't possibly carry on, but it was much too soon to force her into that conclusion. If time allowed, she would have to reach it by herself. But would it be good for her to be here alone, among these stacks of cupboards, tables, chairs and chests? Maybe he could find someone to lend her a hand until Christmas, although it would be for company more than anything. Adopting an optimistic expression, Oliver watched as she cut a new mount, using the big guillotine.

'It's too soon to make any decisions,' he said. 'We'll have to have a holding operation for the moment.' He'd try to pacify the bank. 'I'll be in touch,' he added, and left them to it.

Soon afterwards, Jonathan decided that he could face no more of this today, and he urged his mother to call a halt. They closed up, set the security alarm, and as they were were walking back to Jonathan's car, an elderly woman, on foot, noticed them and hesitated, then advanced.

'Marjorie – my dear – and it's Jonathan, isn't it?' said Prudence Wilmot, who was walking home after collecting some books she had ordered from Mickleburgh's small branch library, whose staff were very helpful, though sometimes she had to go to Fettleton, where there was a large reference section which she consulted on the spot. 'I'm so very sorry,' she said. Aware of Midge's real name, she thought the diminutive might be reserved for intimates and had not liked to use it on so slight an acquaintance. Leaning forward, she gave Midge a big, maternal hug, managing not to hit her with the bag of books.

'The flowers. You sent the flowers,' said Midge. Her eyes filled with tears. 'Thank you. They're lovely. I'm sorry I haven't written.'

'Oh – for goodness' sake – there's no need for that,' said Prudence.

'They are lovely,' Jonathan echoed, shuffling his feet, afraid his mother might disintegrate out here in the street.

'Where are you off to now?' Prudence asked them. 'Would you like to come home with me and have a cup of tea? I live just round the corner, in the High Street.'

Jonathan thought this was an excellent idea. His mother needed what he and Mark could not provide, but which Judy, for a while, had given: female support. He took Prudence's bag from her and they walked together to the end of the road, turned into the High Street, and went down it to Prudence's pretty house in its terraced row opposite the market square

where, except on market day, cars were parked. She found her
key and let them in, shedding her coat and taking Midge's.
'I'll just put the kettle on,' she said. 'It won't take long.'
Tea, the remedy for pain and shock, and for social unease,
as now, where all three were shy, and Midge and Jonathan
embarrassed. Why should bereavement make the afflicted feel
like that? It happened, Prudence knew. You were a worry to
your friends, and maybe all you wanted to do was go into a
wide open space and scream.

Unlike Mark, at this moment entertaining his schoolboy
guests in Deerton, Prudence could offer hers no chocolate
cake, but there were rich tea biscuits and a few custard creams,
which her cleaner liked.

At the back of her sitting room, which overlooked the garden,
Prudence had added a circular conservatory, where she worked;
they could see her desk, and an old manual typewriter. She sat
them down in front of the coal-effect gas fire and, in a very
few minutes, returned with the tea. She poured it out. Jonathan
took sugar.

'Sudden death is always shocking,' Prudence said firmly,
not pussy-footing round the subject. 'And murder is much
worse than death from natural causes, because it need not
have happened.' On various postings, her husband had had to
deal with the aftermath of both. 'I suppose the police haven't
arrested anyone yet.'

'No,' said Jonathan, while his mother, at the moment
incapable of uttering, gulped down her tea like someone
parched. 'And we can't make plans – the funeral – all that.
There may have to be another post mortem.'

'Oh – of course. For the defence, when there is a suspect,'
Prudence said.

And there would be the trial, the newspaper reports, the
reliving of it all.

'Oliver is being marvellous,' said Midge, speaking at last.

'And Sarah, too,' she added hastily. 'They rescued me that night – Saturday – and put me up. It's only Tuesday now,' she went on. 'It feels like months.'

'Oliver called in at the workshop this afternoon,' said Jonathan. It would not do to discuss their financial problems with this comparative stranger, however nice she was, but he could not avoid saying, 'There's quite a bit of paperwork to sort out.'

'I expect there is,' said Prudence. He'd mentioned plans. This pleasant young man and his brother might be full of notions that their mother should be plucked out of her surroundings and popped into a flat. Was she as much as fifty? Hard to tell in her present state, but Prudence didn't think so: quite a long way off, more Sarah's age, she decided. 'I do hope you won't have to sell your house,' she said. 'At least, not yet. Give yourself time if you can.'

Midge believed she could not bear to leave Orchard House, where Daniel's presence lurked round every corner and all his clothes still hung. When she had taken her own coat from the cloakroom that morning, there was his waxed jacket on its hook. She had buried her face in its fleecy lining, smelling him in the fabric.

After two cups of tea, her colour was returning, and she was able to look past Prudence, through the conservatory to the garden.

'That must be lovely in the summer – your conservatory,' she said. 'We've got a sort of utilitarian one, square, with garden chairs and stuff in it. We haven't had much time to sit there lately. I use it for cuttings and things.'

'I've got a tiny greenhouse,' Prudence said. 'I grow tomatoes and a few plants in pots.'

They discussed gardening for a while, and despite her shaky state, most of Midge's remarks made sense. At length she and Jonathan rose to leave.

'Come in any time if you're in Mickleburgh,' Prudence told her. 'I'm usually here.' She hesitated. She scarcely knew the younger woman. Then she added, 'My husband died four years ago. I still miss him.'

She saw her visitors to the door and watched them walk away, then turned back into the house, closing the door. In the sitting room she collected up the tea things and was about to carry the tray into the kitchen when she saw Midge's handbag on the floor, beside the chair where she had been sitting, and almost out of sight.

Prudence picked it up and rushed out of the house, pausing to pull on her coat which lay where she had left it, draped over the banisters. It was cold, and it was getting dark. She hurried up the road towards the Stewarts' workshop, where she knew that Jonathan had left his car. If Midge had not already missed her bag and turned back, she might just catch them before they drove off.

As, panting slightly, she reached the side road, Jonathan's Escort edged forwards to enter the High Street, and Prudence waved the bag. He braked, and amid explanations and apologies, it was transferred to its owner. Jonathan offered to run Prudence the short distance back to her house, but she said it wasn't necessary; it was so close, and his route to Deerton lay in the opposite direction.

She walked rapidly back, and as she drew near her own door, a woman came towards her on the inside of the pavement. Prudence had to pause to let her pass before she could enter. The woman was middle-aged, wearing a black and white flecked tweed coat, her dark hair pulled back from a pale angular face and secured in a French pleat, once so fashionable. Prudence could see her plainly in the light from the nearby street lamp, and knew that they had met before. For a few seconds they stared at one another as, incredulously, Prudence recognised her, even after nearly thirty years.

The woman gave her a cold glance and walked on as Prudence, chilled right through, entered her own house.

She had very good reason to remember her, although it was so long ago. Prudence had seen her across a law court, daily, throughout the trial. She'd worn her hair – fairer then – in that same pleat, though months earlier, at the time of her arrest, it had hung in a long bob below her ears.

She had committed murder, but she had not got away with it. She must have been released years ago, for a life sentence no longer meant just that.

What was she doing here in Mickleburgh? And had she recognised Prudence, who since then had tried, with some success, to forget her existence? Did it matter if she had?

The evil that men do lives after them, Prudence thought. The consequences of that woman's evil deed were terrible, and she could never atone, no matter how many years she spent incarcerated.

Prudence felt quite shaken. Here was, indeed, a spectre from the past. Just as an unknown boy had killed Daniel Stewart and destroyed the lives of those who loved him, so had Wendy Tyler, with a knife, snuffed out another life and wrecked a family, but in her case she had not killed a stranger.

She had murdered Prudence's younger sister, Emily, in a premeditated, shocking way. The evidence had been conclusive: the knife was found, and blood-stains on the accused girl's clothes. There was a motive: not love, but lust. In France it would have been labelled a *crime passionel* and the sentence would have been a light one. It wasn't so here; Wendy Tyler had been found guilty of murder.

If you behaved well in prison, and expressed regret for your offence, you were freed after a period of years. It was alleged by some, and especially the guilty, that by then you had paid your debt to society. As if such a debt – the taking of a life –

could ever be repaid. Wendy Tyler might be unlikely to kill again; perhaps she had genuinely repented, although she had shown no sign of remorse at the time. The newspapers had remarked on it, and it had been palpable in court. Lionel, her lover, stunned, horrified and subsumed by grief and guilt, had rejected her immediately. He had not seen her after her arrest until they met in court, and then he had not glanced at her once. Prudence, seeing this, had felt a sharp stab of pity until a different expression had crossed Wendy Tyler's ashen face, a look of utter hatred. After that, she had revealed no emotion throughout the trial, even after she was sentenced.

Emily had been ten weeks pregnant when she died and the affair between Lionel and Wendy had lasted for five months.

Lionel, attempting to restore his own life, and his children's, emigrated. Wendy would come out of prison one day, he declared, and unless there were oceans and many miles between them, he would not trust himself not to seek revenge.

Or she might, Prudence had thought, remembering that savage face. In this case, love – obsession – lust – whatever it was – had turned to bitter hatred. Prudence and her husband had approved of Lionel's decision and, through various connections, had helped him to find a position with a firm in Toronto. Later, he had moved west, to Vancouver; the whole family had taken out Canadian citizenship and he had met the woman who became his second wife.

Instead of returning to her typewriter, or even consulting the books she had collected from the library, Prudence sat by the fire remembering that dreadful time. Her husband was at the Foreign Office then, so that they were both at hand to offer help to Lionel and the children, who were too young to understand the full scandal of their father's conduct. They were what mattered, not him, but he had to be forgiven, for their sakes. Those were terrible weeks, with the press trying to waylay the children, who were five and seven years old;

they had to be removed from school and went to stay with their maternal grandparents in the Wiltshire house where later Prudence and her husband had spent their retirement. She remembered Lally playing with the dolls' house which Oliver was now restoring. Lally had moved the family of dolls around, hiding the mother doll and using the girl doll as a small adult, which she christened Wendy. One day Lally's grandmother had found the doll Wendy in bed with the father doll, and the mother doll lay in the bath, with a tiny knife from the kitchen poised above her china form.

So the children had understood. Had they seen their father and the girl in bed together? No one knew for sure. In those days counselling, often routine now, was for the disturbed few. Though she accepted that there were crises and tragedies too difficult to face unsupported, and not everyone had wise and patient friends or spouses to share their problems, Prudence considered it had gone too far today; people were not encouraged to brace up and display courage but to crumple. Lionel had been abruptly forced to acknowledge what he had done, and had accepted his own disgrace and responsibility. His second wife, a calm woman, had nurtured him and the children but the marriage had not lasted. Lally was now a television reporter, and her brother Charles was a marine biologist.

Prudence rose and picked up the telephone directory, checking through the Tylers. There was no Tyler, W. in Mickleburgh. That proved nothing. Sickened, she closed the book. Even if she had been listed, exposing Wendy would help no one and would cause fresh pain by resurrecting the old story. All the same, it was wise to know your enemy, and Prudence was very sure that her feelings towards Wendy were still extremely hostile. She would be alert, ready to recognise her promptly if their paths crossed again, and she would, in that case, try to track her down and find out where she lived. She felt sickened. She did not want her peaceful new life contaminated by this presence from the past.

Rapists and child molesters were released into the area where they lived before they were arrested, and this meant many of them were in proximity to their victims, who might pass them in the street. Prudence shuddered at the thought of it. Later, when the Stewart tragedy was resolved and its immediate impact was fading, she might tell Oliver the story, and of her sighting of her sister's murderer. He had been only a young man when it happened, about the same age as Jonathan was now; he might remember the case because, at the time, it was notorious.

Wendy would not have recognised her. They had never met, and Prudence had played no part in the trial, though her photograph as the bereaved sister had appeared in some newspapers. Ten years older than Emily, she did not resemble her at all, even before her hair went white.

Feeling old and sad, Prudence sat by the flickering flames, which never altered their pattern, unlike those in a real fire, but nevertheless they gave out a comforting glow as she recalled those tragic months. Somewhere, there were newspaper cuttings which she had preserved. When she began writing, she had thought she might use the triangular theme for a novel set in Edwardian times. Maybe writing a fictionalised version of the truth would lay some ghosts. Was there, however, another chapter of the real history waiting to be written?

16

It was dusk when the woman nearly knocked into me as I walked along the street. I was walking on the inside of the pavement and she stopped in front of me, so that I, too, hesitated, and she stared at me. Street lighting lit us both, and I saw an old, white-haired woman, neither short nor tall, completely unremarkable, wearing a dark coat. Pausing only for an instant, for I give way to no one, I walked on, but briefly we had exchanged glances and she looked at me with what, if it had not been impossible, I would have said was recognition. Then the moment passed, I went by, and she let herself into the house outside which we had met. Next door, attached, was a large house with a bow window. I would remember it as a landmark.

Because of the intent look she had bent on me, I wondered if she might have been a patient. I put them from my mind as soon as their treatment ends, though I keep their details in my files in case they return; however, I would know them in the street, perhaps not immediately by name, but I would recollect that I had treated them. Some can't exist without an injection of sympathy and interest, and mine is not wholly insincere, because, living vicariously, I like to know about their lives and I enjoy the power I wield, changing their circumstances, often for good, but not always. Some recommend me; if I make them feel better about themselves, they are grateful, even if that has meant a change of job or a broken marriage. Most make up their own minds, which is right; my role is to help them discover what they really want to do, how they wish the situation to resolve.

Jealousy is a powerful emotion. It was jealousy, so people said, that turned me into a murderer; others said it was infatuation, even lust. I saw it differently. I had acted out of love, to open up his way to freedom. By removing her – the obstacle – our path ahead was cleared, uncomplicated. But already he'd betrayed me and what followed was his fault. He led me on – I was young and inexperienced – and he took advantage of me, flattered me, made me feel special, then seduced me.

I was a virgin until then, and they say you always remember your first. It's true for me, at any rate. There have been no others: no more men.

We'd lie in bed – her bed – and plan how we'd run away together, leave her, go abroad and start a new life. It was all just a dream to him, a sort of 'let's pretend' such as you play with children; he was always playing games like that with them. 'Let's pretend we're pirates. Let's pretend we're in a train going to London. Let's pretend we're soldiers.' His ideas were so childish, but they liked the games, Lally and Charles, and I went along with them. I didn't realise that the game he played with me was the biggest fantasy of all. In the end, he did go overseas – to Canada, I found out, after my release. In fact, that silly Emily was an unnecessary sacrifice; my valour was quite wasted. But I have paid for what I did. Now I owe nothing.

After meeting the strange, hostile woman – she was hostile; I sensed it – I went home and put on Bartok. I don't like soothing melodies. Then I thought about those boys and their crime, and the new widow. Would the guilty boy break and confess? I would not have done so. It was more likely that another boy would grass him up. I learnt all the jargon while I was inside, and I still think in those harsh terms. As well as reading murder reports in the papers, I watch television documentaries about prison reform, false imprisonment, and detection. Some of them make me angry; others are simply amusing. None reveal what it's really like to be banged up, forced to socialise, as they put it, with people you would ordinarily go out of your way to avoid. Some inmates form deep friendships which last after their release: not me. I'm a survivor, and I don't need other people; they need me. I'm acquiring plenty who can't do without my cool room and my quiet presence as, with just a word here or there, I direct their thoughts, often their destiny.

I've helped mend several marriages. What's the use in encouraging a plain, dull woman to give up on a philanderer who, in other ways, is an adequate husband, meeting his financial obligations and functioning effectively as a father? She won't meet anyone better, and she'll lose out materially. I help such women, when they consult me in despair – and when they write to my advice column – to accept the limitations of their lives and adopt a hobby. Often it works. To those trapped in violent marriages, however, I advise action, calling the police, who are better than they were at dealing with such cases, with Domestic Violence units deployed in many forces. If such a husband or partner doesn't reform, I counsel leaving him. It's not the fault of the woman, though she often thinks it is. He, by eating away at her confidence, has been the cause of her disintegration. I advise attending a course in assertiveness. People are so polarised; there are those who blame themselves for every misfortune that comes their way, shouldering all responsibility, and others who will never admit that they have brought about their own disasters. Some people are always finding fault with themselves; others perpetually look for it elsewhere and become paranoid, taking offence at the least thing.

The boy who stabbed that man will blame him for interfering in the affray. To blame himself would be too diffcult. He must convince himself that no fault lies with him; he was provoked. The widow will blame herself for not following her husband to the spot in time to save him.

The law will blame the boy, but his background may explain or excuse his violent nature. As we don't know his identity, we don't know if he has already been in trouble with the police, or whether he has been reared in a disadvantaged home, or felt rejected, needing to strike out at someone.

I can't get that old woman encountered in the street out of my mind. I'm curious enough to want to know her name.

Kevin was beginning to feel safe. His friends wouldn't tell on him, because they'd all been in on it with him, and they'd be for it, too. Those other boys wouldn't dare say a word.

He hadn't read the papers or seen any news bulletins about the case; he didn't want to know. He just wanted it all to go away, and it would.

In his hearing, his parents discussed appropriate punishment for lads who were violent. Kevin's father thought a short sharp shock, army-like, would be the answer. He'd always been strict. Kevin's sister, who was older, had had a difficult time when she acquired a boyfriend, with their dad wanting her in by half-past ten and warning her about rape and pregnancy. In the end, she'd gone off with a man who ran a travelling fish van, and now she lived with him near Birmingham, but they weren't married. Their parents thought this disgraceful, so Kevin knew they wouldn't be well pleased if they learned what he had done, even though he wasn't to blame.

His dad would kill him.

If there was nothing for them to go on, the police investigation would slow down. He did wonder about the knife. He'd thought of going back to look for it in Deerton, but if the police hadn't found it, would he? Where else could it be? He slept soundly on Tuesday night, untroubled by guilty dreams, and in the morning set off to school in a defiant mood. He'd tough this out. He was important, a person to be reckoned with: why, the whole of the local CID were out there looking for him, if the truth were known. Too bad it had to be kept quiet.

On Wednesday morning in Assembly, however, the headmaster had some words to say. He referred to Detective Superintendent Fisher's visit on Monday, and the fact that it had yielded no information despite his appeal. It seemed certain that boys from the school were involved, and there were times when loyalty to the community was more important than loyalty to individuals. If whoever was responsible came forward, his confession might earn him later leniency, and equally, if any other students knew who had carried out the attack – the headmaster tried to avoid emotive terms – they should pass on what they knew. It could be done in confidence, he ended. Two police officers were available, in the building.

The officers were in the hall. One of them, Shaw, though he thought the appeal worth making because it would put pressure on the boys who knew the truth, said it wouldn't work. No matter whereabouts in the school he or DC Benton chose to wait, any pupil approaching them with information would be observed.

The tactic, however, had some effect on Peter Grant and Jamie Preston.

'They think we'll tell in the end,' said Peter, and he wanted to, so badly.

If Kevin and the rest were caught, what would happen to them? Neither Peter nor Jamie knew much about institutions for young offenders. They'd get bail, Peter was sure, and they'd clobber him and Jamie, maybe kill them.

All the same, it might be worth finding out what would be done with them. Who would know, apart from the two officers waiting patiently for information which did not arrive?

After school that afternoon, Jamie asked his mother. She was unsure, but when he had gone upstairs to do his homework, she rang Fisher to enquire.

He came round later.

'If I go up and tell Jamie what you've just told me, he'll know I rang you,' Kate had said on the telephone.

Fisher had suggested coming round on the pretext of asking about Jamie's arm, and somehow turning the conversation towards the subject. So they set it up, and when he called, Jamie and Kate were having supper at the kitchen table. It was shepherd's pie, one of Jamie's favourites, and easy to eat with his left hand, with peas and carrots. His mother protested if he took his injured one out of the sling and used it.

'Will you join us?' Kate invited, after Fisher had apologised for interrupting their meal. 'There's enough.' She had cooked some extra vegetables in case he called while they were eating.

'Oh – thanks,' said Fisher. 'Are you sure? Well, why not?'

While they ate, they talked about the chances for various teams in the forthcoming football season, and England's dismal showing in the Test Match series. Jamie wondered why there were no Test Matches involving Scotland and Wales, and why cricket was so peculiarly English. No one really knew the answer.

Helping them to apple pie from Sainsbury's, Kate said casually that the police had been at the school that morning asking for help with the enquiry, but that it was a wasted effort as no one would come forward publicly.

'I know, but it was worth a try,' said Fisher, accepting his plate of pie.

'If you find out who did it, what will happen to them?' Kate asked, offering Fisher crème fraîche.

'Well, if they're charged, they'll be sent to a young offenders' detention centre,' he said. 'Somewhere very secure, where they'll be locked up. They won't get bail, if that's what you mean. They'll be remanded for trial, and that will give us time to assemble our evidence.'

'All of them?' asked Jamie. 'The ones who were there but didn't do it?'

'They were all accessories,' said Fisher. 'One used the knife, but if we knew who they all were, they'd all be locked up, partly for their own protection but also to prevent witnesses from being intimidated. None of them would get bail.'

'I see,' said Kate, and changed the subject.

It was Peter, however, who telephoned. He did it early the next morning, using a kiosk in the centre of Mickleburgh, and wrapping a J-cloth he had taken from his mother's cupboard round his hand. Jamie would not be in school that morning as he had to go to Fettleton Hospital to have his wound examined and the stitches removed.

His efforts, though, bore no fruit, because all he did was dial 999, ask for the police, and then mutter Kevin's name with no explanation.

The civilian clerk who took the call merely logged it, deciding it was a nuisance call. Her request for the caller's name and more details had gone unanswered as Peter had hung up. He spent the day in a nervous sweat, expecting cars with flashing lights and wailing sirens to collect Kevin from his chemistry lesson or his maths class, but nothing happened.

Jamie returned in the afternoon and the two conferred.

'What did you tell them?' asked Jamie, and Peter told him what he had done and how his call had produced no result.

Peter, who had made an enormous effort, felt deflated. 'Maybe it's a good thing,' he said. We don't want trouble.'

'No, we don't,' Jamie agreed. Then he said, 'How can they walk about like that as if nothing had happened? Heck – they killed a man. Or Kevin did. They'd all be locked up,' he added. 'The super – Fisher – he was at our house last night and he said so.'

'They'd get out again,' said Peter gloomily.

'Not for years and years,' said Jamie.

'They might get off,' said Peter. He had heard his parents endlessly discussing the failure of the police to make an arrest and the lack of clues. 'If they kept denying it, the police might not be able to prove that they'd done it.'

'Not if we gave evidence,' said Jamie.

They looked at one another in desperation.

'Well, I have told them,' Peter pointed out. 'If they're too dumb to do anything about it, that's their fault.'

Further action was postponed.

Fisher, too, had delayed the plan to fingerprint the school. It was not a popular idea, and subtler methods might be equally productive.

17

The police had started to trace the movements of the boys in the year above Barry and his friends, but the process was proving slow and unsatisfactory. Not all were in when the police called, and often there was only the parents' word that they had been at home on Saturday night. Some boys had been at clubs or discos where their presence was vouched for by other boys, all dependent on one another's confirmation.

Kevin and Paul had both dodged direct questioning by managing to be out of the house when the police called. Trevor and Wayne, also, individually saw them arrive, and departed through the back doors of their respective houses. The police had a list of boys who must be located to give an account of their whereabouts when the crime was committed.

Trevor's mother was sure her son could not possibly have been involved. True, while she and his father were out on Saturday night, Trevor might well have been seeing one of his friends. When asked who they were, for connecting boys with others could help collate information, she said he had a lot of friends, too numerous to mention. Much the same response came from Wayne's father; his mother, who was a waitress in a local hotel, was working when the police called, and she had been working on Saturday night. His father had been out then, too, with a young woman he had met while doing door-to-door deliveries.

Appointments would have to be made to see the remaining boys, either at home, with a parent there, or at the police station. Each one would eventually be found and questioned.

Fisher and his Detective Chief Superintendent discussed the advantages of an appeal on television by the dead man's family. Such a tactic sometimes paid off, when bare-faced grief was publicly displayed, but Fisher was against it.

'It's too emotional a stunt for Mrs Stewart,' he insisted. 'She's stressed enough, poor woman, and the guilty kids won't be watching.'

'Their parents may be,' was the response.

'If any parent suspects that their boy is involved, no amount of appealing is going to make them turn him in,' said Fisher. 'It takes a bit of doing, when it's murder.'

Rosemary Ellis, seeing Bob and Ginny returning home from school on Wednesday, opened her door and walked halfway down the outside staircase to enquire if there was any news about the case. Were the police near making an arrest?

They had no inside knowledge, they declared. No boys, so far, had come forward.

'Can't they all be interviewed at school?' Rosemary asked.

'Not exactly. It's private premises. A parent or a guardian must be present,' Ginny said. 'I believe there are plans to change this, and the police were hoping to make some special arrangement, but it hasn't happened yet. They've been there appealing to the students.'

'Oh,' said Rosemary. 'Can't you search for knives? Do many of them carry knives?'

'I wouldn't like to say,' said Ginny.

'But why do they do it?'

'It's about looking good,' Bob said.

He had come to this school from an inner city area where many of the pupils he taught lived in rundown flats with fathers who, if they lived at home, had never worked and where there was a serious drugs problem. Drugs were freely available in Mickleburgh, but less openly.

'Society is decaying all around us,' Rosemary declared. 'What has happened to the virtues?' After this remark, she walked back upstairs and went into her flat.

What indeed, thought Ginny.

'Bit intense, isn't she?' said Bob. 'Bit holier than thou.'

'She's quite concerned,' said Ginny. 'After all, she has met Kate, and Jamie was lucky not to be badly hurt.'

'True enough,' said Bob. 'But I wish the little blighter or his mates would spill the beans so that this could be cleared up.'

By Friday night, when there were still no arrests, Peter and Jamie were at a loss, and very worried. After all, Peter had rung up the police the day before, though he hadn't used Fisher's number.

Jamie turned over in his pocket the card Fisher had given him. He could try again. Perhaps he should. If Kevin was arrested, he couldn't attack anyone, and if Paul and the others chose to have a go, well, Jamie and his mates would be ready for them. His arm was much better now and he'd be able to protect himself. He was going to enrol in some type of martial arts activity as soon as he was better – kung fu, or karate. Even so, if he'd already trained in one of those disciplines, could he have saved either Mr Stewart or himself last Saturday?

He might have brought Kevin down, put him on the ground so that Peter's father could get hold of him, but there had been all the others – Paul, small and wiry, and Wayne and Trevor. There had been so many arms and legs flailing about in that struggle, and it had all been over so quickly. His mother said she was proud of him; he'd shown courage, trying to help. Was he showing courage now, wondered Jamie, afraid of what he was beginning to see was his duty. He knew he was keeping silent because he was frightened of the consequences, not because it was dobbing someone in. None of the boys was a friend of his. No way.

Like many an older, more experienced person faced with a moral dilemma, Jamie was bewildered and almost felt like tossing a coin to decide what he should do. In the end, he made a telephone call, like Peter from a public call box, which was easy since he lived in Mickleburgh and could walk to one – in fact, the same one that Peter had used. But he dialled Fisher's number, and he got the superintendent himself.

Jamie spoke gruffly, to disguise his voice.

'Someone rang saying a name but nothing's happened,' was his message. 'From this box, I think.' Then he added, in something more like his usual voice, 'Another person. Not me,' and he gave Kevin's name. Then, heart thumping, he rang off and hurried home.

Fisher, hearing the line go dead, sprang into action, checking all recorded calls. He traced it, in the end, the call that had not been reported.

Only Kevin was, at first, arrested. His was the only name Fisher had been given.

In the presence of his father his fingerprints were taken, but he refused to speak.

His father asserted angrily that the charge could not be justified. Kevin – so far not interviewed as he had been out each time an officer had called round – would account for his movements at the relevant time, and there would need to be an apology of some magnitude for this mistake. Where was the proof?

Kevin thought they must have found the knife, and inwardly he cursed. Why hadn't he made sure it was disposed of? Where had he dropped it? It was still in his hand when they ran away from the scene. But it was fingerprint evidence from the Noakeses' house that the police mentioned. He'd been there, they alleged, causing damage. After a while it emerged that they could prove he was involved in the rampage, but this did not mean that he had stabbed Daniel Stewart. His father demanded to know where was the evidence? Where was the knife?

Fisher and his team would also like the answer. They asked Kevin where it was and now, encouraged by his father's attitude, he said he'd never had one. He tried saying that of course his fingerprints were in Barry's house; they were friends and he often visited.

'Oh yes?' Detective Sergeant Shaw was assisting with the interview. 'That's why they were on a broken vase in Mrs Noakes's bedroom, and a beer can in the lounge?' he said. 'I'm quite sure Mrs Noakes hadn't gone out leaving empty cans from a previous visit of yours in the grate.'

Now Kevin was afraid. His father, sure of his innocence, had refused the offer of a solicitor, and the questions went on and on as Fisher and Shaw described the wrecking of the house, the damage in the bedroom, and said they would ask for samples for DNA matching. Paul had pissed on the bed. Could they prove that?

Kevin had had enough.

'Yeah, well I was there,' he at last conceded. 'It was just for a laugh. We chucked a few things around, cushions and that, but I mostly watched.'

He thought of naming Paul as the killer, to get the police off his back, but he didn't want to cause him grief; besides, if he did, wouldn't Paul – to save himself – say that Kevin had the knife? It seemed they hadn't found it, and unless they did, they couldn't prove anything more than trashing the house. There were the other two, however, Wayne and Trevor. Trevor had come along because borrowing his mother's car was a dare, but if Kevin named him, he'd tell it all to save himself. So why not name Wayne? Wayne was tougher than Trevor, and likely to be more loyal to Kevin. In despair, he named Paul.

'Are you saying he stabbed Mr Stewart?'

Wearily, Kevin looked at the brawny man facing him across the table; he couldn't meet the gaze of the leaner, darker one, the detective superintendent.

'Best ask him,' he drawled. He hadn't really dropped him in it.

But he wasn't released, and now his father did demand a solicitor, who took some time to arrive; when he did, he looked very serious and failed to get bail for Kevin. There was enough evidence to charge him with criminal damage, just to start with, and more serious charges were probable.

His father, baffled, all his bluster gone, said, 'How did you get to Deerton, anyway? You never walked.'

'I'd like to know the answer to that one, Kevin,' said Fisher mildly. No local car theft on the night in question – and there were some – had so far revealed any connection with the crime.

Kevin did not answer.

'Nicked one, I suppose,' said Shaw.

'I didn't,' Kevin said.

'One of the others did, then?'

No reply.

'Are you going to tell us who it was?'

Silence.

'What happened to it later?' Shaw tried.

'Took it back where he found it, didn't he?' said Kevin.

'Who did?'

But Kevin had told them enough. He closed his lips firmly and looked down at the table.

The solicitor suggested that his client needed a rest, and

Shaw took him away to have it in a cell while Fisher turned
to the boy's father.

'Thank you for coming in, Mr Parker,' he said. 'I'm sorry
Kevin wouldn't open up a bit more. It might have helped him
in the long run.'

'He didn't do it. He didn't do the stabbing,' said Joe
Parker. His anger was returning, but now it was directed
towards Kevin, for having been one of the young hooligans
wreaking havoc.

'Well, we'll get to the bottom of that eventually,' said Fisher.
'Now, I'm sending you home with an officer, and we'll be
wanting Kevin's clothes. The ones he wore on Saturday night.
We'll need to examine them.'

'You can't have them without a warrant,' Parker protested.

'I can very soon get one,' Fisher said. 'Do you want to do
this the hard way? What about Kevin's mother? What's she
going to say about all this? Have you thought of that?'

He had, with dread. She'd have to know how serious it
was, and she'd have to find Kevin's clothes, but with any
luck, knowing her, everything he'd had on that night would
be washed and ironed by now.

Fisher had the same thought as Shaw and Tracy Dale set
off back to Mickleburgh with Joe Parker, who sat seething in
the car, his big hands clenched on his knees, his thick thighs
tense, filling out his worn but spotless jeans. This couldn't be
happening. A bit of horseplay, some laddish pranks that went a
bit far – that was one thing, and it was bad if there was damage,
but stabbing someone – being mixed up in a murder – no! He
couldn't believe it of his boy.

All too soon they reached the Parkers' house in its quiet,
respectable street. The police rarely called in this neighbour-
hood, though there had been an occasional burglary. Joe Parker
walked up the path, his gait lumbering, his breathing heavy, and
let himself in through the front door. His wife was in the lounge,

trying to watch television but she couldn't settle, fretting all the time about Kevin.

Joe glanced at her and said, 'They want Kevin's clothes. What he had on on Saturday.'

She stared at him. She knew what it was all about for the police had cautioned Kevin when they took him in for questioning.

'I've washed them,' was her answer, as Joe had anticipated. She rose, and though she was a thin woman, her tread had become almost as weighty as her husband's as she went upstairs with Shaw and Tracy Dale. The basket in the bathroom was empty. She washed every day, she told them, but there was some ironing not yet done. Several of Kevin's shirts would be among those garments, but by now she would have dealt with whichever one he wore last Saturday and it would have been put back in his cupboard.

'What about a coat? A jacket?' Shaw asked.

'Well, he's got several,' Amy Parker replied. 'He's got one with him now.' Then she hesitated. He'd not been wearing his black jacket with the tartan lining and the inside pockets when he went off earlier. He'd had on an old fawn anorak which normally he shunned. Come to think of it, she hadn't seen him in the black one all week, and it was almost new, bought with some of his birthday money in September.

An innate sense of danger made her keep quiet about it. Kevin would have done nothing worse than cause some mess in the Noakeses' house while his companions did real damage; she wouldn't start the police hunting for a missing jacket. There was probably some simple explanation for its absence, like he'd lent it to a friend. Not his new jacket, though; he wouldn't lend that out. She pulled a green anorak from among his clothes.

'He may have worn that,' she said. 'I don't know. I didn't see him go out.'

Tracy took it from her and put it in a plastic bag, which

she sealed. They bagged up his shoes and two pairs of jeans. Downstairs, they went through the washing but everything was as pristine as in a detergent advertisement; there was not a sign of blood-stains anywhere.

'When are you letting him come home?' she asked.

'Not yet, Mrs Parker,' Shaw answered. 'He still has some explaining to do and we have to make more enquiries.'

'He's not a bad boy,' she said, entreatingly, as they left, with Joe following in his own car. He had to be present while his son was interviewed.

'They all think that,' said Shaw, as they drove away. 'It's not their precious lamb who's deep in shit.'

'They're decent folk,' said Tracy. 'They don't need this.'

'Who does?'

Other officers went to arrest Paul, who lived with his mother and stepfather and two younger half-brothers on an estate where several problem families were housed and where the police had already checked on some lads known to them. None had been involved in the Deerton murder. Paul had not been in trouble before, but he was a boy who, like Kevin Parker, had been out each time an officer called to question him.

His wardrobe was not as extensive as Kevin's, and his mother was behind with her laundry, so that a soiled sweatshirt and several pairs of Paul's dirty socks were available, not that the socks were likely to be useful. His mother knew he'd had on his dark jacket – almost black – which she'd picked up at a jumble sale. He wore it now, and at the police station was asked to take it off.

His mother found a neighbour to mind her younger children while she went with him to the police station.

'He'd not do anything like that,' she told the police. 'Not Paul.'

She was afraid he might be into drugs. Not hard stuff, mind, or she'd have done her nut – but a bit of pot and maybe a few pills. She'd never mentioned these worries to her husband, who was down on Paul as it was. She'd hoped that she was mistaken, or, if she was not, that he'd soon chuck it on his own. After all, they got taught a lot about drugs at school.

But the police found amphetamines and two tablets of Ecstasy in Paul's drawer. They told her so.

They'd pin that killing on him. She knew they would. What would his stepfather have to say about that? Luckily he was out just now; she had no idea where he was, but it meant that she'd have time to invent an explanation for Paul's absence. Though if he was charged and went to court, everyone would know, and his brothers and the neighbour had already seen him driven off by the police.

18

The period that followed the arrests was difficult for everyone connected with the case. There was relief over the breakthrough, but detailed information and evidence still had to be gathered. Fortunately, because the boys' identities were protected, there was a media clampdown and even the most tenacious reporter's revelations were limited, but gossip was rife, and the names of the boys concerned were known generally in Mickleburgh.

So far, they had been charged with assault and criminal damage while the police continued to investigate. Murder charges had not followed because there was no evidence firm enough to bring before the court. Fisher and his team were patiently seeking scientific proof as to who had wielded the knife. Kevin was insisting that Paul had done it, while Paul, suspecting but not sure that it was Kevin who had grassed him, declared that it was Kevin. After all, it was the truth.

Blood-stains on Paul's jeans and shoes were eventually proved to match Daniel's blood, and a faint stain had been found on a shoelace of Kevin's, but there was nothing that a competent defence lawyer could not shred in minutes, probably reducing any conviction to GBH. It wasn't enough. Remanded into secure accommodation, the boys were sent to different centres.

Sarah found that time now went so slowly. Though it was not much discussed, thoughts were centred on the trial which lay ahead, and it was so depressing. She had failed to get the job in London and had applied for another, but she had not been short-listed. This was a serious disappointment, though a private one as she had kept quiet about it. She was glad when her routine was broken by a conference in Kent, and went off eagerly to stay in a luxurious hotel at the company's expense. Jonathan and Mark had left Deerton, and Daniel's parents had stayed with Midge, his father helping to repair some of the workshop stock, and his mother giving the kitchen cupboards a much-needed clear out, so that later Midge could not find things where she expected them to be. She was grateful, though; the couple were as sorrowful as she was, and they understood her determination to keep the workshop open while there were still goods to sell and she had framing orders.

While they were in Deerton, Daniel's funeral took place, the coroner having allowed his body to be released after resuming the inquest and pronouncing him the victim of unlawful killing. On a bleak day, he was cremated at an early hour, to avoid possible media harassment and in the presence of just his family and the Foxtons. Tim managed to take time off, and Judy came. It was a very sad little ceremony; poor Daniel's body had lain in the morgue for weeks, frozen, as Midge said bitterly and inaccurately, like a leg of lamb. She could not face a decision about disposing of his ashes, and agreed that his parents should take them home when they went back to Kendal, and scatter them in some lovely spot that they were fond of. Mark drove down to join them for the melancholy ritual, which made him feel much better than the brief, respectful service in the crematorium.

It was Sarah who suggested planting a tree or shrub in the

garden at Orchard House, as a memorial. She went with Midge to buy one, and they chose a rose, Nevada, vigorous and showy, which would grow to a great height and cheer Midge up in the early summer, and she helped Midge plant it. Sarah didn't garden much; she left most of that to Oliver, and the man who came for several hours a week, but she liked to have flowers in the house and, Midge discovered with surprise, seemed to know quite a lot about growing them.

At Christmas, Sarah had again proved her worth. Mark and Jonathan had both come home, but Daniel's parents, though invited, decided that it was better not to travel when they might not be able to return if it were to snow. Often they were cut off in the winter. Sarah and Oliver invited the Stewarts to spend the day in Winbury, and they were grateful. Now there would be no need to keep thinking that the year before, Daniel had been with them, carving the turkey and beating them all at Scrabble. They didn't want to forget, but they did not want to be forced into remembering. Midge thought about him constantly.

She and Prudence Wilmot had become friendly. Prudence had taken to calling in at the workshop now and then, and had helped with paperwork occasionally. Knowing this, and because she was alone and Oliver was fond of her, the Foxtons asked her too. She would help to dilute the Stewarts.

They'd had a very late lunch, after champagne and smoked salmon while everyone opened their presents. It was a bright, cold, invigorating day, and Prudence had decided to walk across the fields to Winbury. She wrapped up well, wearing black trousers and warm boots, carrying a pair of pumps in a plastic bag. She'd made the plan with Oliver the day before, delivering to his office a small pile of gifts for those expected at The Barn House. He'd fetch her if the weather was bad, he said, and drive her back in any case. Her way led beside the river past bare willows which bordered the black water flowing between rimed banks. The air was crisp and clear; it was a day when it was good to be alive.

Winbury was a small village lying in a hollow, with a church, a pub and a post office which sold groceries. There was no school; local children attended a primary school in a nearby village, and the older ones went to Mickleburgh. Prudence often walked this way; she liked to stride about, mulling over the development of her plot or characters as she went, glad that she had such an absorbing and rewarding, though demanding, occupation.

Today, though, she was preoccupied with thoughts of Midge, whose courageous attempts to disguise her misery did not deceive Prudence, who knew she was near breaking-point. It was clear that the business was foundering and she might soon go bankrupt, though no doubt Oliver was keeping an eye on the situation. It was a monument to Daniel's failure, and Midge was unable, on her own, to put it right. Until the case was resolved and the guilty boys sentenced, Midge would know no peace, and what if they were not charged with murder, or, literally, got away with it? It could happen. Prudence knew from Oliver that the police case against the two arrested youths was not strong, and it could be that one of the other two, as yet unnamed, had used the knife, not either of those now on remand.

Wendy Tyler had been on remand for months before her trial. It had been a dreadful time for all of them – Prudence and Emily's parents, and Lionel, not that they had felt much sympathy for him then. Prudence had not seen the woman she was sure was Wendy again. Perhaps she had been only passing through Mickleburgh that day.

Banishing her morbid thoughts, Prudence climbed the final stile by the church and took the footpath leading to the main street. It passed between the churchyard wall and a field where two horses, rugged up against the winter, were eating hay, one of them tossing it up and snorting as he munched. The service was over, but Prudence saw a tall woman walking along the road some way ahead of her. She wore a camel coat and an enveloping type of hat, pulled low over her ears. A dark brown shawl was thrown over her shoulders, muffling her. Prudence slowed her steps as the other woman turned down a side road and went past The Barn House, pausing briefly at the gate and looking up the short drive. Then, not glancing back, or she would have seen Prudence, she walked on.

Rosemary Ellis, attending the service in Winbury church, had hoped that Oliver would be among the congregation. She allowed herself to create a scene wherein, recognising her, he invited her to his house for a Christmas drink. But it was not to be.

She moved away after shaking the vicar's hand and prowled around the graveyard, looking at tombstones, until everyone had gone, including the vicar, who hastened back to his home in another village, for he ministered to three parishes. Then, with no one in sight, she strolled along the road and turned down the lane in which, as she knew, stood The Barn House. She had often walked past it, admiring its old mellow stone and the neat shrubs beside the gravelled approach. Now, she saw a shabby Ford Escort parked outside the door. Perhaps the son's? He was a doctor. Inside, there would be a blazing fire, holly, a Christmas tree hung with baubles, piles of expensive gifts for everyone. Sarah Foxton, a lucky woman who had had it easy all along the line, would be presiding over everything with grace and competence. Conscious of a movement behind her, Rosemary realised that her curiosity might be noticed by anyone approaching and walked on, not glancing back. She had learned to practise iron self-control.

Prudence found the day poignant, and painfully illuminating. Midge and her sons did their best to be cheerful and to help with what was going on, but Sarah was so well organised that she needed little assistance except to carry in the dishes and set them on the long refectory table in the dining room – a low-ceilinged room which faced north and was rather dark, but with lighted candles on the table, it looked festive.

When she arrived, a glass of mulled wine with a kick in it was put into her hand; after her trudge, it was very welcome. Jonathan and Judy were out walking, she was told, but as she had not met them, they must have gone another way. Mark and Midge arrived soon after she did, driving up in the Volvo, Mark looking strained and Midge with bright patches of false colour on her cheekbones, and dark stains beneath her eyes. She had spent a wakeful, weepy night, taking a pill at three in the morning and then lapsing into a torpor. Her sons had tiptoed in, and finding her asleep, had left her to wake naturally; Jonathan, eager to see Judy, had gone ahead to the Foxtons, leaving Mark to follow with their mother.

Even after several cups of strong coffee and a bath, Midge still felt like a zombie, and Mark, anxious and alarmed, saw her gradually adopt a brittle animation which he found as dreadful as it was artificial. She smiled and prattled when they reached The Barn House, almost as if she were drunk. What had she been taking? Mark had seen her with some pills. Surely the doctor hadn't given her anything like speed? Could she have bought something at the chemist's? She was, he realised, very near hysteria.

Some time after the two youths were arrested, Ted Grant had come to see her. He had told her that someone tipped the police off and he would like to think it was Peter, but nobody was saying. He'd touched lightly on his son's expressed fear of revenge. Two other boys had been involved and they had not been traced. Although Kevin and Paul were both locked up in a secure unit, messages could be got out by the determined and if they were allowed to use the telephone, they would be able to organise intimidation.

Midge, required to assuage this decent man's sense of guilt, had done her best.

Gwen Grant, too, had come across to see how Mrs Stewart was getting on. She had brought over freshly baked scones and flowers in an effort to console, and Midge, deeply touched, had wanted to hurl herself into the arms of this kindly woman and sob her heart out. Instead, she strove to be contained, thanked her, and offered tea, which Gwen accepted and then somehow contrived to make, mildly clearing up some of the clutter in the kitchen while she did so.

Now Midge pecked at her helping of turkey with its trimmings. She had drunk her champagne with alacrity, hoping it would put new life into her, and had eaten several wedges of smoked salmon perched on brown bread in an attempt to stop her head from spinning. She felt that she was on the verge of losing all control and it was terrifying. Oliver cast anxious glances at her and was sparing as he refilled her glass. Prudence was shocked at her appearance; it was only a week since she had last seen her and she seemed to have lost several pounds in weight since then. She was much jumpier, more on edge. Perhaps it was the strain of having to face this long holiday, with all its emphasis on family solidarity, often such a myth. Determined not to sit silent, Midge was asking everyone what they were planning to do in the next few days, who was going to the cinema and what would they see, questioning Judy about her course, wondering how Tim was; he was on duty over Christmas but would be home for a brief visit soon. He telephoned during the meal, and had a short conversation with his parents and his sister, and sent his regards to all the others. Sarah said what a pity it was that he couldn't be with them.

'Then we'd all be here,' she said, and Judy kicked her hard under the table, for Daniel wasn't.

Prudence leapt in with a diversion, asking Oliver how the dolls' house was getting on, and he said that it was almost finished. He would give it back to her quite soon, he told her. They talked about it, spinning the subject out for a while, letting the charged atmosphere subside. There were no crackers. Oliver, who rarely insisted on anything with which Sarah did not agree, had decreed that pulling them and wearing paper hats would be too much to expect of the Stewarts. As soon as they left the table, Prudence asked to see the dolls' house, and went with Oliver to his study. Midge followed them.

'I want to see it, too,' she said. 'I think it's wonderful. It was yours, wasn't it?' she asked Prudence.

'Yes. I loved it. I made up stories about the people in it,' Prudence said. 'And my niece played with it when she was little.'

Midge had not heard Prudence mention a niece before. She knew Prudence had a son who held some diplomatic post in Moscow.

'Where does she live?' she asked, and did not listen to the answer as she looked inside at the family of dolls. 'Oh, poor Mr Wilberforce,' she said. 'Whatever has happened to you?'

Sarah, in a fit of malice, had removed him from his position at the table, where Oliver had left him, and had laid him prostrate on the floor.

19

Christmas has always been a lonely time for me, but I am far from unique, and social isolation is surely preferable to the charged atmosphere that can prevail when families, confined together, are forced into false jollity, compelled to co-exist for hours, even days, eating and drinking too much, envying and resenting those they think more fortunate than themselves. However, afterwards, it brings me new patients, those who have found the strain too much and snapped, or almost lost control. I resume consultations the day after Boxing Day, when present and prospective patients are still on holiday and have time to attend; people even come in off the street, with no appointment, hoping I will have the time to see them. The Samaritans and I, and others of my colleagues, are the ones who pick up the post-festive pieces and either put them together again or make the fractured victims understand that their case is hopeless – not that the Samaritans do that: they never give up hope, and actively discourage suicide.

In prison, attempts were made to mark the season. Paper chains were hung, and turkey featured on the menu. I, being one of the religious group, spent hours in church. I sang carols, took my part in anthems, even read the lesson. Soberly, I stood and knelt, appeared to pray, to be devout. It was easy and became a habit, so that I still adhere to it today. It punctuates my calendar. I went to Midnight Mass this Christmas Eve and sang carols. My voice is good, a light contralto.

On Boxing Day I posted my professional card through various letter-boxes, some in the town, but I went out to Deerton, too, and put one through Mrs Stewart's door. There was no mistaking Orchard House; the name was on the gate. It looked deserted. My card bears, in bold type, my initials and my name, with the prefix Dr, to which I am not entitled, but, with the name of the professional association I joined so easily, it inspires confidence.

On my card – postcard size – is printed in italic script my message:

DEPRESSED? TIRED? LONELY?
CHRISTMAS IS FOR FAMILIES. IS YOURS DYSFUNCTIONAL?
DO YOU FEEL ISOLATED? UNABLE TO COPE?
Consult a trained and confidential counsellor.
Fees moderate.

I knew my delivery drop would have some results. Even so, I was surprised when, a week later, Mrs Stewart telephoned.

Kate Preston and Jamie had spent Christmas with her parents, in Devonshire. Kate wanted to escape from the aftermath of the murder and the arrest of the two boys.

After they were charged, Jamie had not wanted to discuss it.

'They were there,' he finally admitted to Fisher, when he was asked for corroboration.

'Aren't you going to say which one of them stabbed you, Jamie?' Fisher had asked him. 'We had a tip-off, you know. Two, in fact, but the first message didn't get through. Both anonymous.' He was steadily regarding Jamie, who looked sheepish.

Fisher had explained that, for want of direct evidence, so far the boys had not been charged with murder.

'They're both guilty, though. The one who stabbed Mr Stewart and the one who aided and abetted him. He's an accessory to murder, and so are the other two, whose names we don't yet know, but we'll trace them now. Guilt by association. You know what that is, Jamie. I don't have to spell it out for you,' he said.

Fisher, who had come to talk to Jamie at home and off the record, deplored the prospect of youths who had hitherto kept out of serious trouble being given long sentences and then, when too old to remain in young offenders' institutions, being sent to adult prisons where they would meet real vice and violence. When finally released, as they would be, whatever the verdict and the punishment, they might emerge as confirmed villains. He wanted to see such youngsters being helped to straighten themselves out, as happened already in some centres; the good work could, however, be undone. Violent youths and children who killed – there were a few – should never, he maintained, be transferred to adult prisons.

He said some of this to Kate, in Jamie's hearing. Kate, in the calm of her parents' cottage overlooking the sea, meditated on his words and whether to open the subject with Jamie. Maybe it was better left, to be faced when they went home.

His grandparents, horrified by the whole business, had understood his dilemma. While he was out kicking a football around with some local boys, they discussed it with Kate.

She told them about the two calls the police had received. Fisher, loyal to Jamie, had not revealed his suspicions about the callers' identities, but Kate shared them.

'Jamie was very brave the night it happened,' Kate said. 'But not quite brave enough to tell the whole story. Neil Fisher – that's the detective in charge of the case – hopes they'll get enough evidence from the forensic scientists to convict the boys they've arrested, but there were two more, and someone stole the car they used. That hasn't been traced.'

'And the whole thing was a sort of gate-crash which went out of control?' asked her father.

'Yes. Mind you, they were bent on mischief – must have been. They took beer with them – there were several empty cans in the Grants' house. By the time they got there, they were probably drunk. Jamie has said he thought Paul – one of them – might have been high on something. Some drug,' she added, in case they hadn't understood.

'And it's a misplaced schoolboy code of honour that's stopping the law-abiding boys from saying enough to convict the others?' asked her father, wanting to be certain.

'Not just that. The two others – the ones still at large – could get at Jamie and his friends,' said Kate. She wondered why the police had not carried out a mass fingerprinting operation to find those boys. Perhaps they still hoped that the arrested pair or the innocent quartet would soon name them.

'Savages,' said Kate's father, a retired merchant seaman.

Jamie succeeded in putting the whole thing out of his mind while he was away. He enjoyed being with boys who knew nothing about it. He slept and ate well, played Scrabble and Monopoly with his mother and his grandparents in the evenings, and went out sailing, well wrapped up, in a boat owned by his uncle, who ran a chandler's shop at a marina not far away.

After they returned to Mickleburgh, just before the new school term began, Peter telephoned when Jamie was alone at home. For a while they talked about what they had been doing during the holiday, and then Jamie asked if there was any more news.

'Can you come over?' Peter said. 'Greg's coming, and Barry. We fancied a chat.'

'All right. Mum's out seeing about something to do with timetables at school. I'll bike over,' said Jamie. 'See you.'

He left a note for his mother, and set off before she could return and tell him he was not to go to Deerton. But she wouldn't do that, he thought; she might have driven him there, though.

He pedalled off. It was very cold, and he wore the knitted cap that had been so useful out sailing, pulled well down over his ears. Usually he scorned gloves, but not today. The exercise soon warmed him up as he tucked his nose inside the zipped-up neck of his fleece jacket, the same one that he had worn that night. It hadn't seemed as cold as this on his uncle's boat, but sea air was somehow different. He enjoyed cycling, and rode fast; he had a good mountain bike which his mother had helped him pay for two years ago. On the journey, he thought of nothing except the speed at which he was travelling and the miles he was clocking up.

It was good to see his friends again. He parked his bike round the back of Peter's house and went in. Peter's parents were both out at work. Ted had plenty to do and not enough time to fit in everything; Gwen, who was a hairdresser, had clients wanting to look glamorous as they celebrated the New Year.

Barry had been glad to get out of his house, where his father, who did not really want to take time off, was restricted because builders' and plumbers' suppliers had all closed down and he could not get materials he needed. He was dealing with emergencies, but, apart from that, was continuing the refurbishment of the house. The atmosphere at home was not altogether friendly, though, as Barry's mother pointed out, all he had done was open the front door to the invaders.

Barry's own desire now was to punch the heads of those responsible. He said so to his friends.

'Well, we can't punch Paul or Kevin,' Greg, who arrived

just after Jamie, declared. 'But maybe we should have told, right away.'

'And got beaten up ourselves? Maybe killed?' asked Barry.

'They'd already done Mr Stewart,' Jamie said. 'They might as well do us too. They'd get no worse punishment. The police did nick them, after all.' He glanced at Peter; neither of them was going to tell the other two what part they had played in this. 'And they'll get more proof,' he added, hopefully.

'But what about Wayne and Trevor?' said Greg, who was having bad dreams about that dreadful night. In these nightmares he was always running home across the garden at the back of Barry's house and then over the allotments that separated his house from Orchard Close, but instead of managing to escape, he was pursued by the four troublemakers, all of them brandishing knives, until eventually he could not run fast enough and they caught up with him and plunged their knives into his body. At that point he would wake up, sometimes, to his mother's dismay, screaming.

'Kevin and Paul will split on them,' said Barry sagely. 'Once they're committed for trial. My dad says they'll know then that it's no good keeping quiet, and if they talk, they may get shorter sentences.'

'But it was Kevin that did it,' said Jamie. 'He was the one with the knife. He stabbed me. I should know.' More and more, he was feeling he should tell Fisher the whole story. He knew he was likely to be called as a witness and that he could not refuse to testify; Fisher had already made that clear. If he did, he might be guilty of contempt of court. 'I thought about it on the way back from Devon,' he said, and, looking abashed, added, 'My granddad got a medal in the war. He was in the merchant navy bringing stuff across the Atlantic. He was pretty brave, I'd say. And then my dad was in the army.' He paused. The others knew his father had been killed on active service. 'He was brave, too,' he went on. 'I can't be a coward. It's just

– if I tell Fisher all about it, it's my mum I'm worried about. If they did me – Trevor and Wayne – would you lot see she was OK?'

The others shuffled their feet in embarrassment and mumbled that they would, and Peter added, 'I can't see that they'd get you, because by then they'd be locked up, too.'

'There'd be their mates. They've got other mates,' said Greg, but he was wondering whether, if Trevor and Wayne were arrested, his bad dreams would stop.

'They wouldn't go for any of us after that,' said Peter. 'It's too serious, this one is. They'll be inside for years and years and we'll all have left school and even college by the time they're out again, if they ever are.'

'My dad said they oughtn't ever be let out,' said Barry. 'Throw away the key, he said. A few years ago they'd have been hanged, he said.'

'Not kids. They didn't hang kids,' said Greg.

'A hundred years ago they got sent to Australia,' Jamie said. 'Even for stealing sheep, or bread, you got transported.'

'Stealing sheep?' This from Barry.

'For food, it would be,' Jamie said. 'They do it still in Wales and places. Sheep rustling. I suppose they get fined now if they get caught.'

'Well, Kevin and Paul won't get hanged and they will be let out one day,' said Peter. 'Not for ages, though.'

'Suppose they get off?' asked Greg. Then they might come after him in real life, not just in dreams. 'People do. Lawyers get them off.'

'Not for killing people,' Peter said.

'It depends on the evidence,' said Jamie. 'They need solid evidence to make it stick. That superintendent – Fisher – said so.'

'And us telling would be it – the evidence,' said Peter, not asking; stating it as fact.

'If we all do it together, we'll be all right,' said Barry. 'They'll believe us, too. We were there, after all.'

They looked round at one another, four adolescent boys, two tall and thin and somewhat uncoordinated, growing fast, one – Barry – short and stocky with a round determined face, and Greg, whose acne was a problem.

'Shall we?' asked Jamie. 'I've got Fisher's number. It's his direct line. Shall we do it now?' He hoped they would say yes, so that he could stop wondering about it and take action. Then it wouldn't be their worry any longer.

Trevor's mother had put her Lada up for sale. She'd advertised it in the *Mickleburgh Herald,* a local paper funded mainly by advertisements, and was now cleaning it out, ready for the prospective buyers she hoped would soon flock to inspect it. She'd use the money for a holiday to celebrate Fred's fiftieth birthday. She had changed her job after Christmas and now worked in a newsagent's in Mickleburgh, where extra staff were needed to sell lottery tickets, and she could walk to work.

She attached a long hose to her vacuum cleaner and plugged it in, then set it to devour the dust, sweet papers and general mess that had accumulated in the car in recent weeks. It had never been a treasured possession, more a convenience to take her to her former job in Fettleton. Some kid might buy it, Trevor had said, though not one who valued his image.

'A girl might. Someone sensible,' his mother had responded sharply. Image, indeed. 'You might help me,' she'd suggested, but there was no sign of him so far.

He emerged while she was scrabbling under the driver's seat, pulling out tissues and a long-lost glove.

And a knife.

She wasn't sure what she'd grasped at first, as she looked down at it, holding it inside a tattered piece of paper – an advertising flyer – which had covered it among the other rubbish. It wasn't an ordinary knife, nor a penknife, but one that disappeared inside its handle: a flick knife. She stood up and stared at it, slowly realising what it was as Trevor, carrying a bucket which he had filled with water and detergent, came to lend her a hand. Seeing what she held, he dropped the bucket.

'Trevor,' she said, very calmly, 'what do you know about this?'

20

She came to see me a few days after Christmas, in the long
fallow period before the world started back to life again. I had
had several urgent callers seeking emergency appointments
and she, it seemed, was one of them. From the window, I
saw her park an old Volvo in the road outside; my consulting
room is in a quiet residential area where it is easy to park
in the daytime, though when I see patients in the evening the
residents' cars tend to fill most spaces.

I waited for her to ring the bell, then pressed the automatic
door release so that she entered my small hall, where three
tweed-seated chairs indicated that each patient was only
one among many wanting my attention. Arranged on a low
table were some magazines – all recent editions, none tatty
as in other waiting-rooms – Good Housekeeping, Country
Life, The Lady, even some motoring magazines: nothing flash
or tasteless. I buy them in a casual manner; I subscribe
to none.

She was early, so I made her wait, though I had no patient
with me. From the start, I have to establish my authority.
After a few minutes – not long – I opened the door of my
consulting room and asked her to come in. Conscientiously, I
smiled down at her: she is very small, five foot two, perhaps,

and extremely thin. I imagine she has lost weight since the murder. It's understandable. She has a raggedy crop of ill-cut dull brown hair.

She was trembling, so I poured water for her, and she sipped it, spilling some before setting the glass down on a Crown Derby saucer placed for the purpose on the corner of my desk.

'Now, Mrs Stewart, tell me how I may help you,' I invited. She found it difficult to speak.

'My husband died. Suddenly. It was violent. He was stabbed,' she said, speaking in jerky sentences, twisting her hands together. 'You probably heard about it. Some boys did it,' she continued. 'In November.'

'How terrible,' was my soothing murmur. 'I'm so sorry. Tell me how it happened. Were you there?' I was not sure if she had witnessed the incident.

'No. He went to intervene – some boys were vandalising a house opposite ours, in Deerton, and one boy – not one of the hooligans – came to us for help. Dan went, and the boys turned on him and stabbed him.'

'I read what was reported in the papers,' I encouraged her. 'It was dreadful for you. Shocking.'

'Yes, and I'm not dealing with it very well,' she said. 'I'm trying to pull myself together and put a good face on things, but I'm not succeeding. I keep on crying and I can't concentrate. I don't want to worry my sons or my friends. I found your card and wondered if perhaps you could help.'

'That's my job,' I told her. 'To guide people towards managing their lives.'

A regular consultation twice a week would be a useful contribution towards my rent, and I would feel good about assisting her, since she was clearly in a state of utter despair. I wanted to be involved in this: I wanted to know as much I could learn of the story, how her circle of friends was reacting, what part that old woman I had seen in Mickleburgh was playing in her life. I had seen this pathetic woman, Mrs Stewart, entering her house more than once when, hoping to learn something about the occupant, I was passing. I hadn't recognised her then, this tiny woman; the newspaper shots of her had been indistinct.

I still didn't know the older woman's name.

She told me the story, more or less coherently, her thin body shaking and her hands tearing at one another. I remember how one shakes like that, in deep stress. I had done it, too. I asked if she was eating, and could she sleep, and she said she had no appetite but tried to force food down. She was sleeping badly, waking up remembering what had happened, reaching out to touch only the empty bed.

I understood her deprivation. I, too, in different circumstances, had lost my lover, my sustainer, but mine betrayed me. Hers was taken from her by a violent hand.

'How do you feel towards the arrested boys?' I asked, genuinely interested.

'I don't know. They're youngsters – fifteen, sixteen – it wasn't personal. They were lashing out – hitting at authority, perhaps,' she said. 'Sometimes I hate them. Sometimes I think they are victims too.'

She told me about the funeral, how it had to be delayed and then how sad and bleak it had been. Emily's had not been delayed long; my defence, content with the official post mortem, had not wanted a second one. She had received hundreds of letters, she revealed, offering condolences, but had not replied to any of them, hiding them in a drawer where her sons would not find them.

'Why don't you let your sons deal with them for you?' I suggested. 'They could send a small printed slip mentioning that you received too many to acknowledge individually.'

She liked this idea, but thought that her sons would be

*shocked that she had left them unacknowledged for so long.
They'd read some of them, she said, those that came soon after
the event, when both young men were still staying with her.*

*'Perhaps some friend?' I proposed, and she said that she
would think about it.*

*Something positive had been achieved. I asked her then
about her friends. Was she receiving adequate support from
them?*

*'Oh yes. My friends have been wonderful,' she enthused.
'Oliver and Sarah Foxton in particular. We'd all had dinner
together that night, the night Dan was killed. They helped me
then. We went to them on Christmas Day, my sons and I. Oliver
is a solicitor. He says I can't keep our business going. It was
losing money even before – before—' Her voice trailed away.*

*'Can you sell it? Do something else?' A pragmatic person
myself, I can often direct others into practical channels.*

*'I could sell the lease if anyone wanted to buy it,' she said.
'But who would? It's not really central and it's not in good
repair.'*

*'A new venture would require its own layout,' I explained.
'It might not suit everyone, but there could be a use for it.
Now,' I added, for I was wearying of her, and I had given her
several excellent suggestions to consider, surely good value
for her forty pounds, 'Your real need is for sleep. When you
are more rested, some of these difficulties will not seem so
immense and you will have more energy to deal with them,
and, of course, my support, if, as I hope you will, you continue
with these sessions. One is not enough, Mrs Stewart,' I added.
'Not when you are the victim of such trauma. I'm going to give
you some herbal remedies which will help you, and I want you
to return in three days' time.'*

*She took the little bottles: floral essences I buy and repack
myself. Some people find them beneficial, and placebos have
their uses.*

She paid in cash, trying to laugh it off, saying the bank might not like her cheque.

I was pleased. I need not put this consultation through my books. It had been an interesting session.

Trevor's mother saw shock and guilt, in equal measure, on her son's face as she held the knife towards him, still resting on the scruffy piece of paper.

'What's the explanation for this?' she asked, her voice icy. Then her hand began to shake and she closed it gently round the knife, still protectively surrounded by the paper. She was remembering that after the shocking murder, Trevor had been out each time the police had called to see him. She had mentioned their visits to him, and he had said they were talking to every boy about the Deerton stabbing. Of course they were; it made sense. 'Come inside, Trevor,' she said.

'It's not mine,' Trevor began, and he turned away, ready to flee from the scene.

'You're not going anywhere,' his mother stated. 'Go into the house. Go on. Now.'

He hesitated, but only for a moment, his stomach churning as, in panic, he obeyed, sliding through the door into the kitchen. She followed him, and laid the knife down on a plate, which she lifted from the drainer.

'It's not mine,' Trevor repeated. 'I don't know how it got there.'

'I think you do,' his mother said. 'You'd better tell me, before I ring your dad.'

His father, a storekeeper in a discount warehouse, had no long Christmas break.

'I didn't touch him. It was Kevin,' Trevor burst out. 'They got the right one.'

'They've got that other boy, too. That Paul,' said his mother.

'It was Kevin had the knife,' Trevor insisted.

'And what had you to do with it?'

'I don't know anything about it,' Trevor blustered, but his mother would have none of that.

'You were there. You said it was Kevin had the knife. You saw what happened. You helped those others trash that house,' she accused. 'How did that knife get into my car?'

'It was an accident – it was just a joke – then this old guy came along,' said Trevor, whining now.

'Some joke,' said his mother. 'I suppose you drove them there. Those others, Kevin and Paul, and there was another, wasn't there?'

She remembered which night it was. She and Trevor's father had made an evening of it, and the news had broken in the morning, but the Lada was in its place when they came home. Trevor had been a bit quiet the next day, she recollected.

Trevor did not answer. He sat facing her, looking sullen, shifting his feet to and fro beneath the table. Then he reached out a hand towards the knife, and she knocked his arm aside with a sharp blow.

'Don't you touch it,' she ordered him. 'Have you handled it before? The truth, now, mind.'

'No,' he said, and added, in a growl, 'Kevin must have dropped it.'

'So you did take it? The Lada?'

Mutely, miserable, he nodded.

'I'm calling the police. Then your dad,' she said, picking up the plate on which the knife rested and taking it with her to the telephone. 'I think you'd rather talk to the police about this than your dad.'

His dad would belt him, and he'd deserve it. Shaking now, partly from shock and fear, but also with suppressed rage, Trevor's mother dialled 999, and when Trevor, desperate now, pushed past her, making for the door, she called him back. 'You're not going anywhere,' she said. 'You'll answer for your part in this.' But he'd named the boy who had used the knife.

The knife was carefully bagged and sealed. Possibly its blade would bear stains of Daniel Stewart's blood, or Jamie's, or even, if they were lucky, identifiable amounts from both victims, but it might also yield a fingerprint. When Trevor's father arrived, not long after the police, Trevor finally accepted defeat and told his story, limiting his own role to that of providing the car and acting as the driver.

'I didn't nick it. I just borrowed it,' he muttered.

'Driving without a licence and insurance,' said Detective Sergeant Shaw, who had arrived to reinforce the uniformed officers who had answered the call.

His father could not believe what he was hearing. His face turned purple, and Trevor's mother's decision to get the police there first, if possible, was justified. He'd have lammed into the boy for his part in this, even if all he did was, as he maintained, take and drive the car.

The police knew, however, from Ted Grant that all four boys had attacked him and Daniel Stewart, though only one had produced a knife. All four had kicked and punched both men as they lay on the ground, and at least one of them had gone for Jamie before he was stabbed by another. They were all accessories. All would face serious charges.

Trevor was taken to the police station for further questioning and, at last, to be fingerprinted. The results of that would put him in the Noakeses' house at the relevant time. Both his parents went with him, while the uniformed officers guarded the Lada until the transporter arrived to take it away for scientific testing. It might retain traces of its passengers on that fatal night, even after such an interval, for the knife had been there, probably dropped by its user in the confusion as they fled, and kicked under the driver's seat. Trevor's mother seldom had a passenger; not much had been disturbed for weeks.

Trevor named Wayne in his statement, and he was arrested later in the day. Neither boy was granted bail, and when Trevor's mother protested, she was told she could be thankful that he would be safe in custody, out of reach of any lynch mob who might want to get their hands on him.

Next day, both boys were remanded to secure accommodation for a week. Like Kevin and Paul, they would be inside until the trial.

Sarah's office had closed down over Christmas but she had brought home with her details of a project for a firm in Swindon which required the reorganisation of its management systems and office layout. Working on it, she grew bored and felt like throwing all her ideas into the wastepaper basket. She'd played about on her computer, drawing shapes and forms, studying the time and motion aspects of various proposals, then costing them as far as she could while unable to contact suppliers who were also closed.

Oliver had not taken the week off. Solicitors were still required to deal with urgent matters, and it was a chance to clear backlogs in the office. While he was there, Fisher, aware that he was supervising the interests of the Stewart family, rang him to tell him about the two new arrests. Now the case was firing up.

Fisher said he planned to break the news to Midge himself, and Oliver decided that he had better be there, too. He wondered if Midge would be at home. She might be at the workshop, although there could be scarcely any business for her to attend to. In order to find out, he rang the premises, but there was no reply. It was safe to assume she was at Orchard House. She would be on her own. Mark had gone back to Scotland for a few days' skiing in the Cairngorms before returning to work, and Jonathan and Judy were also skiing, in Austria, with a university party. Midge had persuaded both her sons to take this break. She said she would need them more when it came to the trial.

Before going over to Deerton, Oliver rang Sarah to explain. 'Shall I come?' Sarah volunteered immediately, glad to have an excuse to interrupt a task she was finding tedious. Since the conference in Kent, she had lost much of her enthusiasm for her work.

'I'll ring you if it seems a good idea,' he hedged. 'Maybe later, if she goes to pieces.'

She might. He had not seen her for several days but she had been so tense and febrile at Christmas, it had seemed as if she might suddenly flare up and fizzle out, like a firework.

Driving over, he remembered finding the father doll, Mr Wilberforce as Midge had named him, lying on the dolls' house floor. What on earth had made Sarah move him? Was she giving him, Oliver, a message? No one else could have done it, but it was unlike Sarah to be fanciful, let alone malicious.

He reached Deerton before Fisher. Midge, who had been warned by a telephone call from Poppy Flower that they were on their way, heard his car and had opened the front door before he reached it. She put a hand on his shoulder and reached up to kiss him. He felt her cool lips on his cheek and hoped it wasn't bristly.

'I miss kisses,' she said, turning back into the house.

'Poor Midge. I expect you do,' he said.

'What's happened, Oliver?' she asked, going ahead of him into the sitting room. 'Did Fisher tell you?'

The fire was low. She poked it ineffectually, and Oliver took the poker from her and added some logs.

'Are you all right for logs and coal?' he asked. The next thing would be that she would succumb to hypothermia; there was no flesh on her bones to keep her warm.

'Yes,' she said. 'Well, tell me, Oliver.'

He put on two more logs. Well dried out, they crackled cheerfully. Apple, he thought; had Daniel cut down an apple tree for fuel?

'He said they'd arrested two more boys. I don't know any more than that,' he answered.

'Oh, I see. Well, that's good. That means there will be a stronger case. They'll know it all now, with all the boys caught,' she said. 'Dan's parents will be pleased.'

'Aren't you?' he asked her curiously.

'Oh yes. Yes, of course I am. I wonder what happened.'

'I expect he'll tell us,' said Oliver. 'Probably one of those decent lads spilled a few more beans. It was bound to happen. They couldn't go on saying almost nothing.'

'Poor kids. How's this going to affect them?' Midge wondered. 'Is it going to blight their lives?'

'I doubt it. Young people are more resilient than we remember,' said Oliver.

What a funny way to put it, Midge thought. He meant, than we remember being. Perhaps she had been resilient years ago, or perhaps your resilience was a finite store and if you dipped into it too often, it ran out. She might ask that counsellor woman what she thought of such a theory.

Fisher soon arrived, and he told them about the discovery of the knife and how this had cleared up the mystery of the car the youths had used. Oliver asked a few questions. The evidence which it was hoped the knife would yield would greatly aid the prosecution, and would mean the four could be charged with murder.

'But they still won't be tried for months, will they?' Midge asked, when Fisher had gone.

'No, I'm afraid not,' said Oliver. 'There will be a preliminary hearing – that might take place fairly soon, as some of the preparation will already have been done –

that's just to commit them for trial. To decide there is a case to try.'

'I see.'

Midge hadn't cried. She seemed almost catatonic, which in a way was more alarming than her feverish gaiety on Christmas Day. Oliver suddenly had an almost overwhelming desire to pick her up and carry her upstairs, and try to comfort her by making tender love to her, but he knew better than to attempt it. To kill a friendship with sexual intimacy would be another murder, and besides, she would be horrified. He knew she felt no reciprocal desire for him; he was good, safe Oliver, her and Daniel's trusted friend.

'I don't think you'd better be here on your own tonight,' he said. 'Will you come back to Winbury with me?'

'What will Sarah say?'

'She'll be delighted. She offered to come over with me just now. I said we'd ring her if you went to pieces,' he said, with a wry expression.

Midge actually laughed.

'I haven't, have I?' she remarked.

'No,' he said. 'Well done. Pack a few things and we'll get going, and while you're doing that I'll dismantle this lovely fire so that we leave it in a safe condition.'

'What a waste,' she said.

'Never mind.'

That night, Oliver took another female doll from his small store, one he had bought the day before. He put her in the dolls' house, hesitating over where to place her. Finally, he arranged her in the armchair in the second largest bedroom, put the child dolls in their respective beds, the mother doll in the drawing room, and the father in his study.

Let Sarah make of that what she would, if she looked inside, he thought. He wasn't sure what he made of it himself.

21

Jamie soon heard about the arrests. Someone had seen the police car at Trevor's house; someone else had seen Wayne being driven off, and outside the chip shop, where the youngsters often gathered, the word had spread.

After making their big decision in Peter's house, Jamie had undertaken the task of telephoning the police, for none of the Deerton boys wanted the call to register on their parents' bills. He would do it when he reached home.

Pedalling back before it grew dark, he passed Oliver in his Rover on the way to Orchard House, but he missed Fisher, whose route from Fettleton did not overlap with Jamie's journey back to Mickleburgh.

While he was out, his mother had come in and had gone out again. She'd left him a note saying that she was going round to Bob and Ginny's, and would be home by six o'clock. If she was later than that, would he turn the oven on. He looked inside and saw a chicken with some foil across it, waiting to be roasted. Jamie pottered about for a while, hanging up his jacket, washing, brushing his hair. Sometimes he wished his mother would find a good bloke and get married again, as parents who split up often seemed to do, he'd noticed, but perhaps it was different if you were a widow. It would be nice for her, he thought, but if the new bloke didn't take to him, it could be tricky. He might have kids of his own who Jamie would have to accept as brothers and sisters. What if they didn't get on? On the whole, he was glad he didn't have to share her with anyone else; they'd been on their own a long time now, and he was old enough to be a help to her, and not a drag. Except for this Deerton business.

He couldn't get out of his head the fact that poor Mr Stewart would still be alive if he had not gone for help, but then Kevin and his mates might have done worse damage to Barry's house – might even have set it on fire. Jamie wouldn't have put it past them. Paul was a really crazy oddball who had boasted that he had done stuff like that – torched a car and got away with it, and other things. Of course, he might have been just talking big; you couldn't always believe what he said. He'd get into real trouble one day, Jamie knew, and then remembered that he had.

He could put it off no longer. Slowly, Jamie went to the telephone. Even more slowly, he dialled Fisher's number.

A woman answered. She said she was Detective Inspector Flower. Superintendent Fisher was out just now, but she would give him a message the moment he returned, or perhaps she could help. Jamie wouldn't tell her why he had rung, nor would he give his name.

Poppy Flower quickly traced the call. She did not ring back. She knew whose that number was; it was written on a pad on Fisher's desk, but though Jamie would be required as a witness, his help in identifying the other two boys involved in the murder was no longer needed for they had already been arrested.

When Fisher returned to the station after his visit to Midge Stewart, he did not call back either; he decided he would go round and tell Kate and Jamie what had happened. It would let the poor kid off the immediate hook. Much would depend now on what the forensic scientists could learn from their examination of the weapon and the car.

By the time he had finished in the Incident Room, it was after seven. Fisher reached Kate's house just as she and Jamie were about to start their meal, and a tempting smell of roasting chicken wafted towards him when she opened the front door. Fisher, a divorced father like those Jamie had been contemplating earlier, who would have collected a pizza on his way back to Fettleton, needed no urging to accept a second invitation to join them. He apologised again for disturbing their evening, but Kate said Jamie would be glad to see him; he had told her what he and his three friends had decided, and she had been relieved and thankful. He had said that he'd already rung Fisher, who was out. They'd agreed that he would try again after supper; Kate had Fisher's home number.

Now he could speak directly to the man.

'Jamie rang you today. You were out,' she said.

'Is that right, Jamie?' Fisher asked. Pre-empted, he thought fast. Should he let the boy give his information or should he, as he had intended, get in first and tell him what had happened earlier that day? He knew immediately that he must retain the boy's trust; if Jamie revealed the full story of that fatal night and then learned that Fisher already knew and had made two more arrests, he might feel betrayed.

'We all decided—' Jamie began, and Fisher interrupted him.

'You and your three friends? Well, before you tell me what your decision was, let me tell you what I came round here to say. We've arrested two more boys. We've found the knife – it's almost certainly the one that was used – and the car they borrowed. It wasn't exactly stolen, as we'd believed.'

'You caught them?' Jamie's face had split into a huge, relieved grin. 'Really?'

'Really,' Fisher confirmed.

'That was pretty cool detecting,' said Jamie.

'Sort of,' Fisher said. 'I can't tell you any more just

now, but let's just say we had a bit of luck when the knife turned up.'

'Oh, great,' said Jamie, still beaming. 'Wow!'

'Wow, indeed,' said Fisher, and he smiled at Kate, who had risen to take a bottle of supermarket Riesling from the fridge.

'Let's have some of this,' she suggested. 'Jamie, you can have some too, or would you rather have a beer? It's a celebration.'

And it was, and he would, and he did.

When Oliver returned with Midge that evening, Sarah felt a mixture of exasperated pity and impatience. Was she going to hang about their necks for ever, like the albatross in the poem?

Forgetting that she had not been enjoying the work she had been doing, Sarah now resented the interruption, sighing as she shut down her computer and put on a smile of welcome.

For the first time in their long marriage, Oliver felt like shaking her. She had everything; Midge had lost the person she most loved in the world, apart from her sons, and had been left financially strapped, whereas if he were to die, Sarah would be well provided for, and, an attractive widow, could have a pleasant life.

She wouldn't miss him all that much, he thought; it was what he represented that she valued.

Speaking sternly, he explained what had happened.

'Well, thank goodness. Now perhaps the police will get on with things and we can put all this behind us,' Sarah said. 'Or you can,' she told Midge. Sarah had already done so, but, as now, it kept being resurrected by events.

'I'm sorry, descending on you again like this,' said Midge. 'Oliver insisted,' she basely added, but she didn't want Sarah to think it was her idea.

She looked like a bedraggled little girl, thought Sarah,

irritated by her forlorn, waiflike appearance, which only too
clearly appealed to Oliver's chivalrous nature. She was so
small. Bulky men like Oliver felt sorry for her and wanted
to protect her while Sarah, though acknowledging that what
Midge had suffered was horrific, wished she would get her
act together. And how like reckless, foolhardy Daniel to dash
straight out into the affray without waiting for the police to
arrive. Didn't they always say you shouldn't 'have a go'? He'd
been brave, she conceded, but rash, and now Midge was faced
with the consequences.

Oliver had had to return to the office. After he had gone,
Sarah made an effort, asking Midge to explain what the new
arrests would mean, and then, settling her down by the fire with
some magazines, she went off to find extra food for dinner, not
that Midge looked as if she was eating at all. She might tempt
her with something succulent, Sarah thought, as ever stimulated
by a challenge, however minor, to her domestic competence.
She put a container of frozen homemade carrot and orange
soup on the top of the Aga, where it would thaw, and also
took some sole fillets from the freezer. While she was peeling
and thinly slicing potatoes, she had an idea which would solve
her dilemma as well as Midge's. She mulled it over while she
decided spinach would go well with the fish. Then she returned
to Midge, who had an open magazine on her lap but was not
looking at it, staring instead at the fire.

'You can plan your future now,' said Sarah briskly. She
sat down opposite Midge, leaning forward, intent on gaining
Midge's attention. She'd take this one by stages, weed out the
other options first.

'How?' Midge asked, her tone bleak. The magazine slid from
her knees to the floor, and as she appeared not to have noticed,
Sarah rose, picked it up and closed it, then put it on a table.

'You'll have to sell the business. The lease – whatever.
Oliver says it's in a hopeless state.' The soul of discretion,

he had not, in fact, gone so far, but by inference Sarah
had understood the extent of its liability. 'You'll have to
get yourself a job,' she said.

'But I've got a job,' said Midge.

'A proper job,' said Sarah. 'What can you do, besides frame
pictures? Can you type?'

'A bit,' said Midge. 'I'm not bad at accounts, though Dan did
most of the book-keeping. I'm not into computers. I suppose I
could learn.'

'Perhaps you could.' Not in her present state, thought Sarah,
who had been thinking that, through her connections, she might
find Midge an office post, but just look at her! No employer
would consider her. She was a mess; she'd have to smarten up
a lot. And she was skeletal. Sarah was at last aware that Midge
was almost past being able to help herself.

'When did you last have a decent meal?' she asked.

'I suppose I had some breakfast,' Midge replied. Had she
had lunch? She'd been to the shop, she remembered, but there
had been no customers. Her novelty value as the victim of a
serious crime had worn off, and in the post-Christmas period,
people were not thinking of framing pictures or buying cheap
second-hand furniture. She had some memory of a banana she
had taken with her. She hadn't eaten it. It must be sitting on the
desk. She'd gone home and then Fisher and Oliver had come. 'I
know I'm a problem to everyone,' she said. 'It seems I may go
bankrupt. You can start again if you do that. But I don't like
that idea. I must pay what we owe. Some of our troubles came
from people who owe us.'

This was doubtless true. Sarah knew about business practice.
This was the moment to make her proposition.

'Why don't you turn the business into something else?' she
asked. 'Use the premises for a new enterprise?'

'What sort of enterprise?'

'Something necessary. A secretarial bureau, incorporating

a staff agency, for instance,' Sarah said. 'You could offer copying facilities, word-processing and printing documents, desk-top publishing, flyers and so on for individuals and small businesses who can't afford the time or staff to do these things themselves. You could supply temps and part-timers, too – full-timers, even. There's no agency of that kind in Mickleburgh. There must be an opening for one.'

'I'd never manage all that,' Midge said despairingly. 'I don't know anything about it.'

'Maybe not, but I do. We could be partners,' said Sarah said, eyes shining. 'I'd get the bank to back us. We might need a loan to get us started. I'd be the more active partner,' she emphasised. 'Just while you get over all this trouble and find your feet. You could be in charge of background matters. Interviewing staff. Working the copier. That sort of thing. You'd soon pick up the rest.'

Midge stared at her. Sarah was away on a wave of enthusiasm.

'But your job. You've got a job. A very good one,' she said.

'I'm getting no further with it,' Sarah said. 'I'd like to work for myself now. I've got a lot of experience. It'd be good. I could go round the local companies, tendering for pamphlets and so on. I'm sure it's a viable idea.' Not often impulsive, Sarah grew more determined with each minute.

'I don't know,' Midge temporised. Could she work with Sarah? 'We'd need to ask Oliver,' she said. Whatever else, it would be better than going bankrupt. That would be letting Daniel down.

Sarah, reinvigorated by her scheme, was not going to let it rest. In her mind, she refurbished the place, knocking down walls, putting up new ones and creating small sub-sections. Leasing arrangements could be made for computers and the other equipment they would need. When she heard Oliver's key in the door, she was ready.

As usual when he came home, Oliver's first action, after hanging up his coat, was to greet her. She was in the kitchen, making a sauce for the sole, and he dropped a light kiss on her cheek. This was ritual. She accepted it without turning her face to his; that was normal, too, but tonight she went straight into a litany about her inspiration.

Oliver was startled. He knew she had applied for a job in London which had not materialised for reasons he had not been given, but he had not imagined she would want to set up on her own. Why not, though? And it would be a bonus if it would help Midge. He instantly foresaw snags in a partnership between them, but if they were anticipated, they might be avoided. He could see that the project might be feasible.

'It's well worth thinking about,' he said. 'How does Midge feel about it?'

Midge, Midge: it was always Midge these days, Sarah thought crossly.

'Is she in any position to turn it down?' she asked. 'It will be the saving of her.'

That could be true. Oliver knew that if he showed too much enthusiasm for the idea, Sarah might lose hers; tactically, and also because it was his duty, he should pick holes in it, point out disadvantages. There might be quite a few. He asked her if she was prepared to leave her current job and risk investment in the new venture.

If she went ahead, and he could find no great objections, he would have to underwrite her, but he must not be influenced by his desire to help Midge. The proposition would have to be thoroughly researched. Sarah could not be allowed to back a failure.

Before he could suggest it, she explained that she would conduct a survey of the likely demand for what she would offer. Of course she knew what she was doing, he admitted; she had been very successful in the last few years and now she would have an outlet for her energy and experience, and be working for herself. He had to give the scheme his blessing.

'How's Midge?' he asked, when it seemed that there was no more to discuss until she produced some facts and figures.

'Shattered, poor thing,' said Sarah, briefly forgiving her. 'I gave her a stiff drink and left her by the fire. Maybe she's gone to sleep. She looks exhausted.'

'I'll go and see,' said Oliver.

Midge wasn't in the sitting room. Perhaps she had gone up to her bedroom; if so, she had taken her drink with her: no glass stood on any surface. Oliver crossed the hall and went to his study. The door was not quite closed, and when he pushed it wide, he saw Midge kneeling in front of the open dolls' house. She was crooning to herself, rocking to and fro, holding close to her the mother doll and the other female doll which Oliver had added to the household.

She heard him, and looked round. Her eyes glittered in her pale face.

'I'm playing houses,' she said. 'You've got a new doll, another woman. Which is the right wife for Mr Wilberforce?'

'It doesn't matter,' Oliver replied. 'You can take your choice.'

His heart was thumping. What spirit of mischief had prompted him to buy the new doll?

Midge put both of them carefully in the drawing room, at either end of the tiny sofa.

'Mr Wilberforce will have to choose,' she said. Then, after a pause, she added, 'I wonder if Prudence had names for them. She's lonely, isn't she? Though she has the people in her books for company. Still, she has to invent all their conversations.' Idly, she picked up Mr Wilberforce and stood him in front of the fireplace from where he could contemplate both female dolls.

Oliver was surprised by her remark about Prudence. Was it true? He watched her as she crouched down, like a child, with the dolls. She did not seem to want an answer, asking him if Judy had played with a dolls' house as a child.

'No,' said Oliver. He had wanted to get her one when she was five or six, but Sarah had rejected the idea, saying that even if she liked it for a while, she would soon be bored with it.

'As we only had boys, it didn't arise in our house,' Midge said. 'I had one, though. Not such a fine one as this, more a modern villa, but I loved it.'

'I'll find another old one and do it up for you, if you'd like it,' said Oliver, astonishing himself. 'I'm going to give this one back to Prudence when it's finished. It's almost done.' He crossed over, reached behind the structure and moved a switch. 'There,' he said. 'The fire is alight now,' and sure enough, in the hearth, warm coals seemed to glow, warming up Mr Wilberforce and his ladies.

'You are clever,' said Midge. 'It's lovely. But do you really want to mend another?'

'Yes,' said Oliver, who knew that when he passed this one on, he was going to miss the interest. 'It's a soothing occupation, and keeps me at home, unlike golf and such. So Sarah won't object.' Though she might, if she knew it was for Midge.

'Did she tell you about her big idea?' asked Midge, who had heard him go into the kitchen. 'She wants to transform the business.'

'So she said,' he replied. 'How do you feel about it?'

'It sounds possible,' said Midge. 'I'm not sure how she'd feel with me as her partner. She'd have to be the boss.'

'As long as you see it that way, it should work,' said Oliver.

'What can I do, if I don't do this?' she said. 'I know you've been trying to postpone the moment when I have to face facts, but it's here now. There's no way I could expand the framing. I'd need a heat sealer, for starters, which would cost a bomb, and it would be very expensive to stock enough mouldings to provide a big choice. You have to buy a huge length when you only want a foot or so. That's why I stick to just a few popular lines.'

'You'd have to have an agreement,' he said. 'A way for each of you to get out, if either of you wanted to. If it did well, you might be able to sell out your part very profitably.'

'Might I? So it wouldn't be like marriage, for better or worse, till death—' here Midge's thin, pretty face, which had briefly worn an animated expression, crumpled.

'Not at all,' said Oliver. 'A divorce could be arranged. Now, let's put the idea on hold and see if dinner's ready. Sarah wants to feed you up. I'll see what she's done about some wine.' Knowing her, a bottle of something white, light and dry would be chilling in the fridge.

'I think I'm a bit tiddly already,' said Midge. 'Sarah gave me an enormous gin and tonic.'

'Don't feel guilty because you can sometimes laugh again,' said Oliver. 'You will heal.'

'Will I? I think I'm getting worse.'

'That's because of the circumstances. Because it's all still going on. You'll get better very slowly. It's like having an amputation and learning to accept an artificial limb. The stump will always be prone to pain, but you'll manage.'

'Dan wouldn't like to be called a stump,' said Midge.

'I don't know. He was thin, but solid. Not a weeping willow sort of chap,' said Oliver. 'Come on, Midge. You need feeding,' and he took her hand and pulled her to her feet.

He was smiling, and Midge was flushed when they entered the kitchen. Sarah, noticing, wondered why.

Oliver did not mention his plans for restoring another doll's house, but he turned over in his mind how to find one which would be a challenge. It must be a period house, elaborate, needing a lot of work so that it would absorb him. He still had connections with the estate agent who had sold Prudence's Wiltshire house; he might know of another dolls' house coming up for sale. It would be worth asking him, before adopting other methods, such as advertising.

Midge's thoughts, however, were more concerned with Sarah's ideas for their joint future than with what she felt was Oliver's sudden whim.

22

Midge had two people with whom she might discuss Sarah's plans, but would it be disloyal to consult Prudence, who had known Sarah for much longer than she had known Midge? Uncertain, she decided that her professional counsellor would be the better, more impartial adviser. Midge could state her fears plainly: worries lest the business relationship damage the friendship between the two families and in particular the closeness between Jonathan and Judy. These anxieties could be dismissed or endorsed, and she might see other possible disadvantages that had not occurred to Midge.

She had slept surprisingly well in the comfortable spare bedroom at The Barn House. Perhaps it was because she was not alone. Sarah and Oliver were just along the passage in their large room with its pale cream carpet and vast bed. You could be two islands in it, Midge thought. She'd even eaten well; the sole was delicious and had seemed to melt in the mouth. Sarah could always run a restaurant, Midge had told her, if their communications centre, as Sarah was already calling it, did not succeed.

A curious calm came over her the next day. Sarah, her office still closed, ran Midge back to Deerton after breakfast, dropping her at the gate and saying she would be starting on the research for their project right away.

Midge went indoors, unpacked her few things, and then rang up the counsellor to bring forward her appointment if it were possible.

She had done nothing about those letters yet, the sympathetic messages of condolence. They were still arriving, now singly and at intervals, from people who had only just heard of Daniel's death.

Sarah would have dealt with them immediately, she thought. She might yet do it, if Midge told her of the problem. On her computer, she'd soon whip up a response and print it off in dozens.

The counsellor allotted her an appointment for the following day.

She came to see me soon after the second pair of delinquent youths had been arrested, seeming relieved that things could move forward now. Like their friends, they had been remanded in custody. As it was all sub judice not much had been mentioned in the media reports, but there was the suggestion that the weapon had been found and I felt sure that each of the four boys would now be blaming the others in order to save his own skin. General complicity was certain to be proved, and they would all go down for some years, even if only one of them was convicted of the murder. A manslaughter verdict was quite possible. After all, it had started as merely a rampage.

She accepted that it had begun that way and that there was no personal grudge against her husband. She was trying to modify her feelings towards the boys in the light of this knowledge, but I told her not to suppress her anger.

'You should release it,' I told her. 'You've a right to hate them, to demand punishment for what they did. There was no excusable provocation.'

'Some would say I should forgive them,' she said.

'Others would suggest that you forgive the sinner, not the

sin,' I answered, always ready with a platitude. 'And no one has the right to forgive on your behalf.'

'Getting angry won't bring Daniel back,' she said. 'Besides, how can I release it? I can't go round hitting people.'

'It's too cold to dig the garden,' I pronounced. 'Manual work releases tension. You could knead bread.'

'I scarcely eat any bread,' she said, taking me literally when I had been speaking metaphorically. 'And I should be working. Only there isn't much for me to do just now. Except the letters. I haven't tackled them.'

Nor would she. I could see her leaving them stuffed in a drawer, to be discovered after her own demise.

Then she told me about Sarah Foxton's plan for a joint operation in the premises now occupied by the almost defunct business she and her husband had run.

'The Foxtons are old friends,' she said. 'He's a solicitor. We had dinner with them the night Daniel died. They've been wonderful to me.'

She was able to say it now. That was an improvement.

'And how do you feel about it?' I asked.

It might be her salvation; a feeble individual to begin with, she had been deeply traumatised by her bereavement. Her husband's attitude appeared to have been paternalistic, protecting her from the full knowledge of their financial difficulties, though she was aware that the business was not thriving. The weak do not survive without support and this project, if it succeeded, could set her on her feet again in so far as that was possible.

'I'm quite intrigued,' she said. 'It would be a fresh start, and we've got the space. If we could get funds. Sarah thinks the bank might help.'

I'd been past her premises, partly curious to see them, partly when I was wondering about that old woman I had seen, whose face keeps coming into my mind. I'd looked up the Stewarts' workplace address in the telephone directory. They hadn't run to the Yellow Pages, only the ordinary local one; an oversight, if they wanted customers. I'd wondered if the old woman could have been on the jury which convicted me, but there were only two women on it, one who was quite young and who would now be middle-aged; the older one had had red hair and freckles; she had looked like a barmaid and perhaps that was what she was. I'd had plenty of time to study their faces during the trial. Neither could have turned into this elegant person. She was always well turned out; I had seen her several times now, though at a distance as I wasn't keen to meet her again face to face.

I decided to encourage Mrs Stewart in this new venture and claim credit if it succeeded, but, were it to fail, I needed to offer some caution to emphasise that she must make the choice, not I.

'Her husband is a solicitor, you said.' A professional man was not likely to encourage a questionable venture.

'Yes. They've been so kind to me,' she repeated. She had told me about them in previous consultations.

'If problems arise, I will be able to help you resolve them,' I reminded her. I should enjoy that; supervising her enterprise would provide me with an interest in the coming months.

'You think I should go ahead?'

'It's your decision. I think you've already made it,' I said, to push her into it.

I wondered if she was at all drawn towards Oliver Foxton. She was vulnerable and he had been kind: a recipe for some sort of sequel.

'Perhaps,' she said, still not convinced. I felt impatient.

'Is there anyone else whom you could consult?' I asked. 'A friend of all three of you, who knows your personalities?'

'Well – yes,' she hesitated. 'I had thought of asking her. She's known the Foxtons for some time, but though I'd met *her a few times, I've only got to know her since Dan died. She's been very understanding. She's a widow, too. Older than me, quite a bit.'*

'Oh?'

'She's a Mrs Wilmot. Prudence Wilmot. She lives in Mickleburgh High Street not far from our workshop.'

Was this the mystery woman? Could Mrs Stewart have given me my answer? I asked her no more questions then. Besides, she'd had her allotted time. I'd find out more about this Prudence Wilmot during my patient's next appointment.

Midge felt guilty as she paid out another forty pounds. This was costing her a lot of money, and she had none to spare, yet it was such a relief to be able to reveal her worries to someone who was listening not from kindness, but because it was her professional duty, and who was not swayed by sentiment or pity.

Driving home, she saw that although she had supposed she was being encouraged to accept Sarah's suggestion, she had been given no firm advice, merely guided towards making up her own mind, but that was what counselling was about: helping you to work through your problems and confront your fears and doubts.

Prudence had told her that she would have to learn to let go of Daniel.

'But it won't happen for a long time,' she said. 'Maybe years. You don't want to, do you? You want to feel he's still with you.'

Midge did. She still expected to see him in the house or garden and sometimes spoke to him, surprised when he did not answer.

She would have to go in with Sarah, she concluded, turning off the main road into the lesser road for Deerton. What was in it, though, for Sarah? Surely she would earn more in her present job, where she was secure? She stood to lose money over this, whether her own or Oliver's. Midge was sure some capital would have to be produced up front to enable the business to be launched. A quarter's rent would have to be paid, for starters, and there would be the cost of adapting the workshop into the smart commercial premises Sarah had in mind.

Had something gone wrong at her own job? Did she want to leave it for some reason of her own? She couldn't possibly have been sacked; she was much too efficient. But if staff were being pruned, no one was safe, as Daniel had discovered.

Baffled, Midge turned in at her gate and had just put the car away when footsteps approached and she saw Peter's mother standing in the drive.

'I hope I didn't startle you, Mrs Stewart,' said Gwen Grant. 'I came to see how you are. You'll have heard about those other arrests.'

'Oh, Mrs Grant – how nice of you – do come in,' said Midge, suddenly glad of the presence of this kind woman, with whom she was linked irrevocably by a violent event. 'Come and have a cup of tea,' she added. She could do with one herself, she who had, for weeks, seldom thought about sustenance of any kind, drinking water if she felt thirsty.

She unlocked the back door with a key she took from a nail banged into the wall of the house and covered with ivy. They had almost always used the back door when going out in the car, as it was so much closer to the garage.

'I hope you watch who sees you with that key, Mrs Stewart,' said Gwen.

'Oh yes,' said Midge airily. She was going to add that strict vigilance wasn't essential here in Deerton when she swallowed the remark. It simply wasn't true.

Gwen followed her into the house and once again put the kettle on while Midge took off her coat, washed her hands and pulled a hasty comb through her hair. There was no fire in the sitting room; ashes lay in the hearth, and it was very cold. To save fuel, Midge had been running the heating very sparingly, but this meant that the house took a long time to warm up.

'Let's stay in the kitchen,' she said. 'It's the warmest room. The Aga's wonderful and keeps the whole house warm.' This was not strictly true, though there was a warm core where the flue ascended.

Gwen Grant's own much smaller, more modern house, less solidly built than this, was nevertheless well insulated by the efforts of her husband and it was snug, with electric heating throughout, expensive but effective. There was no mains gas in Deerton.

'I came to see how you felt. After those arrests,' she repeated as they sat at the table, the brown teapot before them.

'How do you feel?' Midge parried.

'Ever so relieved,' said her guest. 'And for my boy. What a load off his mind. He wouldn't blab, you see. Even though his dad was hurt – and look at what happened to Mr Stewart. He still wasn't going to tell. Kids are strange, aren't they? They won't tell on their friends even if it's something serious, like this. Not that them boys are friends of Peter's. Were your lads like that?' They'd been nice boys, she remembered, and were now agreeable young men. They'd be a great help to their mother, but then they were both away. They had their lives.

'They were never put in such a spot,' said Midge. 'None of their friends ever did anything nearly on a par with this.'

She suddenly felt that she could eat a biscuit. Midge rose and fetched the tin in which there were a few tired Hobnobs. Mark liked them. Mrs Grant accepted one and they both nibbled while they continued their conversation.

'Parents don't always drop their children in it, either, do they? Even when they know they've done something dreadful,' said Gwen. 'Trevor's mother was brave – hard, even – ringing up the police when she found the knife in her car.'

'Is that what happened?'

'Yes. Didn't you know?'

'The police weren't saying much,' said Midge. 'They came to see me – the superintendent did – Mr Fisher. He just said they'd found the weapon and made two more arrests. He did mention the car – said something about them having sorted out what had happened.'

'Well, I can tell you, she was cleaning her car ready to sell it – it's advertised this weekend – but she can't sell it now, of course, because the police have got it. Testing it. She found the knife under the driver's seat. It wasn't her Trevor as used it; we know that. It was one of them first two that got arrested – that Kevin, Peter's saying now – but Trevor took the car. Her Lada. They didn't steal one, like the police thought. She was out – his mum, and his dad – and he borrowed it, he said. Right nerve, he had. Some sort of dare, he told her. She's a nice woman, Trevor's mother. I know her. She doesn't deserve this.'

'No. Poor woman. Her son probably only meant to swank around a bit in the car with his mates,' said Midge.

'That's what she said. And now look at the trouble he's in.'

'Were they drunk?' Midge asked.

'Well, there were those empty beer cans left in the Noakeses' house,' said Gwen. 'It's likely.'

The two women looked at one another across the table – the slightly younger one whose husband, with his own successful business, had not been badly hurt and whose son had been involved on the side of the angels, and the other, now bereft, and barely coping.

'I'm ever so sorry, Mrs Stewart,' said Gwen. 'I feel so bad that we've been lucky over this, and you haven't.' She'd had another bit of private luck, too, which it would be wrong to mention in these circumstances.

'Don't feel bad,' said Midge. 'None of this is your fault, and

it must have been very hard for Peter. At least there aren't two
new widows in the village. And my sons are grown up. Mark's
working, and Jonathan is in his second year at university.'

'He will stay there, won't he?' Gwen asked.

'Oh, he must,' said Midge. 'We'll manage that.' There was
his grant, after all.

'What about the business?' This was delicate territory. Ted
and Gwen knew the workshop; they had pottered in there and
found nothing that they wanted, but Gwen had had a picture
framed, a flower print she had bought at a car boot sale; Midge
had done it nicely and she didn't charge a lot. Not enough,
probably, thought Gwen now.

'Well, it's not going too well,' Midge admitted. 'It wasn't
even before – before.'

'I see,' said Gwen.

'I'm going to have to give it up,' said Midge.

'Oh dear,' said Gwen. 'Still, it'd be a lot for you to manage
on your own.'

'Well – yes. But I'll need another job. I'm thinking about it,'
Midge told her. Then, wanting to get away from the subject, she
said, 'That woman – Trevor's mother – must have had an awful
shock. She did the right thing, of course, but it was brave.'

'I suppose she did,' said Gwen, who was not certain.

After Mrs Stewart left me, I had another bereaved patient, a
man who was plunged into despair by the death of his dog,
which at the time was fourteen years of age. They'd been
mutually devoted, said my patient. The dog was obedient to
his least command, welcomed him, made no demands, gave
him more affection than he received from his family.

I nodded as he told me this, his hands twisting in his lap,
his voice unsteady, so like Mrs Stewart.

This was his first consultation and when I asked him why he
had come to me, he said his wife was unsympathetic about his

*loss and at last had told him to get his head sorted out. Then
he'd seen my advertisement in a local paper.*

'Would you grieve like this if it was your wife who had
died?' I asked him, and he looked astonished.

'I haven't thought about it,' he replied.

'Think about it now,' I suggested, and after a short pause,
out came a tale of resentment towards his wife and how his
love had been diverted to the dog which never questioned him
or went against his wishes.

I asked about his wife. She worked for a local firm, keeping
the books, I gathered; he seemed vague about her actual duties;
and she performed with an amateur dramatic society. Their
daughter was at college, with her own interests. The son was
still at school.

'You feel that none of them have time for you. Is that right?'
I asked.

He agreed, but said that he brought in the income and they
should be grateful.

'Your wife seems to contribute,' I pointed out, and he
had to admit that this was true. They ran a joint account.
Foolish woman, I thought; she should preserve her inde-
pendence.

'You want to control her and she won't allow it,' was my
diagnosis.

'That isn't true,' he indignantly denied.

'She's doing her own thing, and you don't like it,' I insisted.

'Your dog was happy to obey you. Your wife is not.'

I discovered that the dog was an Alsatian, a sizeable dog
to have about the place, whether you are a dog-lover or not.
I'm not.

'He was your wife's dog too? The family pet?'

'No. He was mine – a one-man dog.'

'Who fed him? Prepared his bowls of Chappie, or whatever
you gave him?'

'*She did. My wife.*' When I did not reply he added, '*She doesn't like me in her kitchen.*'

'*Who took him for walks? You?*'

'*When I was at home. I have to travel for my work and can be away for several days.*'

'*So your wife, who didn't want the dog in the first place, unless I have misunderstood you, had to assume responsibility for it in your absence, and look after it? A large, strong dog, which she had to take for walks?*'

'*Yes.*'

'*I see.*'

I longed to tell him what a selfish monster he was, but I had to master my desire. This was a patient whose treatment could be made to run and run, if I controlled the hostility he aroused in me.

'*Have you no other friends? Only the dog?*' I asked him.

'*Work colleagues. I have no need of others. I have my family,*' he said.

But he hadn't: not really. Odd how so many men lack real friends. Perhaps, in the power struggle, women are easier to subdue than men and so they keep a female at home to dominate. And, in his case, for company, a dog.

I sent the man away with a string of appointments booked for when he can fit them in among the other demands upon his time.

'*Are you going to get another one?*' I asked.

'*Another what?*'

Stupid man.

'*Another dog,*' I said. '*Why not?*'

'*She says she'll leave me if I do,*' he answered. '*My wife.*'

'*We'll take it from there next time,*' I promised him.

It could be interesting. Had he thought of acquiring another wife instead of the one he'd got? I'd ask him, in due course.

I wondered why the wife had not sought another husband.

23

Oliver had decided that he must return the dolls' house to Prudence as soon as possible. The temptation to play games with its inhabitants was becoming dangerous, and now he was not the only player. When he found another one to renovate, it would have no occupants; Midge could select some at her leisure.

Returning from the office on the day that Midge had entertained Mrs Grant to tea, he found Sarah home early. She had been to Birmingham again, where her work had been over sooner than she had expected. Everything was going well for Charles and Hugh in their restaurant. Her task there was completed.

'Looks good,' he said, seeing diced chicken, strips of carrots, and chopped herbs all waiting to be assembled. 'There's no need to take so much trouble just for me. I'd be happy with a simple meal and I'll gladly help you with the cooking.'

'It's my job,' said Sarah stiffly. 'Aren't you satisfied?'

'Of course I am. You're a wonderful cook,' he said. 'But you're out all day too, and you have a longer journey than I have, and today I know you've had a train trip.'

'So what?' said Sarah. 'I won't be travelling much when I'm in partnership with Midge.'

She'd already sent in a letter of resignation. Doing so had given her great deal of satisfaction. Would she be entreated to withdraw it?

'Are you sure about that?' he asked her. 'Do you think it will work? Won't you find coping with her in her present nervous state difficult? I don't imagine she's going to improve much until the trial is over, and even then it may take months for her to adjust.' Or years, he thought.

'I thought you wanted everyone to help her,' Sarah said. 'You didn't oppose the idea when we were discussing it. Why change your mind now?'

'I haven't changed it. Not if it's what you really want and if it will make you happy, and providing we establish that it is likely to be profitable. But you can't build your future on a wish to help Midge. There are other solutions for her problems.'

'Yes, and she's looking for them,' said Sarah. She finished laying chicken slices in a dish and added a mixture from a waiting bowl. Then she put it in the oven, closing the door firmly. 'She's seeing a shrink of sorts,' she said. 'When I got back from Birmingham, a road was up near the station and I had to take a diversion. Who should I see coming out of a house ahead of me but Midge? I recognised her at once, and slowed down, but she got into the Volvo without noticing me, and drove off.' Sarah paused. 'I parked in the slot she'd just left and took a look. There was this brass plate on the front door.'

'You went right up to it? Through the gate and up the path?' He could not believe what he was hearing.

'There wasn't a path or a gate. The front door was only a few feet from the pavement, with just a low wall along either side of it. I could read it easily without going too near. I wrote it down,' said Sarah. 'Counsellor, it said, and some initials after it. Some qualification, I suppose. All tasteful. Brass, shiny, well polished, and a glossy front door. Looked all right, if you want to judge by appearances.'

'Oh dear,' said Oliver. 'I wonder if the doctor referred her to this person?'

'Who knows? She never mentioned it to me, if so, but then why would she?' Sarah said.

'What made you stop and investigate?' Oliver asked. It seemed an extraordinary thing for her to do. She was usually too wrapped up in her own affairs to have much time for those of others.

Sarah did not want to answer this. She was astonished at herself. She had, in fact, wondered if Midge had been meeting some man there, though it seemed unlikely, but you could never tell. She couldn't admit this to Oliver. He would be horrified.

'I don't know,' she said. 'I suppose I was just curious. She's seemed so hopeless. At least she's trying to do something about it, which is good.'

Was it, though?

'If she was sent there by the doctor, then that's fine – probably a good idea. But if it's some quack—' His voice trailed off. 'There are some unqualified people about,' he said.

'Well, there were these initials,' Sarah reminded him. 'And it said "doctor". I noticed that. Perhaps we could check in some register.'

'Yes. That's a good idea.'

'I'll do it,' Sarah said. 'The name and address are in my diary, in my bag.'

But she forgot about it.

After dinner, Oliver put the finishing touches to the dolls' house, and the next morning he loaded it into the car before leaving for the office. He'd take it round to Prudence in the evening, and while he was there, he'd tell her about Midge seeing the counsellor, and about Sarah's plans for their partnership. Her views would be worth hearing.

During the day, when he had to deal with two feuding neighbours arguing over a boundary and the trespassing of the bull terrier of one party into the garden of the other, draw up two wills, act for the vendor of one house and the buyer of another, and advise a client who faced a slander allegation, Oliver had allowed himself, at intervals, to anticipate the attractions of a civilised half hour in Prudence's small sitting room. Not wanting to disturb her if she was working on her book, he faxed her to see if his visit would be convenient and soon had an answer, saying she would be delighted to see him. Later, anxious about Midge, he telephoned her at the workshop where she was sorting things out. She didn't intend to stay long. She had no framing orders, and had thought it might be a good idea to list her stock. As she would be closing the business, she would have to sell it for whatever she could get.

This was practical. She was accepting the inevitable and was doing something positive about it. Maybe the counselling had already done her good.

Prudence was pleased to see him, and she was delighted with the dolls' house. At her direction, Oliver put it on a table by the window, and she spent some time admiring it, inspecting all the rooms and rearranging the furniture in accordance with what she remembered from her childhood.

'Emily may have fixed it up differently,' she said. 'She was my younger sister – I was much older – and she played with it, and then her daughter did. My niece.'

'You don't talk about her. Where is she? Your sister?'

'She's dead. She was murdered,' Prudence said. 'It was years ago.'

'Murdered?'

'You'll remember it, perhaps, although you must have been a very young man at the time. It was notorious. A woman – well, she was little more than a girl – who was having an affair with my brother-in-law stabbed her to get her out of the way.

She thought that he would marry her. Of course, he loved my sister, really.' Prudence had had to keep assuring herself of this, in order to be able to speak to Lionel civilly, and help him with the children. She told Oliver a few more details and he recalled the case. 'As we were both married, we had different surnames, so you wouldn't have connected it,' she said.

'Do you know if she's been released? Wendy Tyler?' he asked. She must have been after all this time, unless she had been troublesome in prison.

'Yes, I'm sure she has,' said Prudence. 'She wouldn't have served more than about ten years, if she behaved well, and I expect she did, in order to get out. In fact, Oliver, I think I've seen her. Oh, it's such a relief to tell you! I think I saw her in Mickleburgh just after Daniel was killed. I passed her in the street. I'm certain it was her. I saw that face every day in court, at her trial. Hard, showing no remorse, even making out that Lionel had suggested she do it, which was never wholly disproved though there was no evidence to support it. He denied it, naturally, and I believed him. He never got over his feeling of guilt. Emily was pregnant at the time. It was terrible.'

'How dreadful,' said Oliver. He was horrified. 'Where's he now? Lionel, is it?'

'He took the children to Canada. He became an alcoholic and he died about eighteen months ago. Suicide,' she told him.

'And this Wendy Tyler? Are you saying she's living here now? In Mickleburgh?'

'I don't know. I looked her up in the telephone directory but there's no W. Tyler. She's probably changed her name.'

'Perhaps she was only passing through,' said Oliver.

'I've thought of that,' said Prudence. 'And if it was her, she wouldn't recognise me. I've changed more than she has – white hair and wrinkles – and she wouldn't have noticed me in court. We'd never met. I wasn't a witness.'

'To set your mind at rest, I could try to find out what's happened to her,' said Oliver. 'She's on licence, after all. She's only got to slip up and she'll be locked up again. If she has got a new name, someone must know what she's calling herself.' But she would not be listed in a register of past offenders. There was no such simple record. She was free to move about at will.

'Could you? Without being morbid about it, I think I'd like to know. But really I'm trying to forget about her. I'm not expecting to see her whenever I go out.' She was still standing looking at the dolls' house, noticing the new adult woman doll, wondering why Oliver had added it to the family. She decided not to ask him. 'This smaller girl was meant to be Emily,' she said.

They sat down by the fire and talked about the horror of murder, and the evilness of jealousy, and then Oliver told her about Midge consulting a counsellor. He said that Sarah had discovered it by accident, which was the truth.

'Maybe it's not a bad idea,' said Prudence. 'It depends on the skill and training of whoever she's seeing. But some are so intrusive, and not trained at all.'

'That's what I'm afraid of,' Oliver declared.

24

The full statements which the four victimised boys had now given, together with the scientific evidence – the knife had yielded a clear thumbprint from Kevin and blood-stains found on Paul's clothing matched Daniel Stewart's blood – put both those boys at the murder scene and could prove that Kevin was his killer. Trevor's evidence, admitting that he took the car but denying any part in the violence, contributed. Each guilty youth condemned the others, providing enough corroboration for the Crown Prosecution Service to proceed with murder charges, and after the preliminary hearing, they were committed for trial at the Crown Court.

This was a happier time for Jamie and his friends, now freed from their moral dilemma. They did not talk about the case at school, and even avoided mentioning it among themselves, postponing, in their minds, the knowledge that they must give evidence in court. In case any of them thought of dodging this, Fisher had explained about subpoenas and how they must attend. Kate had suggested to Jamie that, independently of the statement he had made to the police, he should write down what he remembered of that fatal night, because it would be months before the case came up, and his memory might fade. Then he could forget it till just before the trial. He did this, hating the task, but once it was done he felt liberated. Among the innocent boys, his evidence was the most important, because he had summoned Daniel, was at the scene throughout apart from those few minutes, and had been wounded. The others could testify accurately only about the vandalism and the general assault outside.

There was talk of counselling, but it could interfere with their memories of the event and might have to wait; however, the parents all rejected the idea. Their boys could face up to what had happened, Ted Grant robustly declared, and so could he. The headmaster, at the start of the new term, had spoken about the crime in general terms, naming none of the boys concerned but deploring the alleged involvement of pupils from the school in such a dreadful incident. He touched on the importance of being a good neighbour, as the dead man had proved to be, and on the folly of mindless vandalism which could escalate so tragically.

Most of the staff, and particularly Kate, were pleased that he had said so much. The feeling was that once the boys had been convicted, he might go further, but until they had been proved guilty, he must be careful not to seem to pre-judge the outcome of the trial. A verdict of manslaughter for all of them was foretold, even for the one who had used the knife.

'If they hadn't had the knife, they might have thumped the two men and Jamie, but no one would have been killed,' said someone.

There were problems in the school with disruptive pupils, but control was generally maintained. What happened outside school hours was outside staff jurisdiction.

'It's frightening,' said Ginny. 'Some of these kids have no respect for other people.'

'There's respect for animals,' said Kate. 'Those same boys might have gone bananas over a puppy.'

'You're not necessarily right about that,' said Bob. 'Some kids enjoy tormenting animals.'

'Some,' agreed Ginny, emphasising the word. 'Do we know if any of these charming adolescents kept hamsters or rabbits?'

No one did.

'I feel sorry for Trevor's mother,' Ginny said. 'She'll be getting hell from those who think she shouldn't have turned him in.'

'She gets my admiration,' Bob said firmly.

Ginny's remark had been apt. Those who knew who the four boys were – families who lived near them and their contemporaries at school – soon spread the word, and the parents had received hate mail. Slogans had been sprayed on the walls of their houses, and Trevor's mother had been jeered and mocked by two factions: those who deplored the crime and those who called her unnatural because she had surrendered her son to the cause of justice. If adults behaved like this, was it surprising that youngsters were so turbulent?

Some time after she took possession of the dolls' house, Prudence, who had not seen Midge recently, rang her at the workshop and invited her to call in on her way home and stay to supper, if she didn't mind the dark drive back to Deerton.

'I've got something to show you,' she said.

Midge, who had been continuing the dreary task of making an inventory of her stock, with, when she could find the relevant receipt, what had been paid for each acquisition, and whose only relief had been an occasional framing commission, accepted with pleasure, tinged with diffidence.

'Please don't go to any trouble,' she said, not adding that she still had no appetite.

'We'll eat early,' Prudence said. 'Then you won't be too

late getting back.' And she could spend some time on the set
of proofs which had come that morning.

When Midge arrived, Prudence took her coat and led her
straight to the sitting room where the dolls' house stood on a
table in the window.

'Look!' she said. 'Oliver has finished restoring it and given
it to me. I know you've watched its progress while he's been
working on it. I'm so delighted with it.'

'I'm sure you are. It's lovely,' said Midge. 'Can't you just
imagine their lives – the people in the house, I mean. How's Mr
Wilberforce?' At Christmas, when Mr Wilberforce had been
laid out on the floor – perhaps having supped too much of
the Christmas claret, Prudence had suggested at the time –
Midge had explained how, on a whim, she had christened
him. 'Ah – there he is,' she said, and she beamed as she saw
the father doll in the armchair by the fire. 'He's relaxing after
his day in the city,' she declared. 'He's a financial magnate,
isn't he?'

Prudence was enchanted by this sudden burst from Midge,
and, as if her guest were a child with whom she was colluding
in a game, she said, 'I think he's an industrialist who makes
carpets.'

'Was that what your father did? Did you pretend it was him?'
asked Midge, turning to face her, a rush of sudden colour in
her cheeks.

'Yes,' said Prudence. 'And we were the family. My brother
and my sister.'

'You said you had a niece who played with the house. Will
she be coming to see you? Will she see it again? Won't she
be thrilled with it?'

'I hope she will come over one day,' Prudence said. 'She
lives in Canada.' She hesitated, and then said, 'When she was
five years old, her mother was murdered. She was my younger
sister. She was stabbed to death.'

Was it right to tell Midge this? Prudence waited for her reaction.

'Oh! Oh, how terrible!' Midge had now turned pale and sought about for a chair, into which she almost collapsed. 'Oh – I didn't know.'

'How could you? It was a very long time ago.'

'Who killed her? Was it like Daniel?'

'No. It was a premeditated crime. My sister's husband had been having an affair and the woman – his mistress—' She paused. That word was seldom used these days. 'She thought he would marry her if my sister was removed.'

'Oh no! Oh, that's much worse than how Daniel died,' said Midge. 'His death was a random accident. That boy hadn't set out to kill him. But to hate someone enough to want to murder them – oh!' She put her head in her hands and rocked to and fro in distress.

Prudence watched her. Was this a wise way to be proceeding? Would this be damaging to Midge, or would it help her to accept her own grief?

'It was dreadful,' she said. 'My brother-in-law never got over it – never forgave himself.'

'He couldn't have known such a fearful thing would happen,' said Midge. 'Plenty of people have affairs without them ending in murder.'

But some affairs do end in violence, Prudence reflected, and some lead to divorce, and many involve pain and misery.

'He went to Canada,' she said. 'He married again, but that didn't last. He's dead now.'

She would not tell Midge that Lionel had taken his own life. That was too much to expect her to absorb.

'Oh – that's terrible! And what about your niece? Were there other children?'

'Yes. There was an older boy. And Emily was pregnant when she died,' said Prudence.

'Oh, the poor woman! What a shocking thing! She was the innocent one,' said Midge.

'Isn't the victim almost always innocent? Except when it's gangs and drugs?' Prudence said, and added, 'The children are all right – they are survivors. My niece is a television reporter and my nephew is a marine biologist.' She remembered how Lally had called one of the dolls Wendy, and the game she had played with her, and suppressed a shiver.

'And what about the one who did it? The murderer?'

'She was eventually released,' said Prudence. 'I expect she's leading a normal life now. She may have married – had a family. Who knows? She'll probably have changed her name.'

'That's not right,' said Midge. 'Not when she caused so much anguish.'

Anguish: yes, that was the *mot juste*, thought Prudence.

'I rather tend to agree,' said Prudence. 'The argument is that although sentenced to life imprisonment, serving a number of years in prison wipes the slate clean.'

'But you can't cancel that sort of debt. That doesn't bring back your sister or give those children their mother.'

'No. I agree,' said Prudence.

'And those boys who killed Daniel will get out, too, one day,' Midge said. 'They may get married and their wives won't know what they've done.'

'It's possible.'

'Forgive and forget, eh?'

'It won't hurt so much after a while,' said Prudence. 'After quite a long while.'

'Oddly enough, I don't feel bitter towards the boys,' said Midge. 'I blame myself for not going with Daniel and in a way I blame him for being so bloody brave and reckless.' Saying that, she burst into tears.

Prudence produced a box of tissues, and Midge took a bundle from it, blowing her nose and dabbing at her eyes.

'I mustn't keep on crying like this,' she apologised. 'She says I'll have to stop some time. Maybe that should be today.'

'Who says?' asked Prudence carefully. She had set the whole evening up with the intention of trying to prod Midge into revealing that she was seeing a counsellor. Here was the opportunity, arrived at not by her guile but by Midge's own disclosure, for surely this must be the 'she' to whom she had referred.

'Oh—' Midge crumpled up her sodden tissues and took some new ones from the box. Prudence rose to put the wastepaper basket near her, in case she threw the wet mess into the realistic coal-effect gas fire. 'I've been to see this woman. A counsellor.' Midge looked sheepish. 'You may think it's weak and silly of me, but I was weary of boring Oliver and Sarah and everyone, and I thought she might help me sort myself out.'

'And is she helping?' Prudence asked.

'I don't know. I talk about it, and what to do. I suppose mostly she just listens,' Midge declared. 'She thinks it was a dreadful thing to happen, but everyone's agreed on that. None of it brings Daniel back.'

'No – well, nothing can. That is the tragedy. It's so final,' Prudence said. 'And not having had the chance to say goodbye must be so hard. It must seem unendurable, but in the end it is bearable. You've lasted this long, and I think you've been most courageous. The trial will be an ordeal, but you needn't go to it, except if you're needed as a witness, unless you want to. Once it's over, you must try to rule a line under that part of your life and move on to a new chapter.'

'I'll have to go to court. I'll have to see it through to the end. For Daniel,' said Midge.

She might change her mind by the time the case was heard, reflected Prudence. Midge had reached the point of wanting to help herself: indeed, she had never left that position and much of her current agony was due to her own high expectations of herself.

'Be content to make haste slowly,' Prudence advised. 'You can't leap up, miraculously healed and consoled, overnight. Tell me about this counsellor. It's a woman – you mentioned "she" – did the doctor send you to her?'

'No. I found her card pushed through my door one day,' said Midge. 'So when I was feeling pretty desperate, I made an appointment. I've been several times. I'm going next week. Look – I've got her card here.' She fumbled in her handbag, pulled out a battered purse, and took the card from a collection wedged into a small inner pocket. 'She thinks I should go ahead with the partnership with Sarah,' she added, and then, more honestly, 'Well – not exactly – she didn't say, one way or another. She told me I must make up my own mind.' She handed the card to Prudence.

Prudence looked at the card, did her best to memorise the name and the address, returned it, and, on the pretext of getting both of them a drink and out of sight of Midge, wrote the details down. What was all this about a partnership with Sarah? Over their drinks, she asked Midge, who explained, her anxieties obvious as she spoke, although she seemed to consider that the scheme would be her economic salvation. Prudence shared her apprehension. The enterprise might turn out to be a commercial success, but how long would it be before Sarah grew tired of it and pulled out?

'I don't think I've got a choice,' Midge was saying. 'It's this or go bust.'

'You could sell out your part, once it's got going. Someone will want to buy it then,' said Prudence, echoing Oliver.

'Yes,' said Midge. 'I suppose so.' She sounded doubtful.

'Is this counsellor really doing you good?' asked Prudence.

'I don't know. How can I tell? I still can't sleep, and I weep buckets.'

'Why didn't you go to Cruse?' asked Prudence. Cruse specialised in bereavement counselling and did valuable work.

'I never thought of it. I went to her because her card arrived like a sign,' said Midge. 'But you make me feel much better than she does. You understand.'

'I don't suppose she's done you any harm,' said Prudence. 'Let's see if I can coax you into eating something.' She had put a fish pie – light and tasty – in the oven earlier and hoped it would not have dried up by now.

Driving home, after a meal during which Prudence had regaled her with a rundown of the book she was working on, Midge felt comforted. For a wonder, she had actually enjoyed the food. Prudence had given her small helpings and she had eaten everything. Prudence Wilmot was a kind, wise woman and, amazingly, she too had met murder at close quarters. What had she meant when she said that the professional counsellor had done Midge no harm? Did she consider that the sessions had also done no good?

Had they? Midge couldn't say for certain, and they were very expensive.

She hadn't told Prudence about Oliver's plan to renovate another dolls' house; he couldn't have really meant it, and it wouldn't happen.

25

When Mrs Stewart kept her next appointment, I expected to hear her say that plans were under way for her joint venture with Sarah Foxton, but she came in looking subdued.

'This must be my last appointment,' she announced, astonishingly.

My previous patient was a teenage girl who had read about bulimia and had decided that she had it, and must effect a cure. I told her the truth – that the remedy lay with herself and she must cultivate self-discipline, which would lead her to develop self-respect, both of which I would help her to acquire. In my opinion, she is merely suffering from adolescent gluttony. Like many of my patients, she paid me in cash, and I wondered where she'd got it from, but did not ask. That was not my business. I was still musing on my plans to aid the girl when Mrs Stewart, early, rang the bell.

'Why have you decided to discontinue treatment?' I asked her. 'You need a long course – three or four months, at least.'

'I agree with you that I won't be back to normal in five minutes,' she replied. 'I'm sure you've helped me a great deal, and now I must begin to help myself.' Just what I had told my last patient she must do. 'And I can't afford any more sessions.'

'*But I've pencilled you in twice weekly for the coming month,*' I objected. *She was a weak woman; it would be easy to make her change her mind.*

'*I didn't make any more appointments,*' *she declared with, for her, surprising firmness.* '*As I've said, this must be the last.*'

'*I can see that it's the cost,*' *I said coldly.* '*You can resume when you are in funds.*' *I would have liked to show her out immediately, but she had forty pounds for me in her purse, and I would part with her in a professional manner.* '*Now, how have you been since your last visit?*' *I tried to smile, to reassure her lest she think I was offended.* '*Have you firmed up your business plans?*'

'*No,*' *she said.* '*And I'm not going to. It's all off.*' *Then, clearly relieved at having surmounted the difficult hurdle of telling me she was dispensing with my services, she said in a rush,* '*I have a friend who has been very helpful – a Mrs Wilmot – I'm not sure if I have mentioned her to you before. I'm sorry to say I lost control the last time I went to see her, and made an idiot of myself, crying and so on.*'

While she spoke, she gazed at me quite steadily, no sign of tears forming in those large blue eyes.

'*And?*' *I prompted, bored now, but I must see the session through.*

'*She told me about the dolls' house,*' *she said, as it seemed inconsequentially, but patients do have trouble keeping to the point. I steer them back discreetly, as the need arises. Mrs Stewart did not wait for me to give her this guidance but forged on.* '*It's a lovely old one. A model of a large house, which belonged to her and her sister when they were young. Oliver Foxton restored it and returned it to her. She told me about her sister, then.*'

'*What about her sister?*' *Where was this taking us?*

'*How she was murdered. It's so dreadful. Her husband had*

a lover – a mistress – and she killed her. The mistress killed the sister. Stabbed her. She thought her lover would marry her if he was free.'

I was silent, but the pounding of the blood in my veins seemed so loud that I thought Mrs Stewart would hear it.

'What was her name?' I asked at last.

'Whose name?'

'The woman who was killed,' I almost screamed. 'Who was she?'

'I don't know,' she answered. 'I don't know what Mrs Wilmot's name was before she was married, and they would have had different names anyway. What does it matter?'

'I was just curious,' I said, trying to speak calmly. 'A counsellor is interested in everything.' What had got into this meek, depressed creature to make her show this unusual spirit?

'She was called Emily. I remember Mrs Wilmot saying that,' she said. 'The husband is dead, now, too.'

I heard this in silence. This must be the woman who had stared at me so intently in the street in Mickleburgh. I had my explanation. She must have been in court, and she would know my face although hers had made no impact on me.

'Presumably she was arrested and imprisoned,' I said coldly.

'Oh yes. But she would be out by now, walking around, as if nothing had happened,' Mrs Stewart said.

'She would have paid her debt to society,' I stated.

'That's a debt that can't be paid,' she said. 'Money embezzled or goods stolen can be returned but you can't return a life.'

'Loss of liberty is punishment,' I told her.

'It doesn't cancel the crime,' was her answer. She seemed to shake herself, then continued. 'When I heard about this – about Mrs Wilmot's niece who'd played with the house and lost her mother – my own tragedy seemed to diminish. My children are grown up and I had a long and happy marriage, with no other

person intervening. There is nothing to regret, only blessings to remember. I don't need any more counselling.'

She rose to her feet and fumbled in her shabby bag, the usual preliminary to pulling out my fee.

'You haven't had your full time,' I said, but I was shaking. I wanted her to leave.

'I know. But of course I'll pay,' she said, and laid two scruffy twenty-pound notes on my desk. 'Thank you for your help.'

I did not show her out. It was all I could do not to lean forward and bang my head against the surface of my desk. I hadn't expected anything like this; I'd imagined that I'd met this woman – Mrs Wilmot – in some professional capacity – perhaps as a patient, or she could have been a doctor, or someone I had encountered in the normal run of life. She might even have run an exclusive dress shop. I don't buy cheap clothes. Being tall, I have difficulty in finding garments that are long enough.

I sat there, stunned. It had to be the same Emily, the one that I had sent on her last journey. A trick of fate had led me to the same area as that stupid bitch's sister. She may not have recognised me – may have thought she had just seen me somewhere – it's often difficult to recognise people seen out of context – but she could do so if we were to come face to face again. And to think I had walked round Mickleburgh and past her house, on the off chance of seeing her again. No wonder I had been haunted by her stare. But, aware now, I could avoid her. If I were to be exposed, I would lose everything I have built up over the years, my list of patients and my steady income.

What should I do? Should I move away and start yet again? I was in a district hundreds of miles from where it happened, yet this freak coincidence had occurred.

That silly little cow, Mrs Stewart: why did she have to upset me like this, after all I've done for her? Look how much I have helped her! And because she has been offered a business opportunity, even though it's been withdrawn, she thinks she is

*strong enough to stand alone, but I'm the one who's put her on
her feet. Murder and bereavement brought her low, and I have
raised her up. How grateful she should be, and she should have
told me so in fulsome terms instead of those few perfunctory
words uttered before leaving so abruptly.*

*I went out to the washroom, splashed my face in cold water
and made a determined effort to regain command of myself
for I had another patient needing me. Mr Leonard, the man
mourning his dog, had the next appointment. Because stupid
Mrs Stewart had left early, I had an interval in which to
compose myself before his arrival, and, never one to waste
time or give way to my emotions, I made up my accounts and
checked my diary. I had a lot of bookings; there are plenty of
isolated people reaching out for understanding. I've even got
a Roman Catholic priest, who arrives dressed in jeans and a
leather jacket. He is having problems over celibacy and chose
to consult me rather than his superiors. Because of my regular
church attendance, I am familiar with the scriptures and can
discuss his predicament in an informed manner. I see he has
an appointment in the week ahead. I shall have to devise a
structure for the consultation. Simple lust is his dilemma. At
first it was erotic dreams, he told me. Now his base thoughts
and yearnings, as he sees them, have focused on a young woman
in his congregation. He hasn't spoken to her outside the church;
it's all in his head, a fantasy.*

*Why don't you get on with it, I long to say; talk to her,
ask her out, become acquainted? But if he does, he thinks he
will be tempted by the devil – in the guise, one imagines, of
this blameless girl – and have an urge to make a physical
approach. It's all so adolescent, but I must treat him seriously. I made notes on how to channel his vapid musings
into more positive action, then brewed some coffee, which I
needed now, drinking it down while still pensive about Mrs
Wilmot.*

When the dog mourner, Mr Leonard, arrived, it was clear that he was very angry.

'Why, Mr Leonard, what has happened?' I asked, seeing his evident rage. This could be healthy; it could indicate that his mourning had advanced.

'She's left me,' he declared, his voice loud. 'She's gone – packed everything she thinks is hers, though much of it is mine, and moved out to a flat, taking my son with her.'

'What brought this about?' I asked, thinking, good for her, as he is a dreary, unattractive man. I looked at his puffy face, sulky mouth, and small, accusing eyes, and knew that whatever she was like, she was better off without him. I was her benefactor.

'I bought another dog,' he said. 'A new Alsatian with a pedigree.'

'So? She wasn't pleased?'

'It bit her,' he acknowledged. 'But it's only a puppy. It will learn.'

'A dog?' I asked, idly. 'Or a bitch?' I did not care which it was.

'A bitch.'

'Ah.' I made a note. 'And did you leave it in the house when you went to work?' He'd done that with the other dog, my notes reminded me.

'I couldn't take her with me,' he said. 'I had to leave her.' He'd started to refer to the dog by her gender, I observed.

'And what about your wife's work? She couldn't take the dog, either.'

'No, but she has a shorter day than I do, and she doesn't travel. I had to go to Brussels soon after I bought Phoebe – that's the dog – and when I returned, my wife had put her in kennels and had gone.'

I felt like saying, 'I hope you and Phoebe will be very happy together,' but restrained myself.

'And?' I prompted.

'*Well – how am I to manage? I'm left doing all the housework and my own cooking, and there's Phoebe to be considered,*' he said, almost ranting.

'*You chose the dog in preference to your wife, Mr Leonard,*' I pointed out. '*She told you what would happen if you went ahead.*'

'*I didn't think she meant it,*' he replied, almost in a growl, like the dog. '*I thought it was an empty threat.*'

'*Do you want her back?*'

'*I don't want to be alone,*' he said.

'*But you're not alone. You've got Phoebe. You got along better with your other dog than with your wife. You've mentioned no friends, no social life. You have problems with relationships, Mr Leonard,*' I told him, speaking sternly because after all, he had come to me for help and it was my task to guide him towards coming to terms with himself and his own nature.

'*My dog wasn't so difficult – so demanding,*' he complained.

'*You took no trouble to please your wife. You don't need to think about a dog's emotions; all it needs is food,*' I said.

He was thoughtful after I'd said that. I felt sorry for the wife – a most unusual experience as I try to be detached, and normally do not find it difficult, but it is by no means rare for me to dislike a patient. I like very few people, as it happens.

'*Do you think I should go after her?*' he asked. '*My wife?*'

'*That's up to you. Do you want her back, or do you want to keep the dog? You can always hire a cleaner for the housework.*' He could afford my fees. He could pay for a cleaner and a laundry service.

I did not point out that, if necessary, he could pay for sex. That could be the subject of a further session.

He left at last, having written out his cheque, still consumed with self-pity, but less angry. As he walked towards the door I heard him mutter, '*You said I should get another dog.*'

Perhaps I did.

26

As suddenly as she had decided to end her counselling sessions, Midge had made up her mind not to fall in with Sarah's plans. The resolution, reached on the way to keep her appointment, rocked her almost more than relinquishing her consultations in that plain white room with the plain, pale woman sitting across the desk from her, listening impassively to her disconnected ramblings. But like a revelation, Midge had realised that she must not jeopardise her friendship with the Foxtons by submitting to Sarah's brisk dominance. It could never be an equal partnership.

She'd have to get out of the lease in the least damaging way possible, but for that she would need Oliver's help. She'd have to give a reason for her change of mind that would not wound him, or hurt Sarah, and then stick to it. Sarah could still pursue the same scheme, in the same premises, but with another partner; with all her business contacts, surely she would find one?

With that all put in train, Midge would find what work she could. There must be something she was equipped to do.

Driving back to Deerton, her bridges burned, she felt as though a huge weight had been lifted from the top of her head. The dull ache in her chest remained, but perhaps she would get used to it and cease to be aware of it. Once home, she put the car away and then walked round the garden in the glow from the security light over the back door. Mark and Jonathan had decided that as she was on her own, she must have this extra protection, and they had got Ted Grant to fit lights at appropriate spots so that as you walked round the house they came on in sequence. That morning, she had noticed that the small spikes of bulbs, stiff as spears, were already pushing through the frozen ground. They'd bloom eventually; the daffodils would be bright beneath the apple trees, and the cherry would be smothered in pink blossom, but Daniel would see none of this. Last spring had been beautiful; he hadn't known that he would never see another.

Thinking this, Midge felt the warm tears pour down her face again. Where did they all come from, this unending stream? Half blind, she stumbled towards the house to be met by Gwen Grant, who had seen the lights come on and was walking round the side of the house in search of her.

Gwen's bountiful bleached hair stood out round her head in an aureole. She was teetering along in her fashion boots and shiny gold raincoat.

'Oh, Mrs Stewart – dear – Midge, isn't it? Don't cry, love,' pleaded Gwen. 'Come along in and let me make you some tea,' and she put an arm round Midge, leading her in though the back door, this time reaching out to unhook the hidden key herself.

This was the third time Mrs Grant had come round and plied her with tea, thought Midge, stifling an almost hysterical giggle as she allowed herself to be swept inside and guided to one of her own chairs while Gwen put the kettle on.

'My name's Gwen,' Mrs Grant reminded her. 'Now, weak and with sugar, isn't it?'

'No sugar,' Midge managed to reply.

'Well, a biscuit then. You need something sweet, blood sugar, you see,' said Gwen.

Without Midge explaining where they were, she found the tin, with still a few stale Hobnobs left. She'd get some more and pop them round, thought Gwen. She felt quite at home now in this kitchen. In search of milk, she opened the fridge; it was almost empty, and she clicked her tongue. The poor dear was skin and bone and here was proof that she wasn't eating properly.

After they'd had their tea, and Midge's tears had ceased to flow, Gwen explained the reason for her visit.

'We've got a plan, you see. Me and Ted. About the business. Your place. We wondered if you'd be interested, seeing as how Mr Stewart isn't here to do the furniture. We thought, if you were free tomorrow night, maybe you'd come with us to The Bridge for a meal, and then Ted'll put it to you, like.'

Midge stared at her. A plan?

'It's about a job,' said Gwen. 'And about your workshop.' She paused. This was very difficult. She'd told Ted they must give Mrs Stewart some clue about the reason for their invitation or she would be much too embarrassed to accept. 'I told Ted we must explain a bit first. Then you can think about it.'

'Explain what?' Midge was mystified.

'Explain as how Ted wants to expand and have a proper workshop, and he'll need some office help, which I can't give as I've got my own business, you see, and the books have got too much for me now that our Josie's married and gone away – well – we'll explain, if you'll come out with us. We thought we could talk it over during the meal. Our treat, of course,' she ended.

Midge couldn't believe what she was hearing. Miracles did happen, after all.

'You mean you want to take the workshop off my hands and offer me a job?' she said.

'That's it,' said Gwen, beaming at her. 'I think we'd all get along just fine. Details to be arranged.' Gwen intended to move her own hairdressing business into part of the premises, and branch out later into beauty treatment.

Midge managed not to say she would give the workshop away.

'Oh,' she said. 'My goodness.'

'You don't have to decide anything now,' Gwen told her. 'We'll tell you what we're thinking of, and then you can take your time making up your mind. What about if we pick you up at seven?'

'I'll be ready,' Midge said, still amazed. Ted hadn't yet sent in the bill for fitting the lights. What about that, now? She knew it would not come. At least Mark had bought the lights themselves at Argos, so there was no debt for them.

'See, there is light at the end of the tunnel,' Gwen couldn't resist saying.

After she had gone, Midge thought that maybe there was also life after death.

During the night, she wondered if they had devised this plan from pity, and the knowledge that Dan had died and Ted had not. But it was going to cost them. Had they had a sudden windfall?

She was waiting at the gate as they pulled out of Orchard Close. She wore her good coat over a black velvet skirt and waistcoat and a peasant blouse bought years ago on some holiday. She had lost so much weight that her clothes hung loosely on her, but she had washed her hair and put on make-up, adding mascara and brushing blusher on her cheeks.

Gwen was sitting in the back of the Vauxhall, and Ted leaped out to open the passenger door for Midge. She felt reckless and light-headed. No one except her hosts knew where she was going, and it was the first time she had visited a restaurant since the night Daniel died. Well, she had to do it sometime.

I mustn't drink too much, she told herself, and I mustn't cry. I must be calm and level-headed.

She'd been to The Bridge with Dan, but she wouldn't let herself remember that. Not tonight.

'We like this place,' said Gwen as Ted drove into the car park behind The Bridge. 'Our Josie used to work in the bar, when she was studying.'

Now Midge learned that Josie was expecting a baby in the summer. That topic kept them going for a while; Midge sensed that Gwen was anxious, conscious that their social circles did not overlap, but that soon passed as she and Midge drank white wine and Ted had a beer before they ordered. They sat by the log fire in the bar, studying the menu, and Midge let herself be guided into having casseroled pheasant, which Gwen had never tried and also chose, wishing to sample it. Ted, who had ordered steak, related how he had hit a pheasant on the road not many days before.

'Shame. It was a lovely bird but it didn't stand a chance – came out of nowhere,' he declared. He'd got out of the car to make sure it was dead, but had left it on the verge.

'What a waste,' said Gwen. 'It'd have made a nice supper for us.'

'I couldn't have fancied it. Not after that,' said Ted.

He had a tender heart, thought Midge. After a suitable pause to show respect for the slaughtered pheasant, she asked how Peter was, and heard that he was spending the evening with Jamie Preston. They were to do their homework together. Kate would see to it, said Gwen.

'Have they – the boys – got over it?' Midge asked. 'It must have been awful for them.'

'Yes, it was. Funny, weren't they, not speaking up? And just when they'd decided to, the knife turned up,' said Gwen. Neither Peter nor Barry had mentioned Mark's talk with them to their parents. 'But you can understand it in a way. At that age, they can't always see things straight, but it wasn't as if those four were their friends.'

'I expect they were confused,' said Midge. That was the word to use: she was confused, her counsellor had told her.

Further talk about the subject was interrupted by the approaching waitress.

'Here's the girl to say our meal's ready,' Gwen said. 'Come along, Midge. Is that really your name?'

Midge laughed.

'No. It's Marjorie, but I hated it when I was small and I didn't like Marge, and somehow it got turned into Midge and stuck. Not very dignified, but I'm used to it.'

'I'll stick to it then, if that's all right,' said Gwen firmly. 'But in the business, if you agree to our idea, you'll be Mrs Stewart. It's more respectful.'

'If you think so,' Midge said faintly.

'I do. There'll be young girls about, and they must mind their manners,' Gwen said. 'Now, we'll not talk about all that till we've eaten. We want you to enjoy your meal.'

Midge managed to consume the consommé she had asked for, deciding it was the lightest starter on the menu, and she ate some of the pheasant, hiding the rest under the bones. She quite enjoyed the ice cream she had for pudding; Ted had apple pie and Gwen chose chocolate mousse.

Afterwards, while they had coffee, Ted was frank.

'We had a bit of luck,' he said. 'It was just after all that business. Gwen had a win on the lottery – not the jackpot, mind. She and the friend she runs the salon with in Fettleton shared their stakes, and they won a tidy bit between them. They didn't want any publicity, so no one knows about it. Gwen's friend is going to live in Spain, but Gwen wants to keep the salon on, only its lease is up in March and she'd like new premises in a better area. Your place would be ideal – not central, but near enough, and with parking handy. I reckon I could open up the back to get the van in.' He was surprised Daniel Stewart hadn't done that; it would have made loading and unloading much easier. 'If I go in with her, using some of the space for spares and that, we can expand in both directions. Of course, we might need planning permission for a change of use, but they're already commercial premises. I don't think there'll be a problem.' He didn't tell her that a friend of his, a chartered surveyor, masquerading as a customer, had had a good look round and had deplored the misuse of space. The place had a high vaulted ceiling and he thought they could install an upper storey. 'There's a lot of work for a good electrician locally. I get contracts from builders and there's plenty of ordinary jobs, too. I'd hope to get a young lad in as an apprentice, until Peter's old enough, if he wants to join me.'

He beamed at Midge across the table, a confident man, very masculine, sure of his own skill and ability. There was no indecision here.

'How wonderful about the lottery,' she said. 'You did well to keep it quiet. I'll have to ask Oliver Foxton about the lease but I want to get rid of it. I'm sure that part will be all right. He's a solicitor – you know that.'

'We'll need a lawyer,' said Gwen. 'Maybe he'll look after us.' At the moment their winnings were sitting in a building society high interest account growing all the while. 'Then there's your little niche,' Gwen went on. Midge was wondering when they would come to that. 'I mentioned the books earlier. I'm not wonderful at that, so we thought you might take it on. You've been doing some of it, haven't you?' Midge had, until Daniel had tried to stop her discovering the extent of their losses. 'Then, if you fancied the idea, there's a need for a receptionist at the salon.' She'd add style and class, once Gwen had tactfully smartened her up a bit, and she would attract a certain type of customer. 'Some of my ladies will follow me from Fettleton,' Gwen said. 'They're used to me.'

They'd got it all worked out, and Midge could see it shaping up, the place gutted and refitted, with enough capital available to do it properly. There would be room to expand into light fittings and so on, if Ted wanted to. She pictured Gwen's part of the operation, with the row of basins and the overalled figures ministering to the needy heads.

'I think you'd better give me a new haircut,' she said, smiling. 'At the moment I'm not a very good advertisement for the new venture.'

27

'Has she made up her mind yet?'

Sarah looked at Oliver across the breakfast table. It was Saturday morning, and neither was going to work that day, so there was no easy separation. Oliver was planning on working outside, cold though it was. The shed needed clearing out and he could prepare the greenhouse for the tomatoes he would grow there later. Soon he'd have another dolls' house to restore; his estate agent contact knew of one a woman who had bought a house from him wanted to sell privately. Oliver had made an appointment to see it next weekend.

He knew at once what Sarah's abrupt question meant. She was frowning with impatience as she waited for his answer.

'I don't know,' he said. 'You must give her time, Sarah.'

'I don't know why she didn't jump at it,' Sarah complained. 'What choice has she, after all?'

'Several. She could sell the house, get rid of her lease, and move to France. Or Spain or Turkey,' said Oliver, plucking countries from his mind at random.

'Whatever for?'

'She could live more cheaply. Or marry a Turkish waiter,' said Oliver. 'Or both.'

'Now you're being ridiculous,' said Sarah. 'What's got

into you? You don't fancy her, do you?' She said this in so scornful a voice, deriding Midge's appeal as she had done before, that Oliver was incensed. 'You can't,' she answered her own question. 'She's a mess.'

In his head, Oliver counted to ten but reached only six. What if he were to say he lusted madly after Midge? What if it were true?

'You're the one who's talking nonsense,' he retorted sharply. 'It's Midge's future that's at stake, and her income. And her friendship with us. If anything were to go wrong – if you found you couldn't work together or the project failed – all these things would be jeopardised,' he said.

'It's my future and my income, too,' said Sarah.

'You won't starve if it flops,' he answered. 'And what if you get tired of it – or her? You do get tired and bored with things, Sarah. You know you do. Have you got bored with your job? Is that why you want a change?'

'I want to help her,' she declared.

'And yourself. You want someone you can push around, who won't stand up to you,' said Oliver, his tone still heated. 'You've never really been put to the test, Sarah. Even Judy, at her age, knows more about life's difficulties than you do.'

'Oliver! Whatever has got into you? Calm down. You'll have a heart attack if you go on like that,' said Sarah. 'You must be feeling ill, to speak to me in that unkind way.

Oliver took a deep breath and made an effort to compose himself. He did not approve of lost tempers.

'Not at all,' he said, more temperately. 'But I want you to understand that this is a very serious step you plan to take, and you won't be able to throw it away for some whim, if you don't enjoy it later. You have enough business experience to know that.' He paused; then, as she seemed about to speak, he went on, 'My life has been spent trying to make you happy and to please you, and I know I haven't always succeeded, but I'm not going to let you manipulate other people's lives just so that you can feel good.'

'Oliver!'

He turned away, afraid he might dredge up from his subconscious some observation which would do untold harm. Words uttered could not be revoked.

'I'm going to sort out the garden shed,' he said, and left, aware, with alarm, that he had parted from her feeling deeply hostile.

Going to the back lobby to put on his old gardening jacket and his rubber boots, Oliver was dismayed. He and Sarah were almost quarrelling; this was their second sharp exchange and each time it had been because of Midge. Whilst part of him was shocked and startled, he also felt a sense of freedom such as he had not known for years; it was as though he had pulled the stopper from a bottle, let out the genie of his repressed feelings, waved restraint and caution away. This might not be the end of it: Sarah might create a scene when he returned to the house, or she might pursue him down the garden, demanding his apology, though brooding silence and a sulky face were more her line.

Sarah, however, was not prepared to wait. She loaded the dishwasher with her breakfast things – Oliver had already stowed his away – and then went into his study. She'd wreck that dolls' house he had spent such hours on; pull the doors off, dismember the doll family and stamp on the furniture. That would really hurt him.

But it had gone. Preoccupied with her own plans, the cleaning taken care of, she had not been in his study since he took it back to Prudence.

She stared about her, her vengeful impulse thwarted. What had he made of her earlier subversive actions? Had he even noticed? Why should he take so much trouble over repairing a battered toy for an old woman? He'd never made anything for her.

Now it was Midge, Midge, Midge, the whole time. Midge, who was a weak, silly woman who had gone to pieces after Daniel's death. Sarah worked hard at whipping herself up into a mood of jealous resentment. She felt injured and neglected.

Against her will, she remembered the conference she had been to in Kent, not long after Daniel's death. She'd looked forward to it, the first one that involved a night away. The day's meetings had gone well and she had made a presentation which had been commended, but after dinner, when the evening ended, Clive Berry, her immediate superior, had come to her room. He seemed to think he had received an invitation. Sarah had been shocked and frightened as he closed the bedroom door behind him – she had opened it quite innocently when he knocked, thinking he had some message for her for the morning – but he had walked past her, carrying a bottle of champagne, set it down, and moved in on her. That was the wording Sarah's secretary, Daisy, used when describing a sexual approach. It was accurate. Clamped by two powerful arms, a sweating face looming over her, hard, slobbery wet lips pressed against her mouth while a huge tongue probed her lips apart and was thrust down her throat, she had understood that rape was easy because he was so strong. He pushed her against the bed and she fell back upon it, only then somehow managing to bring up her knee and kick him in the genitals.

He had let her go at once, doubling up in agony, and Sarah had made a dash for the door, hesitating there, reluctant to run into the corridor and shout for help. It would be so undignified. She opened it and managed to say, 'Please leave,' standing against it so that she could flee if he refused, but as soon as he could move, he went, picking up the bottle as he did so.

Sarah knew that if her kick had missed its target, the incident could have ended very differently. As it was, he had merely muttered, 'Bloody stuck-up bitch,' and a few more choice epithets. If it had been Midge, who was so small and slight, she might have been overpowered. Rape wasn't always committed by a stranger in an alley.

She had not told Oliver. After all, she had survived without more damage than some bruises on her upper arms, which he hadn't noticed as afterwards she had worn a nightdress with loose sleeves which hid them. However, she had felt humiliated. It had been so degrading; how could Clive have interpreted her friendly manner as an invitation? Since then he had picked on her, going out of his way to find fault with her work. He wanted her to leave, but of her own volition. Well, she was going to do so, and had handed in her resignation letter, saying that she intended to form her own company.

It was rather a pity she wasn't doing that, she thought: she should be setting up her own consultancy, not going in with Midge. Perhaps she had been hasty in proposing that idea, though she thought it was a good one. She might undo it; it wasn't too late. Oliver had just said so, more or less. If she started her own consultancy, she could work from home. She already had a computer; a fax could soon be installed, even a separate telephone line. The outlay would be minimal, and she could take some clients away from Clive.

She'd tell Oliver she had changed her mind, but not today. He must suffer first, repent his cruel words, apologise, and then she might forgive him, but she would not forget his unkindness.

Her morale restored, Sarah set about her Saturday morning chores, which were not demanding. She had just finished when she heard a car outside.

It was Midge.

There was a short ring and a tap of the heavy knocker, Midge's signal. It irritated Sarah that she advertised her presence in this individual way, since a glance from the hall window would reveal her car. Cross, she opened the door.

Midge, heavy with resolution, her courage screwed up tight,

did not notice Sarah's tension as she was admitted, and she did not act with her normal diffidence, starting her set speech at once.

Sarah, giving the door an extra push – it sometimes stuck, Oliver would have to see to it – heard with disbelief what she was saying.

'Sarah – sorry to barge in like this, but in fairness I must tell you straight away, and I didn't want to phone about something so important. Our business deal – your kind idea – it's off. I'm doing something else with the workshop.'

There! It was out; she'd said it. Relief poured over her.

But Sarah's reflexes were swift. She rallied. Frustration would not defeat her fighting spirit, and she said, 'I'd changed my plans, too.'

'Oh?' That did startle Midge. 'So I'm not letting you down, then,' she said. 'That's wonderful.'

The two were still standing in the hall. Pale winter sunlight filtered through the window, casting brilliant slats across the oak table in the centre, on which stood a brass bowl containing daffodil bulbs almost in bloom. Midge smiled nervously. There was no thought in her head that the reverse might apply; that Sarah was reneging on her offer.

'What are you going to do?' she asked, genuinely curious.

Sarah launched into an eloquent explanation of her plans. Midge listened carefully.

'Sounds good,' she said. 'No overheads, and you won't be depending on someone scatty like me. But won't you be lonely?'

'I'll probably need an assistant fairly soon,' said Sarah.

Midge had put her finger on the sole snag. Sarah needed someone to react against, not as company, but as an audience, though she did not think of it in those terms. At work, Daisy, who admired her greatly, fulfilled that role. Still, she'd discomfited Midge, kept the upper hand.

They had never moved from the hall. Sarah opened the door again to let Midge out, and did not stay to witness Oliver, who had seen the Volvo arrive, come round the side of the house and whisk her off to the garden shed, where he had been tinkering with the rotary mower.

There, Midge told him of her plans, and as long as they were subject to various safety clauses and considerations, and an appropriate contract, he applauded them.

Sarah, in a rage, never noticed that the Volvo had not been promptly driven off.

'It's that counsellor woman! She's made Midge change her mind,' stormed Sarah when, towards the end of the morning, by which time the shed was immaculate and the greenhouse ready for spring planting, Oliver returned to the house. Midge had not stayed long. She had a date to show Gwen and Ted Grant round the workshop.

'Midge told me that you said you were pulling out,' Oliver stated. He was calm now; the morning's labours, and Midge's news, had restored his good humour. He was relieved at Midge's decision not to collaborate with Sarah; she had told him she had made up her mind before she heard the Grants' proposal. The opportunity they offered was at least as good a prospect as Sarah's scheme, and she would be under much less strain as a paid member of the staff than as a committed partner. It wasn't always wise to go into partnership with a friend.

'Yes – well, it's true, but she wasn't to know that, coming round and springing it on me,' said Sarah. However, as she had not let Midge give her any details, she was in the dark about her plans.

'I imagine you're thankful,' said Oliver. 'Now you won't be leaving her in the lurch.'

'That counsellor person has a lot to answer for,' said Sarah, keen to milk the subject dry of every drop of disapproval she could squeeze from it.

'How do you know they discussed it?' Oliver asked her. 'I understand the Grants invited Midge out last night and put the idea to her then. She hasn't had time to consult the woman since.'

Who were the Grants? What was the idea? Sarah did not know, and she did not connect the Grants with Daniel's murder as she had paid scant attention to the identities of the various boys, the good ones or the bad.

'I see you've heard all about it,' she said.

'Yes. I saw Midge's car and came up just as she was leaving,' he replied.

'Trust you. You wouldn't let her go without talking to her,' said Sarah.

'No, I wouldn't, Sarah. Not if I saw her, and I'm surprised you didn't call me when she arrived.'

'There wasn't time. She was in and out of the house in seconds,' said Sarah sulkily.

That, at least, was true.

'Well, anyway,' said Oliver pacifically, 'it's all good news. Neither of you is abandoning the other. Let it rest.'

But Sarah couldn't. She was frightened. She had backed off from a plan that could have been successful, and which Oliver would have kept an eye on in the background. Now she had committed herself to a venture on her own, and if it failed, there would be no one else to blame, only circumstances, if they filled the bill.

'She told you what I intend to do, I suppose,' she said. 'Work from home?'

'It sounds a good scheme,' said Oliver. 'There's plenty of room. Later, when you're established, you might do better placed more centrally. You could look into renting an office when you've got going.'

He wasn't even going to disapprove, so giving her grounds for further argument.

'Maybe,' she said. She still didn't know what Midge's fine new plans were, but she was not going demean herself by asking.

Their light lunch was consumed in frosty silence. A telephone call from Judy, now back at university, was an interruption greeted with relief; she rang simply for a chat. Then Tim called to say he had exchanged duties with a colleague and was coming down that night.

'He needs sleep,' said Sarah, putting down the telephone. 'He's exhausted. Their hours are horrendous.'

'Yes,' agreed Oliver. At least she was briefly thinking of someone other than herself.

Tim's rare visits were undemanding as he was always so tired that he spent most of his time sleeping, while Sarah washed and ironed his clothes and cooked his favourite food.

She should have had more children. Then, as Oliver had failed to satisfy her, she might have been fulfilled, with younger ones coming on, needing her expert domestic skills.

He might have liked it, too.

Tim's presence helped them through the rest of the weekend. Though he was tired, he seemed happy and was enjoying his work. Oliver was proud of him, and Sarah's admiration shone from her; here was someone she really loved, thought Oliver, and spared a moment to reflect that it was lucky Tim hadn't brought a girl with him this time. None was mentioned during his brief visit; perhaps he was between women, or he might be seriously involved and not keen to expose a relationship he valued to Sarah's critical inspection.

He left early on Monday morning, and his parents later departed for their own concerns. Sarah, in the office, grimly working out her notice, was sorting through some files when, halfway through the morning, Clive entered, crossed over to her and, leaning close, told her that he wished she was not leaving and couldn't they be friends?

In the open-plan office, in front of other staff, Sarah did not wish to make a scene.

'I'm leaving. That's decided,' she replied.

'Have lunch with me,' he said. 'I'll be in The Verandah at one o'clock.'

The Verandah was in Mickleburgh, not far from the offices of Foxton and Smythe. What a place to choose, if he meant to set up an intimate encounter. But he might not know what her husband did; she had never told him. Coldly, she refused, and said she would stand by her resignation letter. At last he left, and she sent Daisy out for sandwiches. Sarah spent her lunch hour calculating what she must spend on setting herself up in Winbury and how long it would be before she could expect to see a profit. Midge had precipitated her into acting out her bluff, if bluff it was. She was restless and had applied for other jobs, but would she have left without one if Clive had not assaulted her? She could have reported him, made a fearful fuss, but an inner voice questioned whether, although she had certainly given him no encouragement, by not actively distancing herself, she might have seemed to signal green.

She was drinking her coffee when Daisy came rushing in, eager to impart some news startling enough to confound even Sarah. One of the juniors had accused Clive of sexual harassment. She had complained to the managing director himself, and was prepared to sue. What about that? Daisy's blue eyes were enormous in her cheerful face.

'What did he do?' asked Sarah.

So that was why he had invited her out to lunch. He wanted to make sure she didn't support the girl's allegations. If they had a social meal together subsequently, she would lose credibility. What a creep he was.

'Pressed against her by the copier. Touched her up. Made personal comments and improper suggestions,' said Daisy primly. 'He's a sleaze-bag, Sarah. You don't like him, do you?' Just recently, that had been obvious, though they had seemed to get along all right until that conference in Kent, which Daisy had not been to as it was for senior staff.

'I can't say he's my favourite person,' Sarah answered rather curtly.

'He gave me a lift home once, and groped me in the car. I soon hopped out,' said Daisy. 'He said she could leave. Jenny, I mean. Told her she was insolent.'

Sarah, to her own astonishment, for she thought she was never impulsive, heard herself saying, 'I'll back up her story. He harassed me at the Kent conference.'

'No!' Daisy's eyes grew even rounder and still larger.

'Yes.' She felt a glow of righteousness surge over her. 'I'll talk to Jenny. We'd better make a plan.'

She wouldn't involve Oliver in this, and she wouldn't describe the lengths to which Clive had gone; that scene was not for public edification. But if she and Daisy endorsed Jenny's complaint, the management would have to take it seriously and Clive, at the very least, would have to mind his step and grovel.

28

It transpires that one cannot escape one's past. Sooner or later, it rises up, however well it has been buried, however many precautions against exposure have been taken, however much may seem to be forgotten.

I find this in my work. I have been consulted by an elderly woman whose husband, after years of quiet retirement, is visited by dreams of his wartime experiences. His ship was sunk; men drowned around him. He was rescued but he could not save his greatest friend. Guilt and remorse now plague him. I told her that after living through the horror again, his haunting dreams might eventually disappear, be exorcised. If not, he should seek medical aid. It was a sad case, but she said that talking about it had done her good. She came in several times, to report no real improvement in her husband.

Is this happening to me? I find myself thinking about the past more frequently than for many years. It must be because Mrs Wilmot has threatened my security. I risk discovery. That woman is a danger to me. What can I do about it? Wait for nemesis to defeat me? Not without a struggle.

I wrote a letter just the other day, one that should arouse alarm.

*   *   *

Prudence was in Fettleton library when she saw the woman she had recognised as Wendy Tyler again. She had gone there to check some details about Florence in the nineteenth century, where her heroine was a governess whose path had crossed that of the Brownings. She had finished the proofs which had interrupted the flow of the new book and was glad to return to it; Midge's enthusiasm, hearing the outline of the plot, had encouraged her. She still marvelled that people enjoyed reading what she had spent months constructing; they did, for with every book her sales went up, and one had been broadcast as a radio serial.

Wendy Tyler was collecting some books she had evidently ordered. She had not seen Prudence, who was sitting at a table by the radiator, where it was warm. Having accepted the books from the hand of the librarian, Wendy paused at the notice board and studied it; then she left the building.

Prudence did not hesitate. She abandoned the book she had been consulting and followed her, leaving a surprised librarian to come upon it later. Mrs Wilmot was normally punctilious about replacing books or handing them across the counter.

What am I doing, Prudence asked herself, following her quarry into the road. She should have asked the librarian who she was; Prudence was well known in the library, where they were aware that she was a novelist, and the information might have been supplied. She hurried on, following the tall figure who today wore a camel coat, her hair in the same severe swept-back style.

Wendy strode on, past Boots and a delicatessen. Had she more shopping to do, or was she returning to her car? Prudence's was in Safeway's car park; she disliked multi-storey parks and there was always something she needed at the supermarket, entitling her to use its space.

What would she do if she caught up with Wendy? Challenge her? But she wasn't going to overtake; it was all she could do to keep pace with her long strides. Wendy marched ahead through groups of shoppers which parted before her, then closed up in front of Prudence, who marvelled at what confidence she had, arrogantly going through them like a ploughshare. She turned into an arcade which opened between Dixons and a dry cleaner's, and when Prudence went the same way, she had vanished.

Prudence walked the length of the arcade in vain. There was no sign of her. She might be in one of the shops but it was not feasible to enter all of them in search of her. Prudence abandoned the trail and went back to her car.

The woman she knew as Wendy Tyler had seen Prudence reflected in a plate-glass window, and had ducked into the first crowded shop in the arcade while she passed.

It had happened once; it could happen again. Mrs Wilmot would see her and an encounter might be unavoidable.

Seeing her like that, coming up behind me in the street, unnerved me. She might not have noticed me; it could have been chance, but I would not risk finding out if she was following me. I did not want a challenge, or, if one had to come, I would have it in a place and at a time of my own choosing. If she thought she recognised me, she could find out my new name if she set her mind to it; a private detective would, for a price, be able to accomplish that feat. If she does that, I'll have no option but to move on, and to float a new identity.

It's so unfair.

I doubled back after she had passed and returned to my car, driving swiftly away to my consulting-room where Mr Leonard was due in his lunch hour. He had rung me up requesting an emergency appointment.

I calmed myself down, breathing deeply, sniffing some herbs I keep arranged in water on my desk to inspire confidence in my patients. In a short time I was myself again – like Macbeth.

Now why did I think of Macbeth?

I made a mental switch and turned my mind towards Mr Leonard and his canine problems. Or his marital problems. The two were intertwined. He was early, and I pressed the buzzer to open the front door when he rang the bell.

Things started to go wrong immediately. Instead of waiting meekly until I bade him enter, Mr Leonard stormed straight into my consulting room, and he had his large Alsatian dog with him. He had said it was a puppy, but it was enormous and looked more than mature, snarling at me, the hairs on its neck bristling. I'd seen enough of Alsatians in my years in prison to last a lifetime. I was about to ask Mr Leonard to remove the dog and tie it up outside when I saw that he was snarling, too, glaring at me with a maniacal expression on his ugly face.

The desk was between us. I stood behind it, my left hand resting on it, my right hand in my pocket as he began to speak. I was ready if the dog should pounce. I hate all dogs.

'You told me I had to choose. I chose the dog and she left me. My wife left me.' He almost shouted the words in my face, standing up, leaning towards me.

'I know she's left you. You've already told me,' I said steadily. 'You chose the dog.'

I sat down, to indicate that I, at least, was calm. The dog was growling softly, but now, as if to mimic me, it crouched on its haunches, presenting a less menacing appearance.

'Sit down, Mr Leonard,' I commanded. 'Let us talk this through.'

He sat, winding the leash round his wrist, and the dog slumped down, mercifully out of my sight, but I could hear its noisy breathing, punctuated by low, sullen growls.

'There's nothing to discuss. She's gone and it's your fault,'
he said.

*'It was your choice. You chose the dog,' I repeated. 'Why
is your situation worse today than at our last consultation?'*

*'She went off with Frank Hines. A man she works with. I've
only just discovered that,' he said.*

'Perhaps Frank Hines prefers her to a dog,' I said.

*It was a reasonable and obvious observation, but he seemed
to go completely mad, springing to his feet and cursing,
blaming me for the misfortunes of the forty-odd years of his
life. It is strange how reluctant people are to shoulder the
blame for their own mistakes; it's more comfortable to place
it elsewhere.*

*The dog stood up and started barking, and for the first time
in my life as a free woman, I felt physically threatened. That
could not be permitted.*

*I reached into my pocket and removed my knife. I am never
without it.*

*'Mr Leonard, if you don't control your dog, I shall take
drastic action,' I said.*

Rosemary Ellis was very tired that night. She had had a
gruelling day, concerned with the difficulties of other people,
and for once she thought it would be agreeable if someone
were to be concerned with her. But she had never let anyone
come close to enough to do so, not for a long time.

Driving home later than usual, suddenly the prospect of
another meal alone, and a solitary evening before she could
reasonably go to bed, was unappealing. She would break her
routine and eat out. She could go somewhere unpretentious.
What if she called in at The Verandah for dinner?

Why not? Wasn't it time she had a treat?

Oliver Foxton would have gone home by now. There would
be no chance of seeing him if she went straight back to the

flat. It was strange how each small sighting of him seemed to keep her content until the next one. Crumbs, she thought: food for fantasy. She was not coveting him; she did not desire him physically; she feasted only on her glimpses of him.

She was able to park in the market square, not far from the restaurant, and, after locking her car, walked there. Several tables were vacant and she was escorted to a corner, which suited her as she had no wish to be islanded in the centre of the dining area. Asked if she would care for a drink, she ordered a glass of white wine, and when it came, the first sip seemed to rush straight to her head, but it relieved any awkwardness she felt at being there alone, the only solitary diner. She ordered a fish dish; salmon in a sauce which the waiter said was interesting.

While she was waiting for the soup which she had chosen to begin her meal, another woman entered, on her own, and was shown to a table on the far side of the room. Rosemary did not look at her; she lowered her gaze, and waited for her plate to be removed.

Oliver had suggested that Sarah should go with him to inspect the dolls' house he had arranged to see. They could make a day of it, have lunch somewhere, visit a garden centre or go shopping, whatever she would like to do. The dolls' house owner lived in a village not far from Bath.

But Sarah said she was too busy setting up a mailing list for her prospective business and analysing surveys regarding its potential which she had already carried out.

'Can I help?' he offered. The dolls' house could wait. But no, there was nothing he could usefully do.

Except keep out of her hair, he thought.

'Suppose I take Midge, then?' he asked. 'Would that be all right with you? She was so taken with Prudence's that I said I'd find one for her. It might give her an interest. She could look out for the bits and pieces.'

'All right. Take her. Though will she have time for this interest, with her wonderful new career?' asked Sarah, who still did not know what Midge's plans were.

'She may not want to come,' said Oliver. 'I'll ask Prudence too,' he added. Surely Sarah could not be jealous of Midge? The idea was laughable.

But was it? he wondered, as he dialled Midge's number.

He did not tell her the reason for his trip, merely that he had an appointment. She accepted eagerly, and then said, 'Sarah will be coming too, of course.'

'She hasn't time,' he answered. 'But I've asked Prudence.'

'Oh – that's lovely,' Midge said. 'What fun.'

And it would be, he resolved.

29

Saturday was a cold, clear day, the frost that had hung about for weeks still lingering. Midge planned that she and Prudence would amuse themselves in Bath while Oliver kept his appointment. Prudence was already in the car when he called for Midge, and they set off in high feather, with Oliver feeling as if he were playing truant. Perhaps he was. Prudence had thought him wise to include her on the expedition; however innocently undertaken, if he and Midge were seen setting off together, mischief could be made, tongues could wag, and two and two could so easily be wrongly added up.

'Who's this demanding client who requires your presence on a Saturday?' asked Midge, who, without a pang, had closed the shop to go with him.

Oliver had explained the reason for their trip to Prudence. Now he confessed to Midge.

'Oh, Oliver!' Midge knew he'd never say anything he didn't mean. Even so, she protested. 'I can't let you do that for me,' she said.

'He's doing it for himself, Midge,' said Prudence. 'He's lost without his hobby. You're only his excuse. When he's done yours, he'll be hunting about for someone else to mend one for. Let him do it.'

No one mentioned Sarah. All of them knew that she was not the least bit interested in this diversion he had found, but only Oliver knew how bitterly she resented it. He put the matter from his mind. Today was a fiesta.

There was some talk about their destination. They discussed a likely spot for lunch. Prudence consulted various guides Oliver kept in the car, and after a while, looking in the driving mirror, Oliver saw that Midge had fallen asleep.

Lady Fortescue opened the door to them herself.

Her house was beautiful. Oliver had stopped the car outside the gates so that they could admire the pale stone of its construction, and the soft grey tiles on the roof. Then he drove slowly down a straight avenue between two lines of trees, careful not to send gravel scudding over the frosted grass at either side.

'What a gorgeous place,' said Midge.

Its owner must have heard them, or been watching for them, for she was standing at the top of the short flight of steps leading to the entrance as they got out of the Rover and walked towards her.

She was of medium height, plump, with white hair and a lined face; a woman in her later seventies, thought Oliver, who had looked her up in *Who's Who* but had not found an entry for her. He introduced his companions, and she looked sharply at Midge, so that he sensed she might have recognised her. It would not be surprising; after Daniel's death, and again after the later arrests and the committal of the four youths, her photograph had been in many of the newspapers.

'I'm moving from this lovely house,' Lady Fortescue explained. 'My husband died last year and it's much too big for me to stay in alone. I've bought a small house three miles away, as I have friends here and don't want to leave the district. Sadly, I have to dispose of a great deal of furniture.

And the dolls' house, which has been in the attic for more years than I care to think about.'

She led them through the large square hall from which rose a central staircase which divided into two upper flights, and into a small sitting room furnished with two deep sofas and some armchairs covered in rose linen; there was a television set in a corner, but the tables – a mahogany sofa table and two tripod tables – were obviously good. Decanters and glasses stood on a tray on a Georgian pier table against the wall.

'How sad for you to have to move,' said Midge. 'My husband died last year, too, but luckily I can stay in my house, anyway for now. It's not like this, of course.' She spoke quite naturally, without embarrassment. Oliver and Prudence exchanged a glance. A week ago she could not have managed this.

'Ah – I'm sorry. You're young,' said Lady Fortescue. 'Your husband should have had a longer life. Mine was old – over eighty.' She smiled at Midge. 'Sherry?' she suggested.

How civilised, thought Prudence. It was half-past eleven. Several miles away, they had stopped for coffee and what Oliver called a comfort halt, so sherry now was just the thing.

'The house is for Mrs Stewart,' said Oliver, who had introduced them formally.

'Oh?' Lady Fortescue poured sherry into fine glasses and put a small table close to Midge.

'Oliver has just restored one that has been in my family for generations,' said Prudence. 'Midge – Mrs Stewart – has admired it, and he badly needs the occupation as an interest, so here we are.'

'Oliver painted a tiny portrait, smaller than a postage stamp, for one wall in Prudence's house,' said Midge. 'And he's made or mended lots of bits of furniture.'

'Mine will need that,' said Lady Fortescue. Then she continued, 'The furniture I don't need is being auctioned, but I didn't want the dolls' house to go to just anyone. You may think that's silly, but it's the truth.'

'I don't think it's silly at all,' said Midge stoutly. 'You're fond of it. You want it to go to a good home.'

'That's it, exactly,' said Lady Fortescue. 'Have you a daughter?'

'No,' said Midge. 'But I have two sons.'

'And what are they doing?' Lady Fortescue asked.

Midge told her, her colour rising, due partly to the sherry, while Prudence and Oliver sat back, like proud parents pleased to see their offspring performing well.

Lady Fortescue then answered the question none of her visitors had liked to ask.

'We had no children, unfortunately,' she said. 'It was a disappointment.' She set her glass down. 'Shall we go and look at the dolls' house now? It's upstairs in a cupboard. I hid it from the auctioneers who came to catalogue what I want to sell. I didn't want them telling me I could get a fortune for it. I don't want a fortune,' she added hastily.

Oliver intervened.

'May I look at it with you on my own, as this is my little enterprise?' he asked. 'Prudence and Midge just came to keep me company.'

'Certainly,' said Lady Fortescue. 'Help yourselves to more sherry, do,' she added to the two women, and led the way from the room.

The dolls' house was in what must have been her husband's dressing-room. She opened an enormous dark oak wardrobe, almost an armoire, and there it was, resting on a shelf inside, a miniature replica of an eighteenth-century house, shabby and grimed, the wallpaper hanging from the walls of the rooms, and with some woodworm damage, which its owner pointed out.

'How can you bear to part with it?' said Oliver, gazing at it, rapt. Love at first sight, thought Lady Fortescue, touched.

'It's been in the attic ever since I've lived here,' she said. 'It was in my husband's family, handed down – too good for children, in a way, and they weren't originally children's toys, as you know, I'm sure. I was shown it as a bride and told by my mother-in-law that I should have it when I had a daughter old enough to appreciate it. When we came to live here, the right time had somehow passed, and I left it in the attic. It was already decaying.'

'What a pity.'

'Yes. Your friend – forgive me, but she is the woman whose husband was murdered by some schoolboys a few months ago, isn't she?'

'Yes. You recognised her, did you, from the papers?'

'I wasn't sure. But you live near Fettleton, don't you? Where the boys were charged? I noted that crime particularly, because it was so horrific.'

'Yes, it was,' said Oliver. 'Your dolls' house is worth a great deal of money, even in this state,' he went on. 'I couldn't make you a fair offer – it would have to be valued by an expert.'

'And then, if you were to buy it for your friend, she would be embarrassed by the cost of your kindness.'

This was patently true.

'She needn't know that part of it,' he said.

'She'll find out. Someone will let the cat out of the bag. No, the money isn't important. I have more than enough, and there is a buyer in the wings for the house,' said Lady Fortescue. 'He's made a fortune from a microchip device, and he is pleasant. He has a nice wife and some children who will like living here. He can afford to keep it all up and I expect he'll put in a hard tennis court, and a swimming pool. I would, if I were him.' She smiled. 'The surplus furniture will fetch a great deal, too. As I have no children, I don't have to consider anyone except myself.'

She said it sadly. Who would see about arrangements if

she became too frail to manage on her own? A solicitor like himself, he thought; he had carried out the same function for several clients.

'It's very generous of you,' he said.

'It's not. It's selfish. I will get pleasure from knowing you and that poor woman are enjoying it.'

Oliver thought of suggesting that she should come and see the work in progress, or at least the finished article, but refrained. That could wait. He thanked her once again.

'It will please me to think it may help your friend to have the interest,' she said.

'I'm hoping that it will,' said Oliver. 'The trial is still to come, and that will be a hard time for her, I'm afraid.'

'They've got them all, have they? The guilty boys?'

'Yes,' said Oliver. 'After a long stalemate. She stayed with us – my wife and me – after Daniel was killed.' Oliver thought he had better convey to Lady Fortescue the fact that he was married. 'The house I was repairing then intrigued her. She named its occupants. It diverted her.'

'There are no occupants for mine, alas,' said Lady Fortescue.

Oliver was relieved to hear it.

'What's your favourite charity?' he asked her.

She told him. It was a charity for children.

'I'll send them a cheque,' he said.

'Very well. That would be nice. But not more than you can afford. The dolls' house will cost a bit to put in order, after all.'

She opened doors for him as he carried the dolls' house carefully along the corridor and down the wide staircase to the hall, where, on her instructions, he set it on the table in the centre. Lady Fortescue went off, saying she thought she could find a box large enough to hold it.

While she was gone, Oliver called Midge and Prudence to look at his acquisition. Both thought it was wonderful, though they exclaimed about its condition, and Prudence said it would provide inspiration for her next book. One family of participants could live in a house like her own, and another in one like this.

'You've already got the Wilberforces,' Midge declared. 'Now you'll have to give them all real lives.'

'So I will,' said Prudence, eyes lighting up at the prospect. 'That's good. An idea before I'm finished with the current one.' And a rebirth.

They were discussing Mr Wilberforce's family when Lady Fortescue appeared with a large cardboard carton behind which she was almost invisible. When she learned Prudence's profession, she was intrigued. Prudence, who wrote as Prudence Dane, partly to conceal her own identity and partly as a tactic to use a name better placed in the alphabet to catch the eye of a browsing reader, discovered that Lady Fortescue, who admitted that her chosen reading was biography, had read her last book when staying with a friend and had, she said, enjoyed it very much. She went off again, to fetch newspaper to wrap round the house and stop it moving in the box. Prudence followed, to offer help. While they were absent, Midge expressed anxiety about what the house had cost, and Oliver told her what had happened.

'Don't cry,' he warned, as her eyes filled with grateful tears. 'You can later,' he said, and she laughed.

At last it was all packed up and safely in the car. They said farewell, and left, driving slowly down the drive. Lady Fortescue stood watching them till they were out of sight.

'Does she live there all on her own?' Midge asked.

Prudence had learned the answer while they found the newspapers.

'She has a daily housekeeper from the village who doesn't come at weekends unless Lady Fortescue is having guests,' she said. 'It must be very lonely, on her own.'

Going back into the house, Lady Fortescue thought, as she did every day, of the daughter she had borne, and what had happened to her. It was ten years since she had learned the answer.

HOW DOES IT FEEL TO KNOW THAT YOUR BE-TRAYAL LED TO THIS? a typed message, in an envelope delivered by the morning post and enclosing a faded newspaper cutting, had demanded. Below the headline, the murder by Wendy Tyler of her lover's wife was related, and the fact that Wendy Tyler had been adopted as an infant. I MAY COME AND SEE YOU, the letter ended.

Mary Fortescue had checked the details instantly, obtaining copies of further newspaper reports of the crime, eventually employing a private detective to confirm the facts. It was true. Wendy was her daughter, conceived during the war when she, already married, was serving with the WRNS in Ceylon. Mary's husband had been captured after the fall of Singapore; at the time, she did not know if he was still alive. Her brief, ecstatic romance ended when her lover, a naval officer, also married, had been posted away, and then she had discovered that she was pregnant. She had managed to get herself sent back to England and discreetly discharged, saying she had been invalided out, which was true, and implied anaemia and the need for convalescence. She had gone to a remote part of Yorkshire, where she had had the baby, which was adopted after only a few days. It was all over before the war ended and her husband's eventual return. He had never learned her secret, but after it became possible for adopted children to seek out their natural parents, she had grown anxious, and when the letter came, she had feared an overt, determined approach which would destroy not only her life, but her husband's, too. Her daughter would now be fifty-two years old.

There had been no good reason why she did not conceive again; perhaps the problem was with her husband, but they had never enquired. In those days, people did not question fate, as happened nowadays; nor did they believe it was the right of everyone to have exactly what they wanted.

Occasionally, further missives, which she had managed to keep from her husband, had arrived, with messages such as I HAVE NOT FORGOTTEN, and just a week ago Mary Fortescue had received one which said, I MAY COME TO SEE YOU VERY SOON. The earlier ones had borne London postmarks. This one's mark had been Swindon. That was close to home.

Well, she could come now. It didn't matter. Her natural father, who was not named on her birth certificate, had been killed when his ship was torpedoed and he never knew about her birth. There was no one left alive who could be hurt.

Mary found it hard to think of her as Wendy; she had named her Philippa, because her father's name was Philip, and in the newspaper photographs, in spite of the girl's angry, bitter expression, there had been a likeness.

Last night, or rather, in the small hours of the morning, the moment she had dreaded had arrived.

She had been asleep when she heard the noise – the echo of the doorbell being held down with persistence, shrilling through the house, and a loud thumping as the heavy knocker was banged over and over again. An earlier sound had already disturbed her, penetrating her consciousness but not really waking her. The nights were peaceful here, the dawn noises normal country ones: birds, and an occasional bark from a dog. Cars did not race up the drive during the hours of darkness. Even the milkman, in his electric float, did not come until nine o'clock and the postman was still later. Startled, but not afraid – burglars did not advertise their presence in such a manner – she switched on her bedside light, found her slippers and her dressing-gown – a warm woollen one, pale blue – and turned on the main light in her room. All the while the ringing and the hammering continued, not stopping when Mary put on more lights before she came downstairs.

It could be someone who had had an accident, or witnessed one, in the road, and needed to telephone for help, she thought, descending. Hers might be the nearest house. She had convinced herself that this was the reason for the tumult outside before she opened the door and saw the woman on the step.

Mary knew who she was at once.

'There's no need for all that noise,' she said. 'Come in, Philippa.'

30

'That's not my name,' the woman had said, her tone petulant, accusatory.

'No – not now,' Mary had agreed. 'You've had several, I believe. Would you prefer me to call you Wendy? I've always thought of you as Philippa.'

'Thought of me? You never thought of me at all. You gave me away,' she said.

They were still standing in the hall.

'Come along to the kitchen, where it's warm, and I can make you a hot drink,' said Mary, and she led the way, turning her back upon the woman, fighting to breathe evenly and retain the composure she had learned throughout a long life married to an ambitious man. To compensate for his years of lost youth, once he had regained his health, her husband had developed the business which his father had started and had then gone into politics. The fear through all those years that her own secret might be exposed and ruin him had never left her, and it had increased when the first unsigned communication had arrived. Even after he retired from public life he had been active until shortly before his death, and it could have wrecked his final years. Now that danger was past.

'Sit down,' said Mary, indicating a chair at the large pine

table which stood before the Aga. She did not invite her caller to remove her coat, for she did not want her to stay; this morning a man was coming to inspect the dolls' house. She might have to put him off if this woman refused to leave.

This woman. It was odd to think of her like that. This tall woman with the ravaged face, looking older than her years, her hair smoothly coiled back, was once the tiny, red-faced infant for whom Mary had felt a visceral, primitive love transcending any emotion she had ever felt before, the memory of which had never left her. Now, she saw someone she would not have recognised if she had sat opposite her in a train.

Did Philippa feel equally remote from her? Had she an image of her natural mother that conflicted with reality? Philippa was tall, like her father, and her resemblance to him was marked, although he had been only thirty when they met, and she was now much older. Philippa, it was obvious from her expression, hated the world and everybody in it; her father, when Mary knew him, had loved life and humanity.

Philippa, or Wendy, would not sit. Mary, her hand on the kettle waiting for it to boil, watched her pacing up and down the large room with its quarry tiled floor, staring not at Mary but at her own feet: pacing, pacing, thought Mary, as if she were in a prison cell.

'What is wrong?' she asked at last, as she poured water into a teapot. Tea, not coffee, she had decided: it was less stimulating, more soothing; this woman was already tautly strung, at snapping point.

She carried the pot to the table, and set out cups and saucers and the sugar bowl; odd not to know if your daughter took sugar in her tea. She went to the tall refrigerator for the milk, almost crossing the other woman's path as she still paced.

'Do sit down,' Mary repeated, and, ungraciously, her visitor subsided on to one of the chairs. Mary poured the tea with a steady hand.

'Milk?' she asked, the small jug poised above one cup, and, when there was no response, she poured some into both filled tea cups.

'You would add it last,' her daughter growled at last. 'Where I grew up, it went in first.'

'Many people prefer it like that,' said Mary calmly. 'Some think it mixes better. It's a matter of taste.'

'Yes, and it's a matter of taste that you live here in this – this mansion, and I grew up in a suburban street in Birmingham.'

'You were brought up in a good area and your adoptive father was a successful man who prospered after the war,' said Mary. 'Your adoptive parents stood by you when you really needed them.' All this she had discovered, even to the eventual legacy they left her.

'But you weren't there. My real mother. You didn't rescue me.' The tone of this remark was flat, as if the speaker was in a trance.

'I had no idea you were Wendy Tyler,' Mary said. 'And do you really hold me responsible for what you did?'

'You rejected me. You made me search desperately for love,' the other woman said. 'And you made it impossible for me to find it.'

Poor tragic soul, caught in a labyrinth of excuses for her conduct, thought Mary.

'I made the best arrangements I could at the time – more than fifty years ago – to place you in a family who craved a child,' she said. 'Your adoptive father had not been called up for war service, and he was financially secure. I knew that they would love you. If I had kept you, I would have been ostracised – especially as my husband was a prisoner of war in the Far East at the time.' Mary saw her daughter make a sudden rapid movement as she said this. 'Oh yes. I was married but I could not pass you off as my husband's child – something that has happened throughout history in such cases.

And your real father was also married.' She did not mention
his children, this woman's half siblings; no good could come of
that. 'He was killed before you were born and he did not know
I was pregnant.' It was clear that although Philippa/Wendy had
done enough research to track her down, there were limits to
what she had discovered.

'Who was he?' The words seemed to come out reluctantly.

'He was a naval officer I met on an overseas posting. I'm
not going to excuse our behaviour, but it was wartime and
people were under strain. You were conceived as the result
of a great passion,' Mary said. It would not do to call it love.
'Contraception in those days was less dependable than it is
now. Nor was abortion legal then. You look like him,' she
added. 'Except that when I knew him, he was good-humoured
and happy. Clearly, you are not.'

'Would you be, with my history?' the younger woman
demanded, more animated now.

'You loved a married man,' Mary replied. 'You killed his
wife, hoping that he would marry you. That is my understanding of what happened. I, also, had a love affair with a married
man, but I did not wish his wife dead, though I feared my
own husband might be.' She looked at the woman it was so
difficult to regard as her flesh and blood. 'I don't think you
were pregnant, when you did what you did.'

'His wife was,' said the visitor, in a hiss.

'Ah,' said Mary. 'But he took care that you were not.'

'How did you know that?' The question was snapped back
at her.

'I'm guessing. I think you might have wished to trap him.'

Saying this, Mary Fortescue felt a great weariness. She was
responsible for the birth of this bitter woman, yet in her she
could recognise no trace of her own or Philip's character –
but how well had she known him? Theirs had been a two
months' interlude while he was based near her, before he

went to sea again. It had happened all the time during the war, often resulting in hasty marriages which had not always worked out well.

'I hate you,' said Mary's daughter. 'I hate you! Oh, I hate you!'

'And you've come here to tell me so,' said Mary. 'Perhaps you plan to kill me.' The woman did; she knew it in her bones. She began refilling both their cups. Almost without noticing it, the visitor had drunk her tea. Mary had only sipped at hers. Now she took a good gulp, swallowing carefully, anxious not to choke, before continuing, 'If you do, I shan't mind too much, though I should not care for suffering great pain, if you mean to inflict it on me. I am old, and no one depends on me. But I am expecting visitors this morning, and they will be concerned if I do not greet them. By now you will have left traces of your presence in the house. You are not wearing gloves, and I am sure your fingerprints are held on some file. People may have seen your car, and the milkman will be calling soon. The postman, too, will come to the house. I have letters almost every day. I rather think you are on licence and would be locked up again immediately if I died violently and your visit here was discovered.'

The younger woman's stare was glassy now. Suddenly her body slumped, so that it was all Mary Fortescue could do not to rise and go to her, embrace this desperate, angry stranger who was her daughter. But she would not show weakness.

'Why now?' she asked. 'Why have you waited so long to confront me, when I know you traced me many years ago? Are you in trouble? Real trouble? Have you—' she hesitated, wanting to wrap her question in some diplomatic circumlocution. 'Have you made a serious mistake?'

'No,' was the answer, for Wendy Tyler had not stabbed either Mr Leonard or his dog, but both had fled from her presence, Mr Leonard saying she was a danger and ought to be locked up. He might go to the police, though even then it would only be his word against hers.

'Then you are unhappy, and you have made yourself ill by blaming me for what has not worked out for you, instead of examining your own actions.' For the woman was unwell; there was no doubt of it. Mary stood up. 'You must leave now,' she said. 'It's for your own sake, as much as mine. I imagine you have made a place for yourself in society, with a new identity. Go back to it. Don't throw away what you have achieved because you are so full of hatred and resentment.' She moved towards the door. 'As I said, the milkman will be here quite soon, and after him the postman.' Had her visitor called on Sunday, she would have had neither of these excuses to press her to go, nor would she, this weekend, have been expecting guests. 'And my other visitors are due a little later. I must prepare for them,' she ended.

She did not look back to see if the other woman was following her, but walked out of the room, along the passage and into the hall. For want of an audience, her poor, sad daughter must follow, or else perform some melodramatic action. She opened the front door and a blast of icy air blew in.

The tactic worked. Mary saw her daughter walk down the few steps to cross the gravel to her car, a blue Renault, she noticed absently. Mary closed the door at once, and, listening, she heard the car start up. It did not leave immediately, but after a few moments she heard its engine roar and it was driven away very fast.

I offered her no money, she thought, leaning against the door. That, at least, I could have given her, but she was driving a good car, and she was wearing an expensive coat.

She went slowly back to the kitchen and cleared away the tea things, washing them carefully, wiping them, removing all traces of the visit. While she was doing this, the milkman

called, much earlier than usual. He could have passed the
Renault in the road.

Lady Fortescue had some time to compose herself and rest
a little, before preparing for Mr Foxton's arrival. She would
not put him off. He would give her a focus, help her to get
over this intrusion. For that was what it had been, a terrible and
terrifying invasion.

*I had no choice but to turn to her, the wealthy, privileged
woman who is my natural mother. After I produced the knife,
Mr Leonard had left, threatening to inform the police that I
had attacked him, but I had not touched him, nor his vile dog.
At the sight of the knife he had moved swiftly, got control of
the dog and backed off, swearing at me.*

*Prison habits die hard, and I can swear, too. I did so, more
colourfully than he, and told him assaults from patients were
not uncommon and that professional people have to protect
themselves. I pointed out that his dog had growled at me, and
had slavered on the floor.*

*'Don't call again,' I told him. 'All I did was point out your
options. You made the wrong choice, if you wanted your wife
to stay with you.' But of course it was the fact that she had a
lover which had tipped him over.*

*After he had gone, I realised that he had not paid for this
session.*

*I tidied up, cleaned the dog's mess away, vacuumed round and
wiped the surfaces. Then I took his card from the file and scored
it off with a big red line. Discharged himself, I wrote. I made
out his account and put it ready to drop in the postbox on my
way home.*

*The incident was unsettling. I felt restless. Ever since I saw
that woman, Mrs Wilmot, and met her unrelenting stare, I
have not been myself, and when silly Mrs Stewart revealed her
background I knew my unease was justified. She threatened*

my security. Now, two patients had defied me: Mrs Stewart, persuaded, I was sure, by Mrs Foxton, her reneging business partner, to give up her treatment, and Mr Leonard.

I left my consulting room, posted Mr Leonard's account, and drove to Mickleburgh, parking not far from Mrs Wilmot's house. It was in darkness, the curtains drawn. No chink of light was visible as I walked past. Of course, she had money. I had enough independent income to live on, but I had never owned a house. I had always rented. I deserved better. I'd been denied a normal life because I had received such unfair treatment – farmed out as an infant, then betrayed.

Walking along, wondering whether to turn back and ring Mrs Wilmot's bell, confront her, ask her if she had recognised me and if so, what she meant to do, I felt the knife's reassuring hardness in my pocket. Then I noticed The Verandah restaurant. Its softly lighted windows lured me towards them. It would be warm inside. Why should I not have a treat tonight? I needed a pleasant experience after my fracas with Mr Leonard, and, even more, his dog. I went in.

With my meal I ordered wine, and enjoyed it. I seldom drink; it makes me nostalgic. Tonight, though, was different, and it relaxed me. Leaving the restaurant, going out into the night air, I felt a sudden anger because I had been denied so much. It should have been my right to visit pleasant places, to be cherished, nurtured.

She had made it impossible, the woman who had borne me but had surrendered me without a qualm.

I knew where to find her. I would go there now.

On the way, driving through the night, I almost fell asleep, so I turned off the main road into a side lane and found a layby where I pulled in, and slept. With all the car doors locked, no sense of danger came to me, and I had the knife.

I woke feeling frowsty and unclean. A bath or shower would have been welcome. I've appreciated easy cleanliness ever since my time inside. I'd stop when I came to a service area and freshen up, then consult the map. It might be that the motorway, which I had chosen, was not the best route to the village near Bath where she had lived for years in the manor house. Lady Fortescue. A titled woman is my mother. Her husband had been knighted for some service, reference books had told me when, years ago, I traced her. He's dead now. I know that, so I would find her alone, unless she had staff in her large house. She'd played false, I was the result, and she'd got rid of me so that she could continue with her lavish life. Long gone was the childhood dream I'd had of a weeping mother forced to abandon me lest both of us starve.

Leaving the main road, I had some trouble finding the way, but when I reached her village, there was no doubt about which was the manor house. I drove past darkened cottages and a few modern houses. Then I came to huge wrought-iron gates, which were open.

There was no lodge. That surprised me. If she had resident staff I should just have to get past them. I had every right to see my own mother.

The house was in darkness but it must be nearly morning. I drove fast up the drive, my headlights picking out pale tree trunks on either side. A small animal scurried across in front of me, and I pulled up sharp on a wide gravel sweep before the imposing façade which, at my approach, was illuminated by some automatic system. I doused my car's lights, walked towards the door, and rang the bell. A house like this would be alarmed, I thought, and rang again.

No one came. Was she away? Taking the sun in some expensive resort?

I pressed the bell again, then leaned on it, and banged the heavy knocker, up and down, over and over, thumping it.

To me, it seemed like hours before I heard bolts being

drawn. My hand was still raised as the door was opened. She stood there – unless this old woman was the housekeeper – unprotected, no chain holding the door. She stared at me, and knew me instantly.

'There's no need for all that noise,' she said. 'Come in, Philippa.'

She was so small. That was a surprise. She was plump, too, a short, stocky figure in a blue woollen dressing-gown, walking ahead of me towards the back of the house.

I could have struck her then, stabbed her as I had stabbed Emily so many years ago. She, too, would have time to be aware that I had done it. Emily had gurgled, stared at me in shock, then died. She – my mother – would know, too. My fingers, in my coat pocket, clutched the knife. I looked at her grey head – the hair curly, almost white – no rinse, unlike mine which I began to tint as soon as I saw the first grey strands. It would have been so easy.

But I didn't do it.

We went into the kitchen where a green Aga, with four ovens, dominated the room. She put the kettle on as if I was just any caller dropping in. I paced about, wanting to shout at her, to damage her as she had wounded me, but she moved calmly on, setting out pretty china cups and saucers, and a large brown teapot – not a silver one. She used teabags, too, and that almost made me laugh and want to ridicule her: Lady Fortescue using common teabags and a cheap brown pot.

I don't quite know how I came to be sitting down, even drinking tea; it was as though a few minutes had been blotted out, as in an amnesiac fugue. It came to me that I was very thirsty. I drank with eagerness.

I didn't frighten her at all. She wasn't even slightly scared as she told me some romantic tale about my father and their love, and how he had been killed without knowing she was pregnant with me. She said I looked like him.

Suddenly I didn't want to learn any more, and then she was talking about fingerprints and people coming to the house – tradesmen, and visitors – and she was showing me the door.

She called me Philippa.

Before I got into my car, she had closed the door, not even waiting to see me drive away. My mother.

I passed the milk float in the village. My car had been seen, but I had done nothing wrong. It isn't wrong to go and see your mother.

31

Sarah was disappointed and annoyed when Oliver went off with Midge and Prudence, leaving her behind alone. She knew this was unreasonable; he had explained his mission and asked her to go with him, but nothing would induce her to go seeking a silly toy for him to play with, and all as a treat for Midge. She would have been bored to tears while he chatted up some dull woman in an unknown village. She had expected him to cancel his arrangements, and stay to keep her company, but it was true she had pleaded work as an excuse for staying behind. It was also true that she had refused his offer to help her, but she conveniently banished that reflection.

She had gained a weird pleasure from moving the dolls about in the house that was now, thank goodness, no longer in the study. Midge had christened them the Wilberforces; how childish. Well, she'd put Mr Wilberforce out for the count, at least, and she could play games with the next lot of people Oliver installed in the new house, if he bought it. As he would, unless it was a hopeless proposition.

She could always destroy it, as she had contemplated doing to the last one, if she found it all too irksome.

At this thought, Sarah pulled herself up short. Why did such an idea even enter her head? Oliver might be unexciting, but he was reliable and kind, and he had never behaved in the way that Clive had done that night in Kent, when she had been really frightened.

Sarah took her files and went to her computer. She'd concentrate on making her new business a success, and that would show them all, including Clive, just what she could do. And he had a few shocks coming to him, if Jenny went ahead with her complaint.

She was absorbed in her calculations when the doorbell rang – not one sharp ping but a sustained summons, piercing through the house.

Making an impatient sound, Sarah left her desk and went to the front door.

'Yes?' she enquired of the woman she saw standing there, a tall woman in a camel coat, with hair swept round her head in a coil. Had they met? Sarah couldn't place her.

'You're Sarah Foxton,' stated the woman, and before Sarah had realised what was happening, she had pushed past her into the hall.

'I am Sarah Foxton,' she agreed, put out by the woman's tactics, for she was used to holding itinerant vendors at bay, but the woman looked respectable and seemed well spoken. She was annoyed, not alarmed. 'Who are you?' she asked.

'I am Mrs Stewart's counsellor, and you have seriously upset her treatment by cancelling your business project with her,' said the visitor.

She had pushed the front door to behind her, but it had not latched, and now cold air was whistling through the gap. Sarah could not get past her to close it properly, but at the same time, the woman was not welcome, so she made no move to do so.

'Mrs Stewart made the decision herself,' said Sarah firmly. 'And I don't see what it has to do with you.'

'It's very much my concern, if my patient's equilibrium is

likely to be disturbed by outside actions,' was the answer. 'She has ceased her treatment.'

'Obviously that's because she's so much better,' Sarah said. 'I expect you've done her lots of good. Look, I'm very busy now. If you really want to discuss this, can't we do it some other time?' Like when Oliver is here, she thought. Surely it was most unprofessional to discuss a patient with someone else? Wasn't what was said in counselling sessions confidential?

'No, we could not,' said the woman, now advancing towards Sarah, who was suddenly alarmed.

The woman's eyes were glossy bright under the well-defined brows. Her gaze bored into Sarah's, who under the intent stare found herself retreating across the hall. The tall woman continued to move forward until Sarah, at a loss, turned and walked into the sitting room. She told herself to keep calm; this was just a nuisance visitor. A short placatory conversation should be enough to reassure her and she would go.

'Well, let's sit down and discuss it calmly,' Sarah said, and crossed to a wing armchair, not her usual seat but one in which she would be positioned to regain control of the proceedings. Her visitor, however, remained standing. She loomed over Sarah, who gripped the arms of her chair, reminding herself that this person was a specialist who listened to people's problems, not the avenging angel – or devil – she seemed to be at present. 'Mrs Stewart was free to discontinue treatment when she chose,' she said. 'If there's a matter of outstanding fees, I'm sure they can be settled.' Maybe Midge had cried off in mid-course, having pledged to pay for a set number of consultations; it would be just like her to enter into some such foolish agreement.

'Her condition is serious. She is most unstable at the moment,' said the woman.

'She's been depressed. It's not surprising, and it's why she came to you in the first place,' said Sarah. If anyone's unstable, she was thinking, it's you, her so-called counsellor. She decided to attack. 'How is that you know what's best for her?' she challenged. 'Why shouldn't she decide for herself, and ask advice of those who have known her for years, like my husband, who is a solicitor.'

'Oh, I know who he is,' said the woman. 'I've heard about you from my patient. You've had it easy, haven't you? This lovely house. Your high income. Mrs Stewart is the friend you like to patronise, isn't she? To pick up and condescend to when it suits you, and to cast aside when you have other plans. She's had a hard time in recent years, with her husband's business failing, and their debts, and then his death. And when she was counting on you, you threw her over.'

'It wasn't like that,' Sarah said, but was interrupted before she could explain.

'You're a spoiled, ungrateful woman,' said the visitor. 'You have a complaisant husband and you don't deserve him. If he was free, he'd find someone else who would appreciate him – Mrs Stewart, it might be. I'd be doing him a kindness if I did away with you, like that other one. Only I was wrong that time.' She frowned, thinking about it.

'What other one? What are you talking about?' Sarah, until now only puzzled and uneasy, became frightened. She sprang from her chair and moved behind it, and as she did so, she saw a knife appear in the woman's hand. 'Now wait a minute,' Sarah said, and she gripped the back of the chair, holding it before her as a shield. Things like this, women pulling knives, didn't happen in places like Winbury.

But they did. Daniel had been stabbed to death not many miles away, in an even smaller village. He was killed by wicked boys, but she was being threatened by a woman.

A mad woman.

Oliver would not be back for hours. It was no good, this time, expecting him to rescue her, and no one else would do it. She must save herself. She must calm this woman down, make a friendly overture.

'Would you like some tea?' she asked. 'Or coffee?'

'Tea. Coffee. That's what people always give you. She did, too, that other one, this morning. Tea, that was. With sugar. Milk in last. Silly old bat.'

She'd already referred to 'the other one', saying she had done away with her. Had she killed someone earlier today? Some old woman?

'Who do you mean?' asked Sarah, thinking she must keep the woman talking.

'That old bat this morning. My mother,' said the woman.

'Your mother? Would you like to ring her up?' Sarah offered. She could escape and go for help, if the woman used the telephone. But hadn't she implied the other one was dead? Her mother?

'She doesn't want to know,' said the woman.

That was scarcely surprising, if this was her daughter's normal mood; she must be a schizophrenic who had flipped. She was still standing in front of the fireplace, between Sarah and the door, which was ajar. The knife was in her hand, but it was not extended, and she had moved no nearer. She might throw it, like a dart, thought Sarah, ready to duck behind the chair.

'You find that upsetting, then,' said Sarah. 'About your mother.'

'Wouldn't you? To have a child, then give her up and wash your hands of her?'

What could she mean? Had she had a child and had it adopted?

'Have you no patients waiting?' Sarah tried, as a diversion, but she wouldn't have on Saturday, would she?

'Waiting for what?'

'For your advice.'

'Oh. I didn't understand you,' said the woman. 'Patience, I thought you meant.'

It took Sarah a second or two to realise what she meant, but then she felt encouraged. The woman was losing the initiative.

At that moment the doorbell rang again.

'Who's that?' demanded the woman, and she waved the knife around.

'I've no idea,' said Sarah. 'I'd better go and see.'

'Stay where you are,' the woman ordered. 'If you don't answer, they'll go away.'

That was all too likely, but then Sarah remembered that the door, on its sticky latch, had not shut properly. She took a chance and called out very loudly, almost shouting.

'Do come in. Come right in,' she instructed, gripping the chair hard. 'Into the sitting room,' she added, her voice shrill.

Would whoever it was hear her, and obey? If they pushed on the door, it would open easily. She called again, ready to welcome Jehovah's Witnesses, knife sharpeners, dubious pedlars, boys touting for odd jobs. Anyone arriving in the room would break the spell gripping this crazed creature. She listened, her senses sharp, and thought she heard the faint squeak as the heavy old door moved on its iron hinges.

'Come in,' she called again. 'In the sitting room. Please come in.'

She was watching the door of the room, and after what seemed like hours but was, in fact, less than a minute, she saw it open fully and another woman stood there, again tall, but this one was wearing a sober felt hat. It was Rosemary Ellis, the tenant of the upstairs flat behind the offices of Foxton and Smythe. She worked for some welfare organisation based in Fettleton, and was, according to Oliver, painfully shy and awkward but respected in her job. She had a tragic background of some sort – she had been badly beaten up by a lover or a husband, something dreadful, which the charity had hinted at when he checked her reference. Sarah had never been so thankful to see anyone in her life.

'Rosemary,' she cried warmly. 'Come in,' and she emerged from behind her barrier, moving towards Rosemary, hand extended welcomingly. 'Do you know Dr Warwick?' Miraculously, the woman's name had come to her. 'This is Miss Ellis,' she told the counsellor, who had taken her adopted name from the county she had lived in during her childhood years. 'Dr Warwick is just leaving,' she went on. 'Let me see you out, Dr Warwick. What an interesting chat we had. Goodbye,' and in moments Dr Warwick had been ushered out of the house. Sarah pushed the front door firmly to behind her, then leaned her back against it, and slid down, putting her head on her knees. 'Sorry, Rosemary. I'm feeling a bit dizzy. I'll be all right in a minute. Thank goodness you arrived when you did.'

Rosemary gazed down at her. She had been startled when instructed to walk in, and had only faintly heard Sarah's call as the sitting room was right across the hall, but because the door was on the latch, she had obeyed. When she entered the room, the tension between the two women had been almost palpable. She had not seen the knife; it had been pocketed as her foot crossed the threshold.

She had walked to Winbury that morning because the day was fine, and she had decided that she would allow herself to pass The Barn House in case Oliver could be seen working in the garden. Perhaps they might exchange a word across the fence, which in one spot bordered the footpath; she had seen his grey head there one summer's day, when he was cutting the grass.

She knew what she was doing would be seen as ridiculous by any ordinary person; it was a melancholy fixation, but it harmed no one. The exercise she took was beneficial, and she had grown bold enough to have a sandwich in the pub on one occasion. Last night she had dined out; that was a tiny triumph, too. Nothing had gone wrong; no one had snubbed her; the waiter had been polite and helpful. She must do these things which other people found so simple more often.

Oliver was not in his garden, or not where she could see him from the path. She continued past the church and down the street, recalling how, the last time she had done this, on Christmas Day, someone else on foot had approached behind her, and could have seen her pause to look through the gates at the house. No one did this now, but, halting, she saw the garage doors were open and the Rover was not there. So he was out. Probably Sarah was with him, but would they then have left the garage open, with her white Nissan in full view? Perhaps it was safe to do so here in Winbury; it was not a chance she would take. However, a blue car was parked on the gravel where the shabby Escort had been at Christmas.

Last night, the other woman who had dined alone at The Verandah had drunk a whole bottle of red wine. Rosemary, across the room and growing bolder, had seen her speak imperiously to the waiter as she ordered. She had not eaten much; Rosemary had seen her summon him to take away a plate of some barely touched first course. After that she had toyed with whatever she had chosen next, and then she had gone out, only moments before Rosemary received the change from her bill and also left. Walking back to her car, Rosemary had seen her standing still, staring at the attractive house where the Foxtons' friend, Mrs Wilmot, lived. When she saw Rosemary approaching, she had moved on, and had got into a blue Renault car and driven off, passing Rosemary who stood watching her go by.

She wasn't fit to drive after all that wine, and judging by the way she had treated the waiter in the restaurant, she was in a filthy temper. Rosemary had memorised the registration number of her car and had written it down as

soon as she reached home. She was good at numbers; she
did the accounts for the association which employed her and
she lodged it firmly in her mind. When she saw the blue
car, which looked so similar, drawn up outside the Foxtons'
house, some impulse made her walk up to it and check the
number. It was the same car.

The woman, angry and the worse for drink last night, was
probably a close friend of the Foxtons, or a weekend guest,
but her behaviour had been strange. The way she had stared
at Mrs Wilmot's house was peculiar. Rosemary had had the
feeling that she might break a window, which was a ridiculous
idea. No doubt it was her imagination which was running away
with her; she lived too much in her head, and not enough in the
real world.

I'll pretend I'm appealing for the association, she told herself
as she tried to think of a feasible excuse for ringing the doorbell.
There was to be a raffle soon; I'll ask them for a prize, brazen
it out, she thought, with unusual courage. As she waited for the
door to be opened, she expected to see Sarah Foxton appear,
politely masking her annoyance at being interrupted when she
was entertaining a friend. Instead, she had clearly broken up
an altercation.

'I don't know why I did it,' she kept saying later, while they
made a fuss of her.

As soon as the so-called Dr Warwick had departed – they
heard her drive away – and Sarah had recovered from what
was almost a faint, she had declared that Rosemary had saved
her life, and that the woman had been threatening her with a
knife. It was all, somehow, connected with Midge Stewart and
her plans.

Sarah had telephoned the police and Rosemary had given
them the make and registration number of the car. She was
still in the house, plying Sarah with strong coffee, which they
had made together in the kitchen, when the police arrived.

They caught 'Dr' Warwick fairly quickly. She had the knife in her pocket. They were already looking for her because a patient she was treating had complained that she had threatened him.

She was very soon in prison, with her licence revoked, and facing fresh charges.

And Rosemary had been to Sunday lunch at The Barn House, where Midge Stewart and Mrs Wilmot were both present; she had been shown the dolls' house they had bought while 'Dr' Warwick had been threatening Sarah.

Oliver had said he could never thank her enough for listening to her inner warning instinct. 'Dr' Warwick had, it seemed, blamed Sarah for Midge Stewart's cancellation of her treatment, but this was just the trigger which had sent her into a form of mental breakdown. It was a very complex, tragic story, he declared. The enquiries he had initiated into the whereabouts of Wendy Tyler had filled in various gaps, but her connection with Lady Fortescue had not been revealed.

No one knew when, if ever, she would be free again.

She comes to see me regularly. I'm in a hospital now, not prison. I don't know why. They say I need treatment, and she agrees. How foolish.

She sits across the table from me, asking how I am, and if there is anything I need which she may be allowed to send me. She has supplied books and tapes, expensive soap, even clothes. There is no warmth between us, no affection

She's looking older, and seems to have lost weight. I've noticed that. She's moved, she's told me, into a smaller house quite near that mansion which I visited. She never told anyone about that; not wanting, even after all this time, to claim connection with me.

I punish her by sitting silent, never speaking. Once I refused to see her after she had driven all that way, but I like watching her suffer, so I may not do that again. I'll see. It's nice to have that weapon up my sleeve.

Maybe she'll give up – the visiting I mean. Although I didn't touch another person, wounded no one, I shall be here for a long time. It isn't fair.

I've never told anyone who she is, though she says such a revelation can't hurt her now. Maybe that's true. Maybe that's why I haven't made it. She's just a friend, I say. She talks. I listen. After all, I am a counsellor.

If she didn't come, no one would.